Jackdaw

by the same author
SCORPION

Jackdaw

CHRISTOPHER HILL

COLLINS
St James's Place, London
1975

75-105932

William Collins Sons & Co Ltd
London · Glasgow · Sydney · Auckland
Toronto · Johannesburg

First published 1975
© Christopher Hill 1975
ISBN 0 00 221359 1
Set in Monotype Imprint
Made and Printed in Great Britain
William Collins Sons & Co Ltd Glasgow

*To Bryan Forbes
with gratitude*

'Abdication amounts to pronouncing sentence on oneself, and writing oneself down as incompetent, and this is admissible only in old men and idiots. The moment one assumes responsibility for one's destiny, one does it at one's own risk, at one's own danger, and one is never free to give it up.'

From the last letter written by the
Empress Carlotta to the Emperor Maximilian

Prologue

I

Brabant, 1926.
The dog had been barking all the morning. A regular high-pitched yap that echoed through the silent house. She was barking now, standing in the centre of the tiny garden, looking up at the shuttered window of Mathilde's room.

Monsieur Thibaud threw down the paper that he had been pretending to read and glared fiercely at his wife.

'Can nothing be done about that dog?'

Madame Thibaud sighed and made a vague fluttering gesture with her hands.

'She misses Mathilde. Minou is very intelligent. I think she knows that Berthe is going to take her to her new home.'

'She surely can't be going to make this noise all day? Berthe will have to be told to keep her quiet.'

Monsieur Thibaud picked up the newspaper and took refuge behind its large pages.

There was silence for a moment. The dog appeared to have stopped. Madame Thibaud got up and crossed to the window.

'I never thought I should miss Mathilde so much,' she said. 'The house seems dead without her. If only Angèle – '

Her husband put down his paper. 'I forbid you to mention her name,' he said.

'But – '

'I forbid it. That she, of all people, should be so – so – ' There was a pause as Monsieur Thibaud searched for a word sufficiently strong to express his feelings about his eldest daughter.

'So wicked. So basely wicked. As if we did not already have enough sorrow in this house. Trust Mathilde to look after herself. She's well out of the place.'

Madame Thibaud glanced reproachfully at her husband. 'I still think she could have done better if we'd waited. A son of a French country notary is hardly distinguished.'

'One should be realistic. Mathilde is no beauty.'

'But she is young. Twenty-three is young. A girl can wait a few more years. I still think we should have delayed things a little. After all, the Malines were very keen. They would have waited.'

'Of course they would have waited. They needed the money. If you ask me, old Malines would have had to sell his business if it had not been for Mathilde's dowry.'

'Well, then. We could have held on for a better offer. A young notary in the Tarn is no great catch. I'm sure Mathilde could have done better. She's not as bad-looking as all that.'

Monsieur Thibaud shook his head. 'We must be realistic. Mathilde is plain. There is no other way to describe her. She is plain. And apart from that, she has, as we know, certain other disagreeable tendencies. We have to face it, my dear. I do not think she would have had many other suitors. Young Malines is not a bad young man. He may be dull, but he is basically honest. He will make as good a husband as she can expect to find. We have to be practical and face the facts. I know we have had to pay a large dowry, but at least Mathilde will be looked after. We have enough worries and responsibilities as it is.'

Madame Thibaud sighed and nodded. 'Oh, if only Angèle – ' she repeated.

'I don't wish you to mention her name again in my presence. How many times do I have to tell you?'

'But, my dear, you must be reasonable, we have to make some kind of plan.'

'She is not welcome any longer in my house. I don't wish to see her.'

'But she can't just remain locked in her room. We must discuss her future.'

'As far as I am concerned she has no future. She has forfeited any concern that I had for her. As soon as possible she must leave here, and where she goes is no concern of mine. She has brought shame and disgrace to our family. I will naturally fulfil my proper responsibilities, but I now consider that I have only two daughters. She will remain in her room until a decision has been made.'

Monsieur Thibaud's face was set. His wife knew the expression only too well. There was nothing further to be said at this stage. Later on he might weaken somewhat, although she rather doubted it. She sighed again and glanced out of the window at the tiny formal garden. Spring was late this year and the flower beds looked bare and depressing.

Minou saw her and came running up to the window. She began barking again and tried continuously to jump up on the window-sill.

'Now you've made that animal bark again,' Monsieur Thibaud said. 'For goodness' sake get it stopped. Ring for Berthe to shut it away somewhere. Thank heavens she will be taking it away tomorrow.'

'She misses Mathilde,' Madame Thibaud repeated as she crossed to the door. She opened it and called for Berthe. It was some time before the servant's voice answered from the kitchen.

'Madame?'

'Minou is barking and disturbing Monsieur. Will you please shut her away somewhere?'

Berthe appeared from the green baize door that separated the kitchen quarters from the rest of the house. She had been making pastry and her hands were covered in flour.

'Where shall I put her?'

'That doesn't matter.'

'She's barking because she's lonely.'

Madame Thibaud nodded and closed the door. She crossed

to the window and watched Berthe pick up the dog and begin to comfort her. It was a good thing that Berthe liked dogs. She was going to spend a few days' holiday with her brother who had a café in Toulouse and she would take Minou with her. Mathilde and her husband were to pick up the dog on the way back from their honeymoon.

'I don't envy Berthe. Taking Minou on the train all the way down to Toulouse.'

Monsieur Thibaud grunted.

There was a light tap at the door. Madame Thibaud moved to open it.

'Yes?' she said.

'The dog is only lonely,' Berthe said looking enquiringly at Monsieur Thibaud who had retreated again behind his newspaper. 'I wondered if perhaps she could stay here with – '

Madame Thibaud shook her head. 'No,' she said firmly. 'Monsieur is reading. He needs peace.'

'I don't want her in the kitchen with me. I tried it yesterday and it was no good. She wouldn't settle and she was under my feet the whole time. She won't be quiet unless she has company.'

'Put her where you like, but we can't have her in here.' Madame Thibaud was about to close the door when Berthe interrupted her.

'What about lunch?' she asked.

Madame Thibaud looked puzzled. 'Well? What about it?'

'I was wondering how many places I should lay.'

'You know the doctor said Mademoiselle Thérèse should still rest. She will have her tray taken up as usual.'

Berthe nodded her head impatiently. 'I know that,' she replied. 'I wondered about – '

Monsieur Thibaud sighed and put down his paper. 'You will lay two places in the dining-room. My wife and I will be eating alone in future. You may, if you wish, take a small tray up to Mademoiselle Angèle. She will be remaining in her room all day and will only be requiring a simple meal. I would prefer that you do not disturb her. It would therefore be better if you knocked on her door and left the tray outside.'

'Very well, Monsieur.' Berthe glanced momentarily at Madame Thibaud before closing the door. Minou was standing in the hall. She had begun to bark again.

'Sssh.' Berthe stooped and picked the dog up. 'You'll see your mistress soon,' she promised. 'But you must be quiet now.'

Minou snuggled against Berthe's comforting bosom and reached up to kiss her face.

'Poor little dog,' Berthe murmured. 'You only want a bit of love, don't you? Just a little love and comfort. But there isn't much of that about here just now, is there? Never mind. You'll be happy again soon. In a few days' time you'll be with your mistress again. In a new house, with a new master, and in the country. That'll be nice, won't it? Then you'll be happy.'

The dog seemed to understand.

'But you must be good now, and not bark. The trouble is where can I put you while I prepare the lunch?'

She thought for a moment before coming to a decision.

'But you must be good, mind. If you make any noise there will only be trouble.'

She held the dog in her arms as she began to climb the stairs.

The upstairs corridor was quiet. The breakfast tray was still untouched on the chair outside Angèle's room. She had had nothing to eat since the trouble with her parents the previous morning. Berthe paused for a moment and listened at the door. There was no sound. At least the sobbing had stopped. She had been sobbing when Berthe had left the tray for her at breakfast time, but now the room was quiet. She was probably asleep. Berthe tiptoed towards the door at the far end of the passage, and slowly opened it. The room was dark and the curtains were pulled across the window. Thérèse lay still on the bed, her eyes closed. Berthe paused for a moment before gently putting Minou on the eiderdown at the foot of the bed. The dog glanced at Berthe for a moment before curling herself up at Thérèse's feet. Thérèse hadn't moved. She appeared to be sleeping soundly. Berthe paused at the door. Minou had made herself comfortable and her eyes were already closing. Berthe quietly opened the door and left the room. Immediately the bedroom door closed, Thérèse opened her eyes and sat bolt upright. Her movements had disturbed the dog who sat uncertainly at the end of the bed. Thérèse said nothing. She just sat bolt upright glaring malevolently at Minou.

Berthe quietly made her way back down the corridor. As she passed Angèle's door, it opened a crack.

'Berthe?'

'Yes?'

Angèle looked pale and tired. She had been crying. Her eyes were red and swollen.

'Are my parents downstairs?'

'Yes.'

'I think my father is still very angry with me.'

Berthe nodded. 'I think so,' she said. 'You haven't eaten anything. Let me bring you up something.'

Angèle shook her head. 'No, thank you, Berthe. I'm not hungry. Is Thérèse all right?'

'She's fast asleep. Minou was crying. She misses Mathilde. I let her keep Thérèse company.'

'Are you still going away tomorrow?'

'Yes.'

'I wish I could come with you. I can't stay here any more.'

'Can't I bring you up something? Some barley water?'

Angèle smiled and shook her head again. 'No, thank you, dear Berthe. I shall miss you when you're gone.'

'I must go downstairs now. Your parents will be wanting their lunch.'

'Yes, of course. Goodbye.' She reached forward and gently kissed Berthe's cheek before closing her door. Berthe heard the key being turned in the lock.

'Whatever can she have done?' Berthe wondered to herself as she made her way downstairs.

Neither Monsieur nor Madame Thibaud ate much lunch.

Berthe waited by the heavy mahogany sideboard while they pecked at their food. Madame Thibaud eventually made a sign to Berthe to take away their plates.

'I'm afraid we have very little appetite today,' Madame Thibaud said.

'Will you be wanting dessert? I have made a Gâteau Basque.'

Madame Thibaud looked enquiringly at her husband, who shook his head. 'No, thank you, Berthe. I am sorry. Perhaps we could have it tonight?'

'Very well, Madame.'

'It was a lovely lunch, but we are just not hungry.'

Berthe held open the dining-room door as they left the room.

'I think we will both take a rest,' Madame Thibaud said. 'So much seems to have happened to us recently. I think Mademoiselle Mathilde's marriage has tired us.' She paused for a moment, glancing uncertainly at Berthe before she turned and followed her husband upstairs.

Berthe heard their bedroom door close as she began to clear the table.

Angèle also heard her parents' door close. She had been sitting by the window looking out at the depressing little garden. Her parents could see her from their bedroom window. She got up and lay down on her bed. The lack of food had made her feel drowsy. She put her head on the pillow and closed her eyes. The house was quiet. She might have fallen asleep. She never really knew. It had begun to rain outside and the room was dark.

The next thing she heard were the cries. Hideous cries that sounded like nothing she had ever heard before. The cries were followed by screams and then more cries. All coming from the end of the corridor.

Angèle unlocked her door. The cries had died down. There was just an agonized sobbing coming from Thérèse's room. Angèle opened the door.

The blood was everywhere. Blood and black fur. Thérèse lay sobbing on the floor, her face and hands covered in blood. Minou must have thrown herself against the wall in a last desperate attempt to escape. There was a smear of blood across the patterned wall-paper. What was left of her body lay in a corner, scarcely recognizable. Her head appeared to be missing, her body a slashed mass of bloody fur. The room stank with the sickening sweet smell of blood.

Thérèse glanced suddenly at her sister, and for a second Angèle felt terrified. Thérèse's mad eyes flashed dangerously and her hand grasped a cut-throat razor. She slowly got to her feet and approached Angèle. The hand holding the razor reached out towards her and for a second Angèle held her breath with terror. But she stayed still, her eyes fixed on Thérèse.

For a moment Thérèse held Angèle's gaze. Then her eyes dropped and the danger was past. Angèle put out her hand and gently took the razor. She was aware of her parents standing horror-struck at the door behind her, but she paid no attention to them. She took Thérèse in her arms and held her thin shaking body firm.

Madame Thibaud began to sob. Angèle gently laid Thérèse down on the bed, and turned to her parents. Her father was attempting to comfort her mother. He was patting her shoulder and staring with revulsion and horror at the bloody black mess that had been their dog. Suddenly he turned and faced Angèle.

'That's my razor,' he said accusingly. 'Where can she have got that?'

'You must have left it out,' Angèle replied. 'She would have got it from your bathroom.'

Monsieur Thibaud turned to his wife. 'She used my razor,' he repeated. 'She used my razor.'

Thérèse had begun to sob weakly. 'What have I done?' she asked.

Angèle bent over her sister. 'Hush,' she whispered. 'Rest.'

'What have I done?'

'You've killed Minou.'

Thérèse opened her eyes and stared wildly at Angèle. 'Ah yes. That's right,' she murmured.

'Why did you do it?' Angèle asked gently.

Thérèse began to shake her head. 'I don't know. I don't know.'

'Why did you do it?' Angèle repeated firmly.

There was a pause before Thérèse replied.

'Because she was happy. I knew she was happy. She began to play. I knew she was happy because she was going to see Mathilde again. She was happy. Why should she be happy when I'm not?'

'You'll be happy, Thérèse,' Angèle replied. 'I promise you that. I'll see that you're happy.'

Thérèse smiled and closed her eyes. 'Do you promise?' she asked.

Angèle bent and kissed her. 'Yes, my dear. I promise.' She looked up at her parents. 'She's exhausted. These attacks weaken her. She will probably sleep now.'

Madame Thibaud glanced uncertainly at her husband. 'What can we do?' she asked. 'What shall we do?'

Monsieur Thibaud was still staring at the hideous mess on the floor. 'She used my razor,' he muttered.

Madame Thibaud turned to her eldest daughter. 'Angèle, what shall we do?'

Angèle sighed and looked at her parents. She could see Berthe standing behind her mother. 'Tell Berthe to go and fetch Doctor Blanchard,' she said. 'I shall stay with Thérèse.' Neither of her parents raised any objection. They stood impotently for some time in the door watching Angèle, then Monsieur Thibaud put his arm around his wife's waist and led her away.

'Angèle seems to understand these things,' he said. 'It is better that we go.' He gave a short last glance at Thérèse before he went. Angèle was aware of the confused but disgusted expression on his face. She waited until she heard her parents' bedroom door close before she leant over and began to stroke Thérèse's hot forehead.

She was still sitting beside the bed when the doctor arrived. A small bald man with gold pince-nez carrying a black Gladstone bag. He paused in the doorway and looked around the room.

'All this should be cleared up,' he said to Berthe. She nodded silently and went to fetch some water.

Angèle got up and stood aside to let the doctor look at Thérèse. He bent over her for some time taking her pulse and lifting her eyelids. Berthe had returned with a bucket of water and some cloths. Angèle watched her getting down on her knees and silently mopping up the blood.

'Let me help you, Berthe,' she said.

'This will all stain,' Berthe muttered to herself. 'They'll never get these marks off.'

'Let me help you,' Angèle insisted.

Doctor Blanchard snapped his bag shut. 'I would prefer it, mademoiselle, if you had a word with me,' he said. 'Perhaps we could go into the corridor, then we won't be in Berthe's way.'

Angèle followed the doctor into the passage. He motioned her to shut the door.

'These things don't disgust you, mademoiselle?' he asked.

Angèle shook her head. 'Why should they? Thérèse is sick. It is an illness, just like any other. It is no fault of hers. She is not to blame.'

'She does not frighten you?'

'Why should she?'

'She is very strong when she is having an attack. Strong and very violent.'

'Yes, I know that. But she doesn't know what she is doing. She is not responsible for her actions. I am, and I know what she is doing. That gives me a great advantage, and prevents me from being afraid any more. Anyhow,' she shrugged her shoulders, 'I love my sister, and I realize that she is ill and needs me. There is really nothing more to be said, is there?'

The doctor looked intently at Angèle before replying. 'You are a remarkable young lady,' he replied.

'I don't see that, Doctor. My sister is ill. If she had a cold or a poisoned leg would you not expect me to care for her?'

'Of course.'

'Then why should it be different because she has a poisoned mind?'

'You realize she may never get better?'

'Yes, I realize that.'

'And that makes no difference?'

'Why should it?'

'As I said before, you are a remarkable young lady.'

'If you have no further use for me, I would like to help Berthe. It is not right that she should be left to clear everything up alone.'

Doctor Blanchard nodded. 'I must go and talk to your parents,' he said.

He knocked on the bedroom door before entering. Madame Thibaud was lying on the bed with a wet flannel across her forehead. Her husband was standing by the window. They took no notice of the doctor's presence. He had to cough twice before Monsieur Thibaud turned his head and spoke.

'Well,' he said.

'Your daughter is asleep. I will leave you something to give her when she wakes up.'

Monsieur Thibaud nodded his head. 'How could this happen to us?' he asked. 'How did we come to deserve it?'

'It happens in the best of families,' the doctor replied. 'It is an accident of birth.'

'But there was never anything like this in my family,' Monsieur Thibaud murmured, glancing at his wife.

Madame Thibaud lifted up one corner of the wet flannel. 'Neither in mine I can assure you,' she replied firmly.

'Sometimes these things lie dormant for many generations,' the doctor said. 'We do not really understand it yet.'

'What is to be done?' Monsieur Thibaud enquired. 'One thing is quite certain. She cannot remain here. I cannot have these things happening in my house. As if we did not already have enough to contend with.'

Doctor Blanchard nodded. 'I think she should go into a hospital for a time. It is a great pity about Angèle.'

'I have told you, doctor, I will not have her name mentioned.'

'You will not permit her to remain at home?'

Monsieur Thibaud shook his head emphatically. 'I have already made my views clear on that matter. Nothing will make me change them. Nothing whatever.'

Madame Thibaud raised herself up on to the pillows. 'But, my dear, things may be different now. You saw how good she was with Thérèse.'

'Nothing is different. Thérèse must go to some home where she will be cared for, and the other girl must also leave. They must both be out of the house before Auguste comes to stay. Trust Mathilde to have got herself out of this appalling situation.'

Doctor Blanchard stroked his chin for a few moments. 'It could be that I could help you,' he said. 'I might also be able to find a very good place for Mademoiselle Angèle.'

'It couldn't be for too long,' Madame Thibaud interrupted.

The doctor nodded impatiently. 'I realize that,' he said. 'Will you permit me to make enquiries. I could let you know tomorrow.'

'What sort of place are you thinking of?' Monsieur Thibaud asked.

'I would prefer not to discuss it until I have obtained permission.'

'Will she be among decent people?' Madame Thibaud enquired.

The doctor smiled and nodded. 'The best in the land,' he replied. 'Please don't bother to see me out. I know my way and Berthe is busy. I will return tomorrow morning. I don't think you need concern yourselves about Mademoiselle Thérèse. I am confident that she will be in very good hands this evening. I will leave something to help her to rest. Please try to relax and not worry. I will see you both tomorrow. Goodbye. If by any chance I should be needed, please don't hesitate to call me. Goodbye.'

'Goodbye, Doctor.' Monsieur Thibaud watched the doctor leave the room before turning to the window.

When Doctor Blanchard returned next morning, Berthe took him straight upstairs to the Thibaud's bedroom. It was as if they had not moved since he had last seen them. Madame Thibaud was still lying on the bed, and her husband was sitting by the window. They waited for the doctor to speak.

'I understand from Berthe that Mademoiselle Thérèse has passed a comfortable night.'

Monsieur Thibaud nodded hurriedly. 'So I believe,' he replied.

'Also that Mademoiselle Angèle sat up all night with her sister. Berthe offered to let her sleep for a few hours, but she wouldn't hear of it.'

Monsieur Thibaud nodded again impatiently. 'What have you to tell us, doctor?' he asked.

'There is a convent in Brussels not far from here. It is a Nursing Order and the Sisters are very kind. They have offered to take Thérèse. They understand her trouble and she will be well cared for.'

'That is excellent,' Monsieur Thibaud said. 'When will they have her?'

'As soon as she can be moved. I would like to examine her. If I consider there would be no ill effects, she could go there very soon.'

'Thank you.'

'And Angèle?' Madame Thibaud enquired.

'That is what I would like to speak to you about,' the doctor replied. 'Might I sit down?'

'Of course,' Monsieur Thibaud motioned him to a chair. 'Well?'

'You will no doubt have heard of her Imperial Majesty the Empress of Mexico?'

'Naturally,' Monsieur Thibaud replied. 'One presumes she is still alive? One hears nothing of her these days.'

'She is eighty-five now, but apart from her mind, is in excellent health.'

'Does she still live at the castle of Bouchout?'

'Yes. She has remained there ever since she lost her reason sixty years ago.'

'Sixty years in that terrible castle?' Madame Thibaud sat up on the edge of the bed. 'I hear it is a dreadful place. My father went there once when it was a museum before the King gave it to the Empress. He said it was evil. They called it the Castle of the Sleeping Beauty.'

'That is exactly what it has become,' the doctor replied. 'Except that her Imperial Majesty's beauty has faded with the years.'

'What has this to do with our daughter?' Monsieur Thibaud asked impatiently.

'As I have explained, her Imperial Majesty is now a very old lady. One of the great sadnesses of old age is that one continually loses one's closest friends. Her Imperial Majesty has recently suffered just such a loss. A very dear friend and companion of hers has recently died. She also happened to be her Majesty's favourite reader, and the Empress loves to be read to. There is no one to take her place. Her Majesty has asked for someone young. She does not wish to sustain any further bereavements. Like many elderly people, she also enjoys the company of the young.'

'You are suggesting that our daughter become a member of the Empress's household?'

'Precisely.'

'But that is impossible,' Madame Thibaud said. 'Angèle could not remain there for long.'

The doctor nodded. 'Months are equivalent to years when one is dealing with the very old. And apart from that, her Imperial Majesty is completely unaware of time. She frequently believes that she is in her twenties and back in Mexico or

Trieste. She has even on several occasions mistaken me for her late husband, the Emperor.'

'You know her?' Monsieur Thibaud enquired.

'I have been her physician for some years.'

'We never knew that.'

'You knew that I specialized in mental illnesses.'

Monsieur Thibaud nodded. 'Yes, of course. I understand.'

'But will Angèle be safe?' Madame Thibaud interrupted. 'It doesn't seem a suitable place for a young girl in her twenties. Why should you consider Angèle?'

'Because she has a most unusual quality of sympathy and understanding. Mental illness does not repel her. I believe that she would be ideal for the position.'

'When would you wish her to start?' Monsieur Thibaud began to light himself a cigar. His first for two days.

'If you were willing to consider the matter, Angèle would have to meet her Imperial Majesty's senior lady-in-waiting. The Commander of the Castle would also have to be consulted.'

'Not the Empress?'

'A meeting would no doubt be arranged with her Imperial Majesty.'

'But it could only be for a few months,' Madame Thibaud insisted.

'I think it an excellent idea,' Monsieur Thibaud exhaled a cloud of smoke. 'I am deeply grateful to you, doctor.'

'Should we not perhaps ask Mademoiselle Angèle?'

Monsieur Thibaud shook his head. 'She is in no position to refuse,' he replied.

The doctor glanced at Madame Thibaud. She avoided his eyes and pressed a bell on the wall. 'I have rung for Berthe,' she said. 'Perhaps you would wish to see Thérèse.'

The doctor nodded. 'There was no need to trouble Berthe,' he murmured. 'I can easily find my way.'

'It is more suitable that Berthe accompany you,' Monsieur Thibaud replied.

Monsieur Thibaud waited until the doctor had left the room before he spoke.

'This could be an excellent opportunity,' he said. 'Angèle will be mixing with a completely different level of society. The Empress is a member of our Royal Family. She might even come to speak to His Majesty.'

Madame Thibaud was not so enthusiastic. 'I remember what my father used to say about the castle. It is an evil place. It belonged to a Lord of Aremberg, who was called the Butcher of the Ardennes. God knows what wicked things went on there. It is hidden away deep in the middle of thick woods and is surrounded by a huge moat. My father said it never got any sun. It doesn't seem the right sort of place for a young girl. She should be with people of her own age, not shut up in a castle with a mad old woman. It can't be right. There must be somewhere else she could go.'

'Such as?' Her husband impatiently stubbed out his cigar. 'Well?'

Madame Thibaud made a fluttering gesture with her hands. It had become a habit of hers when she didn't know what to do. It was a mannerism that Monsieur Thibaud found excessively irritating.

'You have no alternative suggestion? One thing is quite certain. She is not to remain in this house.'

'No, I have no other suggestion.'

'Very well, then. The matter is decided. When the doctor returns, we will tell him that we would like to accept his offer. You will accompany your daughter to the castle at the earliest opportunity. I hope that you will ensure that she does her utmost to create a good impression.'

'I'm sure she will,' Madame Thibaud replied.

'I really cannot impress upon you sufficiently what an excellent opportunity for advancement this will offer. Angèle cannot afford to turn it down. She will be mixing with the aristocracy. You can't tell me that the Empress does not receive visitors. If Angèle plays her cards right she too will meet them.

It could open up considerable possibilities for her. It is essential that she obtains the post.'

Madame Thibaud remained silent. She sighed and crossed over to her dressing table where she picked up a brush and began to do her hair.

There was a long pause before Monsieur Thibaud spoke. 'There's another thing too,' he said. 'It is probably just irresponsible gossip, but there have always been rumours about the Empress. Rumours about her wealth.'

Madame Thibaud looked enquiringly at her husband.

'They say she brought a great deal of money with her when she left Mexico. She had to persuade Louis Napoleon and the various Courts of Europe to support her cause. There was only one way to have done that, and she was realistic enough to appreciate it. She had to have money. And not just money as we know it.'

'What do you mean?'

'She had to have so much money that the rulers of Europe would listen to her. And they did listen to her, until she went off her head.'

'How could she get this money?' Madame Thibaud asked. 'These are just stories that you have been listening to. Romantic legends that have grown up around the mad old woman in the mysterious castle in the forest.'

'Very possibly. But there is often a grain of fact that germinates into the legend. It would do no harm to find out.'

'You can't honestly believe that the Empress would tell her secrets to Angèle?'

'Stranger things have happened. A mad old woman of eighty-five can be lonely. Angèle has a sympathetic nature. What could be more natural? The Empress forms strange liaisons. Last year it was said that she gave a considerable amount of jewellery to some village woman who went in to make her bed. The woman sold it in Brussels, and it turned out to be a piece of an ancient gold necklace, believed to have formed part of the regalia of the Aztec kings.'

'So the woman is now wealthy?'
'She would have been, but she died soon afterwards.'
'Is this really true?'
'They say it is.' Monsieur Thibaud came and put his hands on his wife's shoulders. 'It would be nice to find out, wouldn't it?'

2

The summons arrived the following morning. A brilliantly polished but ancient limousine bearing the royal coat of arms drew up outside the Thibaud's house, and a letter was handed to Berthe by an elderly gentleman with a huge drooping moustache.

Berthe was uncertain whether or not to curtsey. For all she knew the elderly gentleman might have been the king himself. She hovered uncertainly at the door. Monsieur and Madame Thibaud had had to go out, she explained, but they were expected back for luncheon. The elderly gentleman smiled and shook his head. There was no need for him to bother Monsieur and Madame Thibaud at this stage. They could be given the letter. He would return at the same time tomorrow, by which time perhaps Monsieur and Madame might be kind enough to have a reply for him.

Berthe was certain that they would. The gentleman thanked her and returned to the limousine. Berthe gave an uncertain bob as the car drove away. She rather doubted that the elderly gentleman had been the king, but no one could have been more polite and kind.

When the Thibauds returned, the envelope was lying on a salver in Monsieur Thibaud's study. He picked it up quickly and ripped open the envelope. His eyes quickly scanned the formal writing.

'There we are,' he announced triumphantly to his wife. 'You are to take Angèle to the castle as soon as possible.'

'May I see?' Madame Thibaud took the letter from her husband. It was signed on behalf of her Imperial Majesty, the Empress of Mexico by the Commander of her Château of Bouchout. Her Imperial Majesty had recently suffered a grievous bereavement in the death of one of her ladies-in-waiting. It had been brought to her Majesty's attention that Monsieur and Madame Thibaud's eldest daughter might wish to become a member of Her Majesty's household. Perhaps Madame Thibaud would be kind enough to accompany her daughter to the Château for a preliminary discussion with her Imperial Majesty's Lady of the Bedchamber. One of her Imperial Majesty's limousines would call at Monsieur and Madame Thibaud's house tomorrow morning at eleven o'clock. Perhaps if Madame Thibaud was agreeable she might like to bring her daughter to the Château for a light luncheon?

'What could be more satisfactory?' Monsieur Thibaud said, rubbing his hands together. 'You must acquaint Angèle of the facts. Has she a suitable dress? We don't want her looking dowdy. Perhaps you had better both go out this afternoon and buy some things. You must both look smart and fashionable.'

'Angèle will have to be told,' Madame Thibaud replied.

Her husband shrugged his shoulders. 'Then you had better tell her.'

Angèle was silent for some time after her mother had finished speaking.

'You say this was Doctor Blanchard's idea?'

Madame Thibaud nodded.

'And Thérèse will be looked after by the Sisters?'

'Yes. We went to the convent this morning. They will have her as soon as possible.'

'Will they be kind to her?'

'But of course they will. That is their job. They understand people like that.'

'May I visit her?'

'I'm sure you can.'
'And I will not be with the Empress very long?'
'A few months, that's all. She has recently lost her lady-in-waiting. You can be of great help to her.'
'How can I help an Empress?'
'She is old and lonely. She will need your help.'
Angèle looked at her mother and sighed. 'Very well,' she said.
'You will come with me tomorrow?'
'Yes.'
Madame Thibaud embraced her daughter. 'I'm sure you will never regret it. Now, this afternoon your father has said we must both go into Brussels and buy ourselves new dresses. Isn't that exciting? We can have a lovely time, and spend as much as we like. We have got to look smart for tomorrow.'
'You can buy yourself something. I have really no need for new clothes.'
'What? Oh, don't be so tiresome. Why do you always have to spoil everything? Of course you need new clothes. You will be mixing with quite a different class of person. People of standing with money. You must look smart, otherwise you'll be letting us down, and you don't want to do that.'
'Was that the Empress's car this morning?'
'Umm?' Madame Thibaud fluttered her hands impatiently. 'Oh, I suppose so.'
'I saw it out of my window. It had a crest on the door.'
'Well then, obviously it was the Empress's.'
'It wasn't at all smart. It was clean and shiny, but it wasn't at all smart.'
Madame Thibaud looked sharply at her daughter for some time. Really the girl could be very aggravating at times.
'Well, I shall make myself look nice, even if you won't,' she said, leaving the room.
The next morning at precisely eleven o'clock, the ancient limousine drew up again outside the house. Madame Thibaud was waiting in the hall. She was wearing a rather vulgar but extremely expensive mauve dress. She had chosen the colour

purposely as a mark of respect to the recently bereaved Empress. Angèle was sitting with Thérèse. Berthe tapped at the door.

'Your parents are asking for you,' she said. 'The car is here.'

The elderly gentleman was standing with her parents in the hall. He bent over Angèle's hand when her father introduced her.

'I am delighted to meet you, mademoiselle,' he said smiling kindly at her. 'I have heard most charming things about you from Doctor Blanchard. May I also say how delightful you are looking.'

Madame Thibaud bridled slightly. It was one of Angèle's older dresses, and the silly old fool who looked like a walrus had not made any comment about her brand new dress. 'Perhaps we should be going?' she said.

'Very well.' The elderly gentleman extended his hand to Monsieur Thibaud. 'Goodbye, Monsieur.'

'Goodbye.'

Monsieur Thibaud stood on the step and watched the car drive away.

No one spoke as they drove leisurely through the suburbs towards the country. Angèle was aware that the gentleman was watching her intently out of the corners of his eyes. She turned towards him twice and he smiled reassuringly at her. His face was kind and his eyes were firm but gentle.

After about half an hour, the car drew up in front of some gates. An old man came out of a lodge and opened them, standing back to allow the car to pass through. They drove through a park and then the trees closed in on them and they entered the forest. Angèle shivered slightly in the sudden cold. Then they turned a corner and saw the castle. It was very old, exactly like a castle in a fairy story. A grey grim mass of walls and towers surrounded by a vast moat. The car turned a corner and drove slowly over an old drawbridge and under a massive gateway.

Angèle was aware that the elderly gentleman was smiling at her. They drew up in front of a huge open doorway. A lady was standing waiting for them. She smiled at Angèle as she got out of the car. The elderly gentleman introduced her as the Baroness of Roeselare, her Imperial Majesty's companion and Lady of the Bedchamber. The Baroness took Angèle's arm and led her into the hall.

'I am so glad that you have come to see us, my dear,' she said. 'Doctor Blanchard has told us such nice things about you. I do hope that you might decide to stay with us for some little time. The Empress has great need for someone young and kind like yourself.' She turned to Madame Thibaud who was following. 'Your daughter is charming, Madame,' she said.

They had lunch in a small dining-room that looked out over the water. Both the Baroness and the elderly gentleman did their utmost to make Angèle feel at ease, and tended rather to ignore Madame Thibaud.

When they had eaten, it was suggested that Madame Thibaud might like to see the park. Angèle was taken into a small adjoining sitting-room.

'Sit down, my dear,' the Baroness said. 'I wanted to have a few words with you alone. I suppose you know the sad story of her Imperial Majesty's life?'

'I know some of it,' Angèle replied.

'She is now a very old lady, and she cannot live much longer. Her mind is greatly disturbed, but you must not let that worry you. Sometimes she will say strange things, troubling things, but you must ignore them. She will also act strangely, sometimes with violence. This too, must be ignored. She is never dangerous. When she is violent, she behaves like a child, and she must be treated as such. Treated with firmness but with kindness. At other times, she is almost normal and it is possible to have an intelligent conversation with her. But then, quite suddenly, she can change. She has been deeply upset by the recent death of her lady-in-waiting. She desperately needs the company of someone kind and sympathetic. Someone like you, my dear.'

The Baroness smiled at Angèle.

'Doctor Blanchard has told us all about your youngest sister.

He was deeply impressed by your love and kindness towards her. She is young, and the doctor thinks that with treatment she might improve. The Empress is old and will never change. We arranged for a place to be found for your sister in a nearby convent where the Sisters understand these things. She will be well cared for there. Naturally, too, you will be able to visit her whenever you wish. The Empress is eighty-five; she is feeble and prone to catch cold. She could die at any time. She needs you so much, my dear. Will you come and meet her?'

'I would like to,' Angèle replied.

'Good.' The Baroness stood up and moved to the door. 'Do not be afraid. You may see and hear strange things, but do not be afraid.'

'I'll try not to be,' Angèle promised.

'Bless you.' The Baroness took Angèle's hand, giving it an affectionate squeeze. She opened the door and led the way down a long corridor hung with ancient shields and flags. There was a door at the end which had been thickly padded with felt.

'The Empress hates noise,' the Baroness explained. 'Sudden loud noise can cause her great distress. It is essential to speak softly to her. She has excellent hearing. Always speak softly and never move suddenly. You will notice that all the doors of her apartments have been padded and the handles removed. This is to prevent noise. Do not be afraid. You will never be alone with her. There is always someone watching.'

The Baroness pushed open the door. A woman was standing at the other side.

'Is her Imperial Majesty well today?' the Baroness asked.

The woman nodded. 'She is holding an audience in the Throne Room.'

'Oh, good. Come along, Angèle. Follow me.'

The Baroness led the way to another padded door at the far end of the room. The woman had followed them. She pushed open the door and stood aside to let the two women through.

It seemed at first to be pitch dark. Then gradually Angèle's eyes accustomed themselves to the darkness. They were in a large room with draped curtains right round the walls. The only light came from two candelabra at the farther end where a dais had been built for an ornate gilt throne covered by a dusty velvet canopy emblazoned with the arms of the short-lived Mexican Empire. There were no windows, and the room smelt dirty and musty. As they approached the throne, Angèle could see that the Imperial crest was covered in cobwebs.

An old woman sat erect and proud on the throne. She was wearing a long black dress with the ribbon of an Order across her flat chest. She had a gilt crown on her head and was playing with a bag on her lap.

The Baroness swept a low curtsey and signalled to Angèle to do likewise. The old woman gave them a quick glance before emptying the bag into her lap. A glass bauble rolled across the floor.

'Your Imperial Majesty,' the Baroness said in a firm quiet voice. 'Might I present Mademoiselle Angèle Thibaud.'

'These aren't real, you know,' the Empress said, playing with the baubles in her lap. 'They're not real.'

'Mademoiselle Thibaud might come to live with us.'

'These are not the real ones. This is just rubbish. Rubbish.' The old woman gazed intently at Angèle for several moments. 'These are just rubbish. Everything is rubbish now. Everything. Life is rubbish.'

'This is not one of her good days,' the Baroness whispered. 'We won't stay long.'

'You'll stay as long as I intend,' the Empress said in a clear commanding voice. 'You seem to forget whom I am. I am not only a Princess of the Blood Royal, but I am also an Empress by marriage. Never let that be forgotten. I am also the daughter of his Majesty the King of the Belgians. I am not some vulgar upstart like that Spanish bitch.'

'Oh dear,' the Baroness sighed.

'Who is she talking about?' Angèle asked.

'The late Empress Eugénie. Her Imperial Majesty regards the late Empress as her greatest enemy.'

'She wore paint, you know. And so did he. He wore paint and dyed his hair and he kept prostitutes. He called himself the Emperor of the French, but he was nothing but a Nouveau Riche. He was afraid of me because I was royal.'

'I believe your Imperial Majesty is holding an Audience this afternoon?'

The Empress nodded. 'Yes, I am. How clever of you to know.'

'Then we must not take up any more of your Majesty's time.' The Baroness took hold of Angèle's hand and together they walked backwards to the door. Angèle gave a last glance at the mad old lady counting out her mock jewels on the dusty gilt throne before the padded door closed behind them.

'Not one of her good days,' the Baroness said to the woman. 'Come along my dear.' She led the way back down the long corridor, pausing at the end to turn to Angèle.

'Well?'

'She has been very beautiful,' Angèle said.

The Baroness nodded. 'She had lovely eyes.'

'How could she have been Empress of Mexico?'

The Baroness shook her head sadly. 'That was just it. She couldn't. But don't you know her story?'

'Not really.'

'Then come with me to my sitting-room and I will tell you.'

The Baroness spoke solidly for about a quarter of an hour. When she had finished she glanced at Angèle, and saw that her eyes were full of tears.

'Well, my dear,' she asked. 'Will you come and help us look after her?'

Angèle looked up and smiled at the Baroness.

'After all you have told me, how could I refuse,' she replied.

'Bless you. Then let us go and tell your mother.'

Madame Thibaud and the elderly gentleman had just returned from a drive in the park.

'It is all so beautiful,' Madame Thibaud enthused. 'I was

expecting a rather grim place, but the park is enchanting.' She looked enquiringly at Angèle.

'Your daughter wishes to join us here,' the Baroness said.

'I'm so glad.' Madame Thibaud embraced Angèle on both cheeks. 'I feel sure you will be happy. It is a lovely place, and you will meet such nice people. Did you see the Empress?'

'Yes, Mother.'

'My dear, how exciting. I suppose I might not be permitted . . .'

'Her Imperial Majesty is rather tired today,' the Baroness interrupted firmly. 'And now I expect you will be wanting to return home. You will no doubt have various preparations to make. When do you think Angèle will be free to commence her duties?'

'When would you like her to?' Madame Thibaud enquired.

'As soon as possible.'

Angèle turned to her mother. 'I would like to come tomorrow,' she said.

'Isn't that a little soon?' Madame Thibaud asked.

'I would like to come then,' Angèle replied firmly.

'And we would like to have her then,' the Baroness added.

Madame Thibaud fluttered her hands. 'Oh, very well. But we will have to see what my husband says. The final word must rest with him.'

'Naturally,' the Baroness nodded, and led the way towards the car. 'The car will call at your house tomorrow morning at eleven o'clock. Then if Monsieur Thibaud has any objections we can perhaps discuss them.'

'Goodbye,' Madame Thibaud held out her hand to the Baroness. 'Perhaps you would be kind enough to give my regards to the Empress.'

The baroness nodded. 'Of course. Goodbye, Angèle. We will look forward very much to having you with us.'

The car swept sedately out of the courtyard and across the drawbridge. A curtain fluttered in one of the tower windows as the Empress watched the car disappear amongst the trees of the park.

3

'You look sad,' the Empress said. 'Are you?'

Angèle smiled and shook her head. 'No, not really,' she replied.

The Empress leant across and whispered in Angèle's ear. 'Love makes time pass. Take care that time does not make love pass.' She clasped hold of Angèle's hand and held it firmly. 'They tell me that you will not stay with me for ever.'

'Who told you that?'

'One of those ugly women that sit by the door. I hate those women. Why do they come here?'

'To look after you. To make sure that you are all right.'

'All right? What does that mean? They are plain common women. I do not like their accents and I do not like their clothes.'

'They are women from the village. They speak with the local accent and they do not have a great deal of money.'

'That is why they are here, is it not? They come for money.'

'They have to earn money to live,' Angèle explained.

'They are greedy. They all of them ask questions.' The Empress suddenly let go of Angèle's hand.

'Questions? What sort of questions?'

'But you are different. You have never asked. My brother did, though. He never stopped asking.' The old lady folded her arms tightly across her thin chest and rocked herself backwards and forwards in her chair. 'But I never told him. I never told him.' She began to laugh softly to herself, rocking backwards and forwards. She began to rock harder and harder and her laugh became louder and louder until she leant back and shouted at the top of her voice. 'I never told him. I never told him anything.'

The high vaulted roof rang with the mad old woman's laughter.

The woman sitting by the padded door got up from her chair. 'That's enough, now,' she said firmly. 'We don't want to make too much noise, do we?'

The Empress turned around sharply, quelling the woman with a regal stare. She turned back to Angèle, and gestured towards where the woman had sat down again at the far end of the huge room.

'She's only a commoner, you know. There's not a drop of good blood in her. What right does she think she has to address an Empress and the daughter of a king in such a way? People have been shot for less.'

Angèle nodded placatingly.

'They shot my husband, you know. Did you know that? He was shot by those vulgar Juarista. They were just uneducated Mexican peasants, and they shot a Hapsburg.'

'Don't think about all that now,' Angèle whispered. 'Why don't you rest? We could go for a drive in the park later.'

The Empress smiled and shook her head. 'You are a dear girl,' she said. 'You shine like a jewel in this dark place. Do you like jewels?'

'Of course,' Angèle replied. 'Everyone likes jewels.'

'Everyone wants them, too,' the Empress replied. 'Except you.'

'I don't know what you mean.'

'Perhaps you don't. A lot of other people do, though. These village women, as you call them.' She glanced quickly at the woman sitting in the shadows. 'They're not all village women, my dear. I'm not such a fool as some people would like to believe. I know that village women have hard hands. And they have red faces as well. But sometimes the women that come here have soft white hands, and their faces are pale. Those are the ones that hover around me asking questions.'

'What sort of questions?'

The Empress laughed. 'There was one here recently. She had

the whitest hands of any of them, and she asked me the most questions. So I pretended not to understand. I even answered some of her questions. And then I gave her something. I was very clever, you see. She thought I liked her, thought I didn't see through her little games. So I gave her a present. Like I gave a present to those two women who called themselves Empresses. They used to hang around me, too, pretending they cared. That vulgar Spaniard had tricked me at first. I thought she was a friend of mine. I thought she believed in my husband's Empire. But she was shallow, like that womanizer she married. When I went to her for help, she looked the other way. So I gave her a present for her son.

'Then the other one came here later on. She came in with her tight dresses, so closely corseted she could hardly move. She came in here, into this room, filling it with her perfumes and airs and graces. She talked a lot of nonsense about doctors, and some rubbish that she'd picked up in Vienna. I let her go on. Her husband hadn't done anything for us. The Emperor was his brother, you know. But they wouldn't help him. Even his mother wouldn't help. I tried to see her, but she just shook her head and talked to me about duty. Duty! As if anyone needed to talk about duty to me, the daughter of a king. She was not even a ruler. She was just a duchess, married to a weakling, not fit to wear the crown. How dare she talk to me of duty!

'Elizabeth tried. But she was half mad, you know. The Wittelsbachs had bad blood. I let her go. But not before I gave her something. Something for that carrot-faced son of hers. She took it, too. They both did. They were both as greedy as each other. I remember them both putting out their hands and taking what I gave them. 'This is for your son,' I told them both. They each had only one son. But they both lost them, didn't they? Both their sons died.'

The Empress laughed again.

'I think you should rest now,' Angèle said firmly. 'It is not good to excite yourself. You will only get tired. You must rest.

If you don't, we won't go for a drive later.'

The old lady stopped laughing and sat quietly in her chair.

'I want to go for a drive,' she said.

'Then you must be good,' Angèle replied. 'I will leave you to sleep now.'

'When are you going for good?' the Empress asked. 'I know you are. One of those women told me.'

'That was very foolish of her.'

'But you are going. Are you not?'

'I can't stay here for ever, can I?'

'Why not? I have to. Why cannot you?'

Angèle bent down and kissed the old lady's forehead. 'Hush now,' she whispered, 'and rest. I will come back in a few moments to see that you are asleep.'

The Empress patted Angèle's arm. 'You are a dear girl. I shall miss you. When you go, I should like to give you something. Several things. Beautiful things. Things that will make you rich. Would you like that?'

'Very much,' Angèle said soothingly. 'Now rest.'

The old lady relaxed and closed her eyes. Angèle tiptoed across the vast stone floor. She paused at the door and looked back over her shoulder. The Empress was already sleeping. The woman by the door watched Angèle leave.

The Baroness was in the corridor outside.

'How is she?' she asked.

'She has been talking too much. But she is sleeping now.'

'What was she talking about?'

Angèle smiled and shook her head. 'Nothing,' she said. 'Just a lot of nonsense.'

It was time for the woman to be relieved. She could hear her colleague's heavy footsteps approaching. She pushed open the door.

'Any news?'

The woman nodded and glanced at the sleeping Empress.

'She's been talking to that girl. She's going to give her things when she leaves.'

'But she wouldn't take them.'

The woman grunted contemptuously. 'Don't you believe it,' she said. 'I heard her. She can hardly wait to get her hands on them.'

1975

I

London.

'Elizabeth is looking absolutely marvellous. God, you're a lucky man, Grainger.'

Tony turned around to face the man who had spoken. It was a thick coarse voice, slurred by alcohol. The man was like his voice, gross and red-faced, his shirt stretched tightly across a beer drinker's diaphragm. Tony had never seen him before in his life.

'She's a real stunner, I don't mind telling you.' The man put his hand on Tony's shoulder. 'It's all wrong, you know. Why should an ordinary bloke like you have such a terrific wife? S'all wrong. S'things like that make one believe in socialism.'

Tony roughly shook off the man's hand. 'Excuse me,' he said, and walked to the other end of the room. A waitress came past with a tray of drinks and he helped himself to two. He watched Elizabeth as he quickly drank the first drink and handed the glass back to the waitress who smiled at him.

Elizabeth was still talking to the man. She had a glass in her hand, but she hadn't touched it for the past ten minutes. She was laughing. The man had just leant over and whispered something to her. Tony could hear her laugh from across the room.

'Tony, dear. Why are you on your own?' Susan had just come into the room. 'I've been watching you. You're being naughty and stand-offish. I know it's a bloody awful party, but you might help by talking to people occasionally.'

Tony smiled. 'I'm sorry. Who shall I talk to, then?'

'Well, you see that rather plain woman over there in the corner?' Susan pointed towards the far end of the room where a woman was standing alone. 'She's been like that all evening. Actually, she's quite nice. Just rather shy. Be a darling and go and chat to her, will you? You'll be doing your poor old hostess a good turn at the same time.' She stood and surveyed her roomful of guests. 'God, what a load of shits they all are!' she said.

Tony slowly walked towards the woman in the corner. Elizabeth had just taken another drink. She was standing closer to the man now. He was tall and dark, and had to stoop to hear what she was saying. They laughed again, softer this time. The man took hold of her hand and held it while he spoke. She made no attempt to withdraw it.

He stopped for a moment to light himself a cigarette and watched them. They were both very alike. The man was expensively dressed, and he certainly hadn't got his tan in London. He looked as if he had plenty of money. They fitted well together. They were both rich, beautiful and self-assured. Whatever they did, they would do well. He could imagine them naked together. It wasn't always easy to picture people making love, but somehow with Elizabeth and that man, it was difficult not to. Tony inhaled on his cigarette and realized how much he hated them. Both of them. It came as rather a surprise. He snapped his lighter shut and approached the woman standing by herself in the corner.

She was about his own age. Nice but boring, he thought. Her hair was drawn back from her face in a severe and unflattering style and she was wearing a plain but well cut dress that was obviously designed to serve several functions. He noticed one of her ankles was bandaged.

'My name is Tony Grainger,' he said. 'Can I get you something to drink?'

She smiled and shook her head. 'No, thank you. Actually, I'm just plucking up enough courage to leave. What does one do? I can't just walk out, can I? Only I haven't seen our host or hostess since I arrived.'

'Are you a friend of Susan's?'

The woman shook her head. 'No. I'd never met her until this evening. I occasionally do a job for her husband.'

'What do you do?'

'I suppose I cook. I've just started my own business. Doing lunches for executives. It isn't very exciting, I'm afraid. What do you do?'

'I'm a writer.'

'Now, that is exciting. I should love to be able to write.'

'So would I.' Tony laughed.

The woman looked puzzled. 'How do you mean?'

'I should like to be able to write a good book.'

'What sort of books do you write?'

Tony shrugged his shoulders. 'I'm not quite sure really. I wrote my first one about three years ago. It was quite successful. That was a thriller. But I didn't want to get stuck with them, so I have been trying to do something else.'

'Are you writing now?'

'I'm waiting to hear from my publisher.'

'It must be terribly difficult. And such a gamble, too. To do all that work, and not know whether it will even be accepted.'

'Yes. You're much better off. At least you know your lunches are going to be eaten.'

The woman laughed. 'I wish I'd met you earlier,' she said looking at her watch. 'I haven't spoken to a soul here, except for a word with Julian Harbord. And now I have to go. It really is a pity. Will you excuse me?'

'Who is Julian Harbord?'

'He's one of my clients. That's him over there.' She pointed to the man with Elizabeth. 'He's terribly handsome, don't you think?'

'I suppose so,' Tony nodded. 'What does he do?'

'He's a merchant banker in the city. Makes a great deal of money.'

'What's he like?'

'Not bad. Quite nice.'

'Is he married?'

'No. A man like that doesn't need to be. He's certainly found himself an attractive woman this evening. She's lovely, isn't she?'

'Yes.'

'I wonder who she is?'

'She's my wife,' Tony replied.

'Oh dear!' the woman exclaimed. She looked hastily at her watch. 'I really must go. It was so nice meeting you. Goodbye.'

'Goodbye.' He stood and watched her make a hurried exit. One or two other people had also begun to drift away. He stubbed out his cigarette and walked across to Elizabeth.

'I think it's about time we left,' he said.

She gave him a quick look. 'Do you now?' she replied.

'It's getting late. I think we ought to go.'

She looked at her watch. 'It's precisely twelve minutes past eight, and that isn't quite my bed-time.'

Tony sighed. 'Come on, please, Elizabeth. I would like to go home.' He noticed that Julian Harbord had walked away. He had attached himself to a group in the corner of the room. Elizabeth had made no attempt to introduce him.

She lit herself a cigarette. 'I'm quite enjoying myself,' she said. 'If you want to, go home. I don't mind.'

'I think it would be nicer if we went together.'

'But I'm not ready to go yet. I'm enjoying myself. I haven't just been spending my evening skulking about in corners like some adolescent schoolboy. If you haven't enjoyed yourself, fair enough. Go home. But don't expect me to come, just because you're bored. I think that's rather one-sided, don't you?'

It was always the same when she had had too much to drink. The only thing to do was to humour her.

'Yes, I suppose so,' he replied softly. 'Will you say goodbye to Susan for me.'

'If I see her.'

'I'll leave you the car. I can walk or get a taxi.'

'Very well.'
'See you later, then.'
'Yes. Goodbye.'
He turned when he reached the door. She had joined the group in the corner.

She didn't get back until very late. He was asleep when he heard her key in the lock. He looked at his watch. It was nearly one o'clock.

'You're late,' he said.

Elizabeth nodded and went into the bathroom. 'I stayed on there to supper,' she said. 'I didn't ring because I thought you might be asleep.'

'I did some revision on the book.'

'But it's finished.'

'I'm not entirely happy about it.'

Elizabeth came back into the bedroom. She had put a nightdress on. That was always a bad sign. She seldom wore one, but when she did, it meant she didn't want him to make love to her. She sat on the edge of the bed and began to massage some night cream into her face.

'We haven't said good night,' Tony said. 'I can't kiss you with all that stuff on your face.'

'I thought you were tired.'

'Not too tired to make love to you.'

'Just too tired to stay at a party that I was enjoying. Just too tired to be polite and civil to my friends.'

'Did Susan mind my going?'

'I shouldn't think so for a moment.'

'Then there was no harm done, was there?'

'None at all,' Elizabeth replied as she got into bed.

'Are you angry that I left?' Tony moved over in the bed and put his arms around her. Her body was tense and unyielding. 'I'm not angry,' she murmured. 'I'm just bored, that's all.'

'Bored by me?'

'Frankly, yes.'

'I'm sorry. It was my fault. I'm not much good at cocktail

parties. I'm a bit worried about this book. I can't afford a failure.'

'You should have thought all that out when you gave up your job. I really haven't any patience with that sort of talk. You had a perfectly good job as an architect, and you chose to throw it all away to write. Now you start worrying because you're afraid you can't. Can you wonder that I get bored?'

He moved away to the other side of the bed. 'It isn't quite as simple as that, is it? You were as keen as I was that I should write.'

'Write, yes. But not go on moaning that you can't. That irritates me.'

'You don't seem to understand,' Tony replied quietly. 'It is difficult for me when I don't make sufficient money.'

'Oh?'

'I don't wish to have to be supported by my wife. Not for much longer, at any rate.'

Elizabeth laughed. 'You like to feel strong and dominant, do you? The big strong hairy male with his poor submissive little mate. Is that it? It breaks the rules if the little woman has all the money, does it? The strong hairy male feels he can't climb aboard so easily. Is that it?'

Tony turned over in the bed. 'You don't understand,' he said. 'Everything has always been so straightforward for you. You've known all your life that you need never worry. You've always had plenty of money, plenty of admirers, everything you could possibly have wanted. You've never known the meaning of insecurity. To you it's just a word in the dictionary. Well, you are most fortunate, I assure you. Good night.'

Elizabeth shrugged her shoulders and reached out for a cigarette.

He hated her habit of smoking in bed. She hadn't done it recently. He heard the match strike and smelt the acrid smell of sulphur. He thumped the pillows and curled himself into a semi-embryonic position. He was asleep when Elizabeth finished her cigarette.

When he woke up, the other side of the bed was empty. He could hear her running the bath. He got up and softly tried the bathroom door. It was locked.

He yawned and went into the kitchen to make some orange juice. He saw that Elizabeth had already had some. The orange skins were lying on the table. She had only made enough for herself. He glanced at the clock on the wall. It was nearly ten. He had overslept.

Perhaps he had been rather selfish last night, he thought. Perhaps he had left a bit early. It hadn't been Elizabeth's fault that he hadn't mixed very well with the people there. Perhaps he had also been rather rude to Susan. He was quite fond of her in small doses. He would not have liked to have hurt her feelings. There was a phone in the kitchen. He picked it up and dialled her number. It was answered almost immediately.

'Susan? It's Tony. Tony Grainger. I'm sorry I left early last night. I hope you didn't mind?'

'No, dear. Not a bit. I'm sorry it was all such a bore. It was my fault. I had to get several people knocked off my list. Really I think cocktail parties are about the most insulting form of hospitality one can offer. Anyhow, it was nice of you to ring.'

'I'm sorry I missed the supper.'

'Supper? What supper?'

'Didn't you have supper after the party?'

'No, darling. We had to go on somewhere else. Thank God everyone had gone by nine o'clock. Where the hell did you get the supper idea from?'

'Nowhere. Sorry. I must have got confused.'

There was a pause at the other end of the line.

'Is Elizabeth all right?'

'Yes, she's fine,' Tony replied. 'Goodbye, Susan.'

' 'Bye, darling.'

He went to the fridge and took out some oranges. There was a sharp knife on the table. He began to cut the oranges in half.

Elizabeth had come out of the bathroom. He could hear her moving about in the bedroom.

The telephone rang.

'Mr Grainger?'

'Yes.'

'Hold the line will you? I have Mr Dennis for you.'

Mr Dennis was his editor. Tony never ceased to be infuriated by his publisher's habit of ringing him up and then keeping him hanging around at the end of the line.

'Tony?'

'Yes.'

'John Dennis here.' As if the bored Etonian voice could possibly have belonged to anyone else. 'How are you?'

'Fine.'

'I've been reading your manuscript.'

'Yes?'

'It's interesting. I quite like the idea. But I don't think you've quite got it organized.'

'In other words, you don't think it's good enough.'

'I wouldn't exactly say that.' If they taught them nothing else at Eton, Tony thought, they certainly taught them the art of gracious evasion. 'I just don't think it is quite the sort of thing we handle.'

'You won't publish it?'

'It's not our kind of book. But, Tony, listen. Don't be discouraged. The first one was so good. It had an excellent quality of ruthlessness. We liked it a lot. The second book is always the most difficult, you know. So don't be discouraged. Try to recognize your limitations. Don't aim too high.'

'Would you like me to revise it?'

'No. Forget about it. I know that sounds hard, but believe me, it's good advice. Always remember that nothing is ever wasted. All writing is experience. Try and go back to the quality and simplicity of the first book. Try for that hard ruthlessness. That's what we want. Can you start soon?'

'I hope so.'

'Well done. Give me a ring any time if you want to discuss anything. Goodbye.'

There was a click from an internal extension. He realized that Elizabeth had been listening from the bedroom.

She came in to the kitchen about ten minutes later carrying a copy of *The Times*.

'I wanted to use the phone and overheard some of your conversation with John Dennis,' she said. 'I hope you don't mind.'

Tony shook his head.

'There's an advertisement in this morning's paper that might interest you. A house to let in France, suitable for a writer. You've often said that you find it hard to write in this flat. This could be the solution. And you speak excellent French.'

'Where is the house?'

'Somewhere near Albi.'

'Would that suit you?' Tony asked.

'It wouldn't have to. I shan't be going.'

'Are you trying to get rid of me?'

'I'm simply trying to help you in your work. You say that it's impossible for you to write here. I see your point. It isn't big enough. You don't have a room to yourself, and I don't see why I shouldn't have my friends in when I like. We didn't take the flat for you to write in. We took it when you were an architect, and worked regular hours from nine to five. Frankly, it doesn't work any longer with us both in all day. And as it happens to be my flat, I don't see why I shouldn't entertain in it. The solution is simple. You need to write another book. And you must do it somewhere else. Am I not right?'

'I suppose so.'

'Very well then. This is the solution. You can take the house by the month.'

Tony read the advertisement. It gave a London number. 'There's nothing here about letting it by the month,' he said.

'Well, they will,' Elizabeth replied. 'I rang them up. They're sending some pictures of the house. It's in a village called Laurac-sur-Tarn.'

Tony went to fetch a map. 'It's right on the Toulouse-Albi road,' he said.

'Well, so what? You're going to write a book, not watch traffic.'

The pictures arrived next morning. A typical old French farmhouse hung with wistaria, and surrounded by barns grouped around a small courtyard. There was even a *pigeonnier*.

'It looks delightful,' Elizabeth said. 'I feel quite envious.'

Tony rang up the owners and asked about the traffic. They assured him that the house stood some way back from the main road, and faced the other way. They were quite agreeable to his having it by the month. A woman from next door would keep it clean for him. He agreed to take it.

He rang up a travel agent, and booked himself a single flight to Toulouse. There was a plane leaving the next day.

2

The Tarn.

He could hear the traffic as soon as he got out of the train from Toulouse. A continuous rumble in the distance. The house was only about ten minutes walk from the station. He had been given the directions.

Laurac was not a particularly pretty village. It had been built mainly in the last century. The station was in the typical French country style with an avenue of trees leading towards the village. No one had got off the train with him. A young man had taken his ticket and disappeared into the station. The place appeared to be deserted.

Tony began to walk slowly down the avenue towards the village. He passed a school on his left. A few children were playing in the playground. They took no notice of him as he passed by. It had begun to get hot.

JACKDAW

The avenue ended at a crossroads. The village centre was on his left and he could see a garage and a small supermarket with fruit and vegetables displayed outside. Farther on was the church, an ugly red brick structure with a ludicrously pretentious steeple. The road on his right led away from the village and out into the country. He put down his suitcase and glanced at the map he had been given. The house was straight on, just past the post office.

Apart from the children, he hadn't seen a soul. The place appeared to be almost dead, except for the continuous noise of the traffic in the distance. It got louder as he walked along the road. He passed the post office on his right, a hideous modern white building with a glaring red roof. A woman was standing at the door. She watched him silently as he passed.

He could just see the roof of the house ahead of him. He recognized the tower of the *pigeonnier*. The road curved round to the left and joined the main road.

A huge container lorry thundered past him. There was no path so he was obliged to climb up on the grass verge. The road stretched in a straight line across the flat open countryside with an unending stream of fast heavy traffic passing between Toulouse and Albi. Fortunately the house was on the righthand side of the road from where he was standing. Tony felt that he would be taking his life in his hands by attempting to cross. He walked through the gates and entered the courtyard.

The photographs had been distinctly flattering. The house glowered at him. Even the wistaria managed to look disapproving. He had been told the key would be under a stone by the door. He stooped and picked it up. It was gigantic. He had been warned that it was a double lock and would be hard to turn. It certainly was. Even when unlocked, the door was stiff. It was as if the house was reluctant to accept him. The hinges creaked complainingly as he pushed the door open.

He found himself in a tiny hall with a steep flight of stairs ahead of him. The door on his right was open. He put down his suitcase and walked into the room. It was dark and smelt strongly of soot. He crossed to the window and unfastened the shutters. Suddenly the room was flooded with the strong sunlight.

He was sweating from carrying the heavy suitcase from the station. He took off his shirt, threw it across an old wooden settle and stood in the room looking about him.

It was a beautiful room with a flagged stone floor and a magnificent open fireplace. The furniture was old but adequate. There was another window on the far side of the room. He crossed over and forced open the shutters. He realized his mistake instantly. The window opened on to the main road. The room was immediately filled with the roar of the traffic. He quickly closed it and refastened the shutters.

There was another room on the other side of the hall. It was a small dining-room which led into a big kitchen. Upstairs were two bedrooms with a connecting bathroom. The house was ideal, except for the constant roar of the traffic. The woman from next door had obviously been in recently. The place was clean, a bed had been made up in one of the bedrooms and the gas and electricity had been turned on. He began to unpack his things. There was a table in the bedroom which would be perfect for working at. He moved it away from the window so as not to be distracted by the view and laid out his paper and pens. He always worked best in the mornings. He would start first thing tomorrow. Meanwhile he would go and explore the village after he had had a shower.

There were two ways into the village. He could take the longer way by the quiet road to the station, or the direct main road that led straight there. He took the direct road, walking through the rough grass at the side of the road in order to avoid the traffic. It wasn't long before the village began, at first a few straggling houses and then a terrace with shops until the road widened into the village square by the church.

The main road continued to the right and the village spread out on the left. The square was relatively peaceful. There were several shops, a hotel and garage all dominated by the church with its ugly steeple. A road led past the church towards the crossroads near the station. A quarter of an hour's walk and he had virtually covered Laurac-sur-Tarn. He bought himself some basic provisions at the small supermarket and wandered back to the house by the quiet road.

He tried to work during the afternoon, but his brain was tired and no ideas came. He found the continuous roar of the traffic distracting. It was very hot. He took off his shirt and sunbathed in the small courtyard. Eventually he dropped off to sleep.

He must have slept for about a couple of hours. It was cold when he awoke. The sun had moved behind the *pigeonnier*, which cast a shadow across the courtyard. He shivered and looked at his watch. It was nearly eight o'clock. He felt cold and hungry. He got up and went into the kitchen. He had only bought some cheese and charcuterie. It was about time he had a good meal. He had seen a menu outside the hotel in the village. He got dressed and walked down to the square.

The hotel had once been attractive. It was a long low building with a verandah covered in vines. But some recent owner had done his utmost to ruin it. The outside had been painted pink with green windows, and plastic gnomes capered amongst plaster windmills in the tiny garden. Tony looked at the menu. There was a choice of chicken or veal.

The outside of the hotel had been made as ugly as possible, but it was nothing to the inside. The floor was covered in green vinyl and the walls papered with a design that defied description. An opaque glass door led into the bar. A woman was serving drinks to some old men. She looked up as Tony entered.

'Monsieur?'

'Can I eat here?' Tony asked.

'But of course. The dining-room is down the passage.' She pointed to an archway leading out of the hall. A group of men were seated at a table playing dominoes. Tony was aware that everyone was watching him. He thanked the woman and walked towards the dining-room.

It was almost empty. A fat man who looked like a sales representative was noisily gulping soup in the corner. He broke off a piece of bread and avidly used it to wipe his plate. Tony sat down at a table.

A young girl appeared at the door. She gave Tony a distracted look before disappearing. The fat man belched and began to pick his teeth.

Tony glanced at his watch. It was almost nine o'clock. He was just about to get up and ask the woman in the bar whether he could be served when another woman came in and presented him with the menu. He ordered chicken with a bottle of the local wine.

It was an excellent meal, and cost him less than the equivalent of two pounds. As he left the dining-room, he collided with the young girl whom he had seen earlier. She gave him a terrified look before scuttling away into the kitchen.

He was tired after the meal, and took the quick way back to the house along the main road. The traffic thundered past, headlights blinding him. It was certainly a dangerous walk at night. He felt quite relieved when he finally reached the gates of the house.

The traffic continued until well into the night. He lay in bed and listened to it thundering past. Eventually it eased off at about three in the morning, and he was able to get some sleep, only to be woken up when it began again at six. It was hopeless. He would never be able to work in the house with all that noise.

He tried during the next day. He went down to the village in the morning and bought some wax ear-plugs, but he hated the feel of them and eventually threw them away. In the afternoon he went for a walk beside the river Tarn. But no ideas came. Nothing at least that was suitable for a book. He felt lonely, and wanted Elizabeth. He lay on his bed and imagined her lying beside him, thought of her smooth softness, of the places he liked to kiss. He wanted to take her in his arms, wanted to arouse her. He realized how much he missed and needed her.

There was a telephone downstairs. He put a call through to

London. The operator told him there could be anything up to an hour and a half's delay. He went into the kitchen to make himself an omelette and open a bottle of wine.

The call came through quicker than expected. The line was bad and Elizabeth's voice was faint.

'How are you getting on?' she asked. 'What's the house like?'

'The house is fine. But the traffic is terrible. It's right on the road. I can hardly hear myself think for the noise.'

'You always seem to have something to complain about, don't you?' she said. 'Have you thought of a plot?'

'Give me a chance. I've only just got here.'

'Well, you'd better get on with it.'

Tony changed the subject. 'I miss you. Why don't you come out for a weekend? I could meet you at Toulouse.'

'You've gone there to work. Or at least I hope you have. Anyhow, my mother's coming to stay.'

'That should be nice for you.' Elizabeth's mother and he had disliked each other from the start. At first he had done his best to get on with her, but now all pretences had been dropped and the two of them were barely civil to each other.

'She's coming up for Wimbledon.'

Tony grunted.

'Well, I mustn't keep you from your work,' Elizabeth said. 'I hope it all goes well. Goodbye.'

'Thank you. Goodbye.' He slowly replaced the receiver.

He tried to work all next day, but found it hard to concentrate with the noise. He realized that it would be impossible to work in the house. He would have to try to find somewhere else. It was a pity that he couldn't have taken a room in the hotel, but it was right on the square and if anything, the traffic could be even louder there. But they might know if there was somewhere else nearby. He would go down there again tonight and ask. Meanwhile he lay on the bed upstairs and listened to the traffic thundering by.

The woman behind the bar shook her head. 'No. There's nothing in the village,' she said.

'Are you sure? Not even a room I could have?'

'No.' The woman moved away to the other end of the bar. Tony turned to a group of men sitting at the table.

'Would any of you know if there is a quiet house in the village I could rent. I'm a writer and I've come here to work. But the noise of the traffic is impossible. Surely there must be somewhere quiet that is away from the main road?'

The men glanced at each other for a moment before one of them spoke.

'There's nothing like that here,' he replied.

The woman came out from behind the bar. 'Will you be wanting dinner?' she asked.

'Yes, please.'

'Would you mind having it now then?' she asked. 'It's the chef's night off.'

'Very well.' Tony nodded and made his way to the dining-room. He passed the young girl in the hall. She had been standing by the entrance to the bar. She gave him an agonized look as he went into the dining-room.

The fat man had gone, to be replaced by a young man reading a paperback. He looked up and nodded at Tony as he sat down. The service was quick tonight. He had finished the meal in half an hour. The young man, too, had been served quickly. He put his paperback in his pocket and left the room. Tony heard him going upstairs and unlocking his bedroom door. The hotel was quiet except for the murmur of voices from the bar.

'Monsieur?'

Tony looked up. The young girl was standing by the door. She glanced behind her before speaking again.

'Monsieur?'

'Yes?'

'You were asking about a house?'

'Yes. That's right.'

The girl timidly approached his table. She looked behind her again at the door. 'I know one,' she said. 'It's very quiet. I can take you there.'

'When?' Tony asked.
'When I've finished work. There's not much to do. It's the chef's night off. I can meet you by the church in half an hour.'
'Thank you.'
'But don't tell anyone, will you?'
He promised her he wouldn't.
The girl vanished into the kitchen. Tony got up and went into the bar. He ordered a brandy. The men at the table stopped talking as he came in. One of them got up to fetch a pack of cards, then sat down again and began to deal them out to his companions. One of the other men glanced up and caught Tony's eye, then quickly looked away again. Tony was aware that they had been talking about him. He sipped his brandy and waited for the half-hour to pass.

It went very slowly. He was aware of an atmosphere of constraint in the room. Hardly anyone spoke. The woman behind the bar dried the glasses and stacked them away behind her. An old man slowly got up and went out into the street. The men at the table continued their game.

It was time to go. Tony got up and walked to the door. He was conscious that several of the men were watching him.

The square was deserted. The sky had clouded over with a weak moon struggling to emerge. He could just about make out the mass of the church at the farther end. He strolled slowly towards it. He could see the girl waiting in the shadows. She stepped forward timidly as he approached. 'It's not very far,' she said. 'Just past the crossroads.'

He followed her down the road towards the crossroads. They continued straight on.

'Where does this road go?' Tony asked.

'Nowhere really. Just out into the country. But we don't have far to go.'

They walked past a couple of old barns and allotments to where the road curved around to the right.

'There it is,' she said.

Tony was just about able to make out a tall house with pretentious gables. There was a small garden in front which was beginning to look overgrown.

'It's very quiet,' the girl said. 'There's never any cars come past here.'

Tony nodded. A pale moon came out from behind the clouds and shone for a moment on the grey walls and closed shutters.

'Do you want to go in?' the girl whispered.

'If I may.'

She stooped to pick up a key from under a flowerpot and unlocked the front door, standing aside to let Tony enter. He stepped inside and waited for the girl to open the shutters. The wan moonlight shone through the windows and Tony saw that he was in a long hall with a sitting-room on his right. The house was fully furnished in the French provincial style of the twenties. The girl went ahead of him through the house, opening up the shutters. There was a dining-room at the end of the hall with a kitchen beyond. On the other side of the sitting-room was a tiny study with a roll-top desk. Upstairs were three bedrooms and an old-fashioned bathroom and lavatory. Above the bedrooms were several attics.

'Do you like it?' the girl asked. 'It's very quiet.'

Tony nodded. 'I think it's exactly what I'm looking for.'

The girl looked pleased.

'Who does it belong to?' he asked.

'My mother.'

'She doesn't live here?'

The girl shook her head. 'We live in the village.'

'Does no one live here, then?'

'Not now.'

'Then I could take it for a few months perhaps? How much would it be?'

'You would have to ask my mother. If you've seen all you want, I'll shut it up.'

Tony waited in the garden while the girl closed the shutters. 'Can we go and see your mother now?' he asked when the girl joined him.

'Yes.'

They walked back down the lane towards the village, turning left at the crossroads. The girl led the way past the station and up a narrow path to a group of old cottages by the river. She pushed open a door and led the way in. The door was low and Tony had to stoop. He stepped into a long low room with a big open fireplace.

It was like stepping back a hundred years. The uneven floor was covered with sacking and the only furniture was a bare wooden table with three decrepit chairs. The whole place smelt damp and musty.

A woman was sitting on a box by the fire. She slowly turned her head as they entered.

'Monsieur would like to take the house,' the girl said.

The woman shifted slightly around and looked at Tony. She had been quite pretty once, but her face was tired and she looked ill. Her hair hung greasy and lank about her face. 'Who are you?' she asked suspiciously.

'My name is Grainger. Tony Grainger. I'm an English writer, and I'm looking for a quiet place to work. I've taken a house on the main road, but I can't work there because of the traffic.'

The woman nodded. 'You won't find any noise at that house. It could be too quiet for you.'

'Nothing could be too quiet,' Tony replied.

'When do you want it?' the woman asked.

'As soon as possible.'

'It'll have to be cleaned. I'll do it for you tomorrow.'

'Thank you very much. What is the rent?'

The woman scratched her forehead. 'Would a hundred francs a week suit you?'

'Very well indeed.'

'Then I'll get it all ready for you in the morning. You can move in during the afternoon.'

'Will I need any linen or anything?'

The woman shook her head. 'Everything's there,' she said.

Tony thanked her and moved to the door. The girl ran and opened it for him. 'Good night,' she said, smiling at him.
'Good night. And thank you.'
She stood at the door and watched him go.
'You shouldn't have done that,' the woman said.
'Don't worry,' the girl replied. 'Nothing will happen.'
'What a dreadful place to live in,' Tony thought as he walked back along the quiet road. 'What on earth were they doing there, living in that squalor, when they had another perfectly good house to go to.'
He was just about to get into bed when another thought occurred to him. The girl worked at the hotel, and these French villages were close-knit communities. The people in the bar must have known that the house was empty. He wondered why they hadn't told him about it

3

He walked down to the house in the afternoon. The front door was open. He went into the sitting-room. He hadn't been able to see it clearly last night in the dim moonlight. Now, in the strong afternoon sun with the shutters open, he saw that everything in the room was at least fifty years old. It was like one of those set scenes one sometimes saw in museums. 'A French provincial drawing-room circa 1920.' There was even an aspidistra in a pot behind the lace window curtains.
He heard a noise from the kitchen. The girl was on her knees scrubbing the stone floor. She looked up with a start as he entered. Tony noticed that she looked frightened.
'I'm sorry if I startled you.'
The girl paused and recovered herself. For a few moments she was unable to speak. Whatever it was had frightened her badly. She ran her hand across her forehead.

'Have I come too early?' Tony asked.

The girl shook her head. 'No. I'm nearly finished. All the other rooms are done. I've made the bed up for you in the front bedroom. I shan't be much longer.'

He thanked her and carried his suitcase upstairs. The bedroom door was open. It was a large room occupying the whole front of the house. A big walnut double bed stood in the centre of the wall opposite the large window. He sat down to test the mattress. It was beautifully comfortable. He could lie in bed and look out across the fields. There was a narrow wrought-iron balcony. He got up and walked out on to it.

It was so quiet. The house faced away from the village, so that he might almost have been in the country. There was an uninterrupted view of fields stretching away into the distance. The field opposite had been planted with barley. To the left, the land climbed towards a small wood. He could just see the roof of a house through the trees. Apart from that, there was nothing. Just the open countryside. The only sounds were the birds in the trees. It was exactly what he wanted.

He turned back into the room. There was a faded photograph over the bed. It was a wedding portrait. Rather a plain couple, Tony thought. The woman especially so. The young man was looking pompous and self-important. His bride one would almost call ugly. The only attractive thing in the picture was a dog. A black poodle sitting at the bride's feet, looking up at her.

There was a tap at the door. The girl came shyly into the room.

'I've finished now,' she said. 'If you like, I'll come every day to clean up for you.'

Tony paused.

'It won't cost you anything more,' the girl said eagerly. 'I've got nothing else to do in the mornings. I could just come in for an hour to make the bed and do any washing or anything.'

'That would be very kind.'

The girl turned to go, but Tony stopped her.

'You say this is your mother's house?'

'Yes.'

'Then who are they?' He pointed to the photograph. 'The woman isn't your mother, is she?'

The girl glanced quickly at the picture, then shook her head. 'No. She used to live here. She died not long ago and left the house to my mother.'

'She was a relation of yours?'

'No. She had no family. We used to do washing and odd jobs for her.'

'So she gave all this to your mother?'

'Yes.'

'It's a fine house. Why don't you live in it?'

'Oh, we couldn't do that.' The answer had come instinctively and quickly. The girl had never spoken so positively before. She caught Tony's eye and looked away. 'My mother does several jobs in the village. She would feel too isolated out here. Too far away from her work.' She had resumed her hesitant way of speaking.

'Tell me about the woman who lived here. Did you know her well?'

The girl looked uneasy. 'She was a widow. Her husband died some time ago. He was a notary with an office in Albi.'

'She wasn't very pretty, was she?'

'No.'

'Was she nice?'

'Not many people liked her,' the girl replied. 'I must go now. I have to lay the tables for dinner down at the hotel. Shall I come back tomorrow morning?' She smiled shyly at him. It was a sweet smile. She would have been quite pretty if she'd only taken a bit of trouble over herself.

'I'd like that,' he replied.

The girl seemed pleased. 'Until tomorrow, then,' she said.

He went out on to the balcony. The girl turned at the gate and looked up to wave at him. He stood and watched her as she walked back towards the village.

He felt that he would be able to write in this house. The small study was a perfect place, and the big desk was very comfortable to sit at. The only problem was the lack of plot. Several ideas ran through his mind, but none of them were suitable. He began to plan a semi-autobiographical short story.

But the house fascinated him. He put his few provisions away in the old-fashioned refrigerator and prepared himself some lunch, carrying it into the gloomy dining-room. Why did they always make their dining-rooms so dark, he wondered. The curtains were a heavy brown material and the window faced out on to the overgrown lawn where a monkey puzzle tree blocked out most of the light. A large oil portrait of a man hung over an ornate mahogany sideboard. It was a bad painting and was hung in such a way that the frame leant out into the room. The man had a sour discontented expression not unlike the woman in the photograph upstairs. He looked as if he could have been her father. It was one of those pictures where the eyes followed wherever one went. Tony ate his lunch at the heavy mahogany dining table while the man in the painting stared at him.

It was hot after lunch. He undressed and lay naked on the large bed with the window open so that a breeze wafted through the room. From where he lay, he could see across the barley to the house amongst the trees. It was too hot to sleep, but it was a great relief to be away from the traffic. He felt slightly guilty, lying around on the bed when he should have been working. He remembered that he must ring Elizabeth. He needed to tell her that he had moved. He'd better also let the people at the post office know so that they could re-direct any mail. And he hadn't unpacked either.

He got up and slipped on a pair of briefs. There was a large chest of drawers in the corner of the room. He opened his suitcase and took out a pile of clothes. He opened one of the heavy drawers.

It was full of things. Women's things. Old-fashioned underclothes and petticoats. He opened another drawer. That too was full. All the drawers were. He crossed to an ornate wardrobe on the other side of the room. That too was full of dresses. The house was still full of the woman's things. Nothing had been cleared away.

He went downstairs to the small study and opened the drawers of the desk. They too were full. Full of papers and files. Likewise a chest in the hall and another chest of drawers in the sitting-room. They were all full of papers and personal possessions jumbled up together. Whoever the woman was, she appeared to have been an extremely untidy person, although the rest of the house was very orderly. He felt curious to find out more about her.

He was just finishing his breakfast next morning when he saw the girl coming up the path. He heard her open the back door. He got up and took his coffee into the kitchen. The girl was at the sink. She turned and smiled at him.

'I brought you some bread from the village,' she said. 'I can always do any shopping you want. Just give me a list and I'll bring you whatever you need. We can do your washing for you, too,' she added.

'That's very kind.'

'Did you sleep well? There wasn't any noise was there?'

Tony shook his head.

'There you are,' the girl said. 'I knew you would like it here.'

'Tell me about the woman who used to live here,' he said.

The girl looked uncomfortable for a moment. She picked up a saucepan and began to clean it. 'I already have,' she finally replied.

'You haven't told me very much. What was her name?'

'Madame Malines.'

'How old was she?'

'About seventy I should think.' The girl had done the washing-up very quickly. 'I'll go and make the bed,' she said.

'What did she die of?'

The girl paused for a moment at the door with her back to him.

'She was old. I've told you she was over seventy.'

'Did you know all her things are still here?' Tony asked. 'Nothing's been taken away. All her clothes are still in the drawers.'

'Does that matter?' the girl asked. 'Do you mind?' She stood at the door, still with her back to him. 'I can clear a few drawers for you.'

'It seems strange that she had no friends. That she just left everything to your mother. Did she have much money?'

The girl turned to face him. 'Not much. My mother didn't get any. Madame Malines didn't have a bank account. She didn't believe in banks. There was some money in the house. She left it to the church.'

'Had she lived here long?'

'Ever since she was married.'

'And she had no friends?'

The girl shook her head.

'It seems strange to live in a village like this all one's life and not make friends.'

'I've told you. Not many people liked her. They liked her sister, but not her.'

'She had a sister?'

'Yes. She died about two years ago.'

'Did she live here, too?'

'Not in this house. Nearby.'

'She wasn't married?'

'No.'

'Why didn't people like Madame Malines?'

The girl paused for a moment before answering. 'Oh, I don't know. She was mean and greedy.'

'And untidy.'

The girl looked up sharply at him. 'What do you mean? She was a very tidy person.'

'Well, she doesn't seem to have been very tidy with her things. I opened several of her drawers. Everything has been thrown in any old how.'

'But that isn't so,' the girl replied. 'Everything was left neatly.'

'Then someone's been mucking about then,' Tony said. 'And it wasn't me. You'd better come and see.'

He led the way upstairs to the bedroom and opened several of the drawers.

The girl stared at the untidy mess. Tony could see that she had gone pale and was looking frightened again. It was some time before she moved.

'I'd better make up the bed,' she said at last.

'So long as you don't think I made all that mess,' Tony said.

The girl shook her head. 'No,' she replied. 'I know you didn't.'

Tony glanced at his watch. 'I'm just going down to the post office. I'd better let them know that I've moved so that they can re-direct any mail.'

'I can tell them if you like,' the girl offered. 'I've got to pass there on my way to the village.'

'No, don't bother. I like to walk. And anyhow I must ring my wife as well.'

'I'll lock up when I've finished. You know where we keep the key, don't you? Under the flowerpot by the front door.'

Tony nodded.

He glanced up as he shut the front gate. The girl was watching him from the bedroom window. She moved away when he caught her eye. He walked down the lane towards the cross-roads.

The post office was empty. There was a bell on the counter. He rang it and waited for someone to come. A door opened at the back and a middle-aged woman emerged. She looked enquiringly at Tony.

'My name is Grainger,' he explained. 'I've recently come to stay here for a few weeks.'

The woman smiled and nodded. 'You're the English writer. You've taken the house on the main road.'

'That's right. How did you know?'

The woman laughed. 'Laurac is a small village. Everyone knows everyone's business.'

'I see. Then I shall have to be careful, won't I?'

'You will if you don't want people to know what you're doing.'

'I moved yesterday. I couldn't work in that house with the noise of all that traffic. I've found myself somewhere better. I thought I ought to let you know, so that you could re-direct any mail.'

The woman nodded and picked up a paper and pencil. 'What house have you moved to?' she asked.

'I don't know its name,' Tony replied. 'It's where Madame Malines lived.'

The woman glanced up at him, her pencil poised over the paper.

'You're living in the Malines' house?'

'That's right.'

She shrugged her shoulders and wrote down the address. 'Very well,' she said. 'I shall see that you get your letters.'

'I suppose you will be shut tonight. I must ring my wife in London. Unfortunately there isn't a telephone in that house.'

'You can always ring from the hotel,' the woman replied.

Tony thanked her and walked out into the sunshine.

The woman watched him go before returning to the room at the back. A man was sitting by the window reading a paper.

'That was the English writer,' the woman said, closing the door behind her. 'He's moved into the Malines' house.'

The man glanced at her for a moment and shrugged his shoulders. 'Rather him than me,' he replied. The woman stood at the window and watched Tony walking back to the house.

The girl had gone and the house was locked up. He lay down on the lawn in the shade of some trees. He tried to think of a plot for a book, but his mind raced over a number of things. He had a great deal to think about.

Later in the evening he wandered down to the hotel and put through a call to London. He could hear the phone ringing in the flat, but there was no reply. Elizabeth was out.

He went into the bar after he had eaten. The girl was nowhere to be seen. It must have been her night off, but the woman was behind the bar. Tony ordered a coffee.

'I thought you told me there wasn't a quiet house to let in the village,' he said as she handed him the coffee.

'That's right.'

'Well, I've found one. Madame Malines' old house. Just past the crossroads.'

'You're living there?'

Tony nodded. 'And it's very comfortable. Just what I wanted. Why didn't you tell me about it? You must have known it was empty.'

'Oh, I knew it was empty. I just didn't think you would want to live in it, that's all.'

'Why ever not?'

The woman shrugged her shoulders. 'I just didn't think you would want to live in it,' she repeated. She began to stack up a tray with glasses. A voice called from the kitchen. 'I'm coming,' she replied loudly. She picked up the tray and carried it out into the kitchen. Tony could hear her talking to someone. He was able to catch a word or two. They were talking about him.

The bar was empty except for an old man sitting alone by the wall. He nodded at Tony as he sat down . . .

'Monsieur is living in the Malines' house?'

'That's right,' Tony nodded.

The old man shook his head. 'That's a bad place, that is,' he said.

'Why?'

'She was a bad woman. Bad and greedy.'

'In what way?'

'In every way. She was mean. She had a mean face and a mean mind. No one liked her. We all hated her in the village. People only put up with her because of her sister. They were as different as chalk from cheese. You wouldn't have thought they were sisters.'

Tony got up and took his coffee over to where the old

man was sitting. 'Tell me about her,' he said. 'Did you know her?'

'Of course I knew her. Everyone knows everyone else in a village like this. Her husband died some years back. He wasn't a bad fellow. But she gave him a terrible time. Wouldn't leave him alone. She was at him from morning to night. Nag, nag, nag. She never let him alone.

'Anyhow, he died, lucky fellow. So Madame Malines wrote off to her sister who was living in Belgium. They were a Belgian family, you see. The sister had never married, and was still living in her parents' house. They were dead, though. Been dead some years I believe.

'Anyhow, the sister sold up and came down here. A lovely lady she was. As nice and kind as the other was mean. Then she died. About a year or so ago.'

'And Madame Malines was left on her own again?'

The old man nodded. 'That's right.'

'Left on her own until she died.'

'You can put it like that if you like.'

'What do you mean?' Tony asked.

'Saying she died. I prefer the truth myself. When something happens, I don't believe in telling a whole lot of lies. Madame Malines didn't die. She was murdered. And a very nasty murder it was, too.'

4

The woman had come back into the bar.

'Let me get you a drink,' Tony said to the old man. 'What would you like?'

'Eau-de-vie.'

Tony went up to the bar to order the drinks. The woman looked disapprovingly at the old man. 'You shouldn't listen to all his talk,' she said. 'He's old and talks too much.' She handed Tony the drinks.

'What about you?' he asked. 'Will you have a drink with me?'

The woman shook her head. 'I never drink,' she said.

Tony returned to the old man and handed him the brandy. 'How was she murdered?' he asked.

'She was stabbed. Over and over again. They say it was a terrible mess. There were bits of her all over the room She was hardly recognizable.'

'Did they find out who did it?'

The old man shook his head. 'They never found her for about a week. She lived alone, you see, and didn't have any friends. No one liked her, you understand. So no one missed her. It was the butcher who found her. He used to call at the house every week to collect her order, and when he got no answer he went inside. It gave him a terrible shock. She was upstairs in the bedroom, lying on the bed, with blood all over the place.'

'She was murdered in the front bedroom?'

'That's right.'

Tony shivered. 'And they never discovered who did it?'

'Well, they had a good idea. There was one of those "pop" festivals on in Albi at the time, and the village had been full of those long-haired fools. A lot of them had been on the drugs, and they were careering around the village half-naked, making a terrible noise. Quite a few of them had been in trouble with the police over drugs and things. They made a thorough nuisance of themselves, I can tell you. You've never heard such a noise. They were dangerous, too. They went mad in Albi and broke into a couple of shops. Like lunatics they were.'

'And you think they killed her? Why should they? What reason would they have?'

'They'd probably heard all the stories.'

The old man had finished his brandy. Tony picked up the glasses and took them back to the bar. 'Same again,' he ordered.

The woman frowned and refilled them silently. 'You shouldn't listen to all his talk,' she said when Tony had paid her. 'He's a terrible old gossip.'

'Is he telling me lies, then?'

The woman shrugged. 'Some things are better left forgotten,' she said.

Tony took the glasses and returned to the old man. 'What stories?' he asked.

The old man sipped his drink. 'There'd been all kinds of stories,' he said finally. 'They say there were valuable things hidden in that house.'

'What kind of things?'

'Oh, I don't know. All kinds of things. She was a greedy woman. Wanted everything she could lay her hands on. Never satisfied, she wasn't. Like an old jackdaw. When anything caught her fancy, she had to have it. She wouldn't rest until she'd got it either. They say that's why she got her sister to come and live here.'

'Was her sister wealthy?'

The old man glanced quickly at the woman behind the bar. He leant across to Tony and whispered. 'They say she had jewels and things.'

'Jewels?'

The old man nodded. 'She'd used to work for some old queen or other, I forget her name. Madame Malines used to go around the place boasting about it. How her sister had been friendly with this mad old queen. She was off her head and lived in some castle up north there, and used to dress herself in jewels and gold necklaces and stuff like that. Anyhow, they say that when the sister left her job, this old queen gave her a lot of her jewels and things. Madame Malines knew all about it.

'Then, when her husband died, she persuaded her sister to come down here. It certainly wasn't that she was fond of her, because they didn't see all that much of each other. If you ask me it was because of the jewels. When the sister died, Madame Malines was the first to go through all her things. You can't tell me she didn't find what she was looking for. Sharp as a flint she was when she wanted anything. Sharp and greedy. Just like a jackdaw. That's what we called her in the village. The jackdaw.'

The old man gulped down the last of his brandy. Tony was just about to ask him if he would like another when the woman came out from behind the bar and approached the table. She picked up the old man's glass.

'It's time you were getting home,' she said. 'Your daughter will be worrying about you.' She fetched his stick from where he had left it on a nearby chair. 'Come along now. It's time you were off.'

The old man grumbled under his breath. The woman helped him to his feet and went to open the door into the street. She held it open and waited for the old man to leave. He nodded at Tony before shuffling out into the night. The woman watched him go.

'It doesn't do to encourage him,' she said. 'These things are better not talked about.'

'Are they true?' Tony asked. 'Was he telling the truth?'

The woman began to wipe down the table. 'I don't know what he was saying. And I don't want to know either.'

'He was saying that Madame Malines was murdered, and that people think she had valuable things hidden away in the house. Is that true?'

'I don't know,' the woman replied. 'Do you want another drink? Because if not, I might as well shut up. No one else will be coming at this time of night.'

'No, thank you,' Tony replied. 'Good night.' He walked towards the door. The woman followed behind him and opened the door. He paused on the step and turned to her.

'Was he right about Madame Malines being murdered?'

'Yes. He was right about that.'

'Murdered in that house? In her bedroom?'

The woman nodded. 'But things like that are best forgotten. Good night.' She shut the door and bolted it from the inside.

Tony slowly crossed the square towards the church. He

paused half-way across and looked behind him. The woman was watching him from one of the windows.

He was tired when he reached the house. He let himself in to the silent hall. It seemed somehow altered now. He imagined the ugly old woman living there alone. The ugly old woman that nobody seemed to like. She would have stood where he was standing now at the bottom of the stairs. Like him, she would have gone upstairs to her bedroom, the room that was now his. She would have been wearing one of those dresses that were hanging up in the wardrobe. Like him, she would get undressed and climb into the big bed, turn out the light and wait to go to sleep.

Had she gone straight to sleep, Tony wondered, or had she just lain there in the dark room? Perhaps she had heard a noise? A window or a door being forced open. Or perhaps one of the hippies had been hiding somewhere in the house, waiting until she went to bed. What secrets was the house hiding? Had the old woman taken her sister's jewels? Was that why she had been killed? The jewels were hidden in the house. The girl had said that Madame Malines didn't believe in banks. Therefore she would have hidden them somewhere in the house.

Tony remembered the untidy chests and drawers. The girl had been surprised by their untidiness. She hadn't expected it. They had been disturbed recently. That was why she had looked so frightened. Someone had been in the house searching through all the old woman's things. And it had happened recently. A chill of fear passed through Tony's body as he realized something.

The old man had said that the hippies had killed Madame Malines. But he had been wrong. The hippies had been and gone. Their 'pop' festival was over and done with. But the old woman's things had been searched recently. Whoever had murdered her had apparently not found the jewels. So he had come back to look for them. Tony wondered whether he had found them, because if not, it could only mean one thing. He would return to continue his search.

Tony shivered and for the first time drew the bolts across the front door. He went through the dark house bolting all the windows and the back door before he went up to bed.

He was unable to sleep. He lay in the bed, Madame Malines' bed, and thought about her. He wondered whether she had been frightened. Had she expected to be attacked? It seemed strange that she had gone around the village boasting about the jewels. Almost as if she had been asking for trouble.

The house was silent. He turned over and tried to think of other things. He pictured Elizabeth asleep in their bed in the flat, and wondered whether that cow of a mother of hers was in the spare room. He imagined Elizabeth lying on her side in their double bed. She might have an arm outstretched across the empty space beside her. He wondered if she missed him. They bickered a lot during the day, but it was a different matter at night. They had always been perfect together in bed.

He had often wondered why she had married him. She was very attractive with a large private income. He had been a struggling architect with no money and a secret ambition to write. He had nothing except his looks. He had asked her once why she had married him, and she had smiled.

'I like dishy men, and you're a very good lover,' she had said. 'People who are good in bed can usually do most other things well. Provided they want to, of course. And you are a bloody marvellous lover.'

Tony could see her now in their bed. Perhaps she too was restless, wanting him. Perhaps she had just turned over, displacing the sheet and revealing her breasts. Like him, she always slept naked. He pictured her beautiful nipples. They had neither of them wanted children, and her body had remained like a young girl's.

He rolled over again in the bed. Christ, how he wanted her.

He must have finally gone to sleep because he was awakened by the sound of a powerful car passing the house. Its lights threw a frantic dancing pattern across the bedroom ceiling. He heard it disappear into the distance up the lane. Funny, he wondered drowsily, everyone had told him the lane didn't lead anywhere. And yet the car didn't return. Probably just some couple having it off together in a quiet corner. He turned over and went to sleep again.

He was awakened again about an hour later by the car returning. Again the frantic darting lights across the ceiling as it roared by. 'Bloody inconsiderate bastards,' Tony thought to himself. 'I hope he makes her pregnant.' This time it took him about an hour before he got back to sleep.

He overslept and was awakened by a timid tap at the door. It was the girl bringing coffee and croissants.

'I thought you might like your breakfast in bed,' she said, handing him the tray. 'You were tired. Have you been working hard?'

Tony yawned and ran his fingers through his hair. 'No,' he replied. 'I've been listening to all the gossip about Madame Malines.'

'Oh.'

'They tell me she was murdered here.'

There was a pause before the girl answered.

'Yes.'

'In this bed?'

'Yes.' The girl looked agonized. 'But she was a horrid woman. I know that is an awful thing to say about someone who is dead, especially when she left this house to my mother, but she only did that out of spite. She was mean and horrid. No one was sorry when she was killed. Things like that only happen to unpleasant people. It's nothing for you to worry about.'

'Who do you think killed her?'

'Those young men, of course. They were hanging about the village for days. Terrible, they were. You should have heard their language. One of them had a huge knife, and you should have seen his eyes. Wild they were. Like the eyes of a lunatic. They said afterwards that he'd been on the drugs. Drugs make people do terrible things, you know.'

'What about this story of the jewellery?'

The girl looked evasive. 'I don't believe any of that,' she said. 'That's just talk. Madame Malines was no fool. She wouldn't have had things like that in the house.'

'But you said yourself that she kept money here. That she didn't believe in banks.'

'There wasn't much money. Only about ten thousand francs. That wasn't much to someone like Madame Malines.'

'Then who has been searching the house? And why were all the drawers disturbed? Why should anyone want to do that if they weren't looking for something? What were they looking for if it wasn't the jewellery?'

A look of fear had passed across the girl's face. She turned away from him and walked towards the door, pausing for some moments with her hand on the door knob.

'I asked my mother about that,' she replied eventually. 'She had done it. She was looking for some washing that had been wrongly delivered.'

The girl left the room without looking around. Tony felt certain that she had been lying. There was only one way to find out. He got out of bed and quickly dressed.

He could hear the girl in the kitchen. He tiptoed down the stairs and quietly opened the front door. He paused for a moment and listened. She was doing the washing-up and hadn't heard him. He silently shut the front door and walked quickly down the lane towards the village.

He paused outside the door of the old cottage. A woman was watching him from across the street. He knocked at the door. The woman leant over her front gate staring at him. He knocked again. He could hear the mother's footsteps inside. She was muttering to herself as she pulled the door open.

'Oh! It's you,' she said.

'May I speak to you for a moment?' Tony asked. 'It's very important. I won't keep you long. May I come in?'

The mother stood aside reluctantly. He stepped into the gloomy room.

'I want to ask you something about the house. Someone has

been searching through Madame Malines' things. Your daughter said that you had done it. That you were looking for some washing. Was she speaking the truth? It's important that I should know.'

The mother turned her back on him and went and sat on a chair at the table. It was some time before she spoke.

'I should never have let you go there,' she said finally. 'It was wrong. It would be better if you went. It was all my daughter's fault. She should never have told you about the house. She said we needed the money. God knows we do, too. But she shouldn't have taken you there. Money isn't everything. It would be best if you went.'

'Was it you who went through the old woman's things?' Tony insisted.

'Why don't you go?'

'All I want is an answer to my question. Was it you who disturbed those things?'

The mother turned and looked at him for a moment. Then she turned away and shook her head. 'No,' she replied. 'I wouldn't go near that house.'

'Why not?'

'Because it's evil, that's why. It's a bad house. And it always has been, ever since I can remember. She was a bad woman. Greedy like a jackdaw. Nobody liked her. She deserved what happened to her. I should never have listened to my daughter. She was only trying to help, but the young don't always understand what's best. I was wrong to let you go there.'

'But why? It's exactly what I want.'

She shook her head. 'No. You'd better go. It's not good that you should be there. No good will come of it. I'll give you your money back, and you can go. I've been told that you've been asking questions. We don't want that here. We want it all forgotten. You must go.'

'But why?' Tony repeated. 'I like the house. It's what I want. Why won't you let me stay?'

'Because it isn't right for you to be there. No one should be there. There'll only be trouble. Someone will only find out.'

'Someone?'

The mother looked away quickly.

'What do you mean by "someone"?' Tony asked.

'Nothing,' she replied evasively, shaking her head. 'I didn't mean anything.'

'But you did,' Tony insisted. 'You said "someone". Who did you mean by that?'

The mother turned and faced him. 'Go away from here,' she shouted at him. 'Go away! We don't want you here. Go away and leave us in peace.' She turned suddenly and looked over his shoulder towards the door, an expression of terror on her face. A shadow fell across the floor at their feet. There was someone at the door. The woman collapsed sobbing at the table.

Tony turned towards the door.

The girl was standing there in the strong sunlight, her face in shadow.

'I followed you down,' she said quietly. Her voice sounded different, more authoritative. 'I thought you wouldn't believe what I told you. But you shouldn't have worried my mother. She has enough on her mind as it is.' She came into the room and put her arms around her mother's shoulders. 'You must forgive her. She is tired. She works too hard and she worries a lot. Perhaps it would be better if you went.'

Tony nodded and walked to the door. 'May I stay in the house?' he asked.

The girl glanced at him for a moment. 'We'll see,' she said. 'You can stay there at present. We'll see what happens.'

'Thank you.'

The girl was bending over her mother as he quietly shut the door.

He stopped in the village on his way back and bought some things for lunch. He felt it was about time he got down to some real work.

The girl had left the front door open in her hurry. He entered the house and closed the door behind him. It was cold in the hall. Cold and eerie. For the first time he felt afraid in the house. There was something different. Something had changed.

He heard a sound in the kitchen. He realized that he was not alone. He could hear footsteps on the stone floor of the kitchen. He stood transfixed with terror as they approached. Whoever it was was coming into the hall. He could hear the footsteps in the dining-room.

The girl had forgotten to open the shutters in there and the room would have been pitch dark. But whoever it was seemed to know their way past all the furniture. He stood silently in the hall as the footsteps came nearer. Then the handle of the door was slowly turned and the door opened.

A figure emerged from the dining-room. Someone was standing in the shadows at the end of the hall. He was able to see a dim shape in the darkness. He waited as the figure slowly came towards him down the hall.

5

A woman stepped out of the darkness.

'I'm sorry. Did I startle you?' She stood looking at him hesitantly. A pleasant looking woman in her middle forties.

'I'm sorry,' she repeated. 'I must have given you a shock. The front door was open and I thought you might have been in the kitchen.'

'That's quite all right,' Tony said. 'Can I do anything for you?'

The woman smiled shyly at him. 'That's really what I came to say to you. I live nearby, you see. I heard in the village that you had taken the house, so I called in to see whether you had everything you wanted.'

'That was very kind of you.'

'They told me you were alone. Sometimes a man on his own

needs help. If there is anything I can do, please let me know.'

'You are very kind.'

She moved past him to the door and paused for a moment in the strong sunlight. 'I think it's going to be very hot.' She took out a pair of sunglasses from a pocket in her skirt. 'Do you like this kind of weather?'

'Very much. But it makes me feel lazy, and that isn't good for my work.'

The woman smiled and put on the glasses. She was pretty in an unspoilt homely way. Tony noticed that she wore hardly any make-up.

'They told me you were a writer.'

'That's right.'

The woman nodded and turned to go. She began to walk towards the gate. Tony was aware that he didn't want her to leave. 'Where do you live?' he asked.

She pointed to the house amongst the trees. 'Up there.'

He could see that she wore no wedding ring. 'Won't you stay for coffee?' he asked.

She smiled and shook her head. 'You are very kind, but I must get back. There are several things that I have to do. Goodbye.'

'Goodbye.'

She had almost walked out of sight round the corner of the lane before he realized that he hadn't asked her name.

He turned back into the house and walked down the dark hall to the study. It was cold in there. The room must face north. He sat down at the desk and began to write.

He worked for about an hour, pausing several times to light a cigarette or look out of the window. The room was freezing. It felt as if it had never got any sunshine. He got up and tried to open the window. The clasp was stiff and rusty. It had obviously not been opened for some considerable time. After a great deal of struggling, he eventually managed to move it and forced the window open. A blast of warm air entered the room. He sat down and began to read through what he had written. It was bad. He scrumpled the paper into a ball and threw it violently into the waste-paper basket. What had happened to him, he asked himself. Why couldn't he write?

He got up yet again and walked to the window. The garden was warm. He was a fool to spend the day shut up in the depressing little study. He could write just as well in the garden. In fact, he could hardly write worse. He started to close the window.

But it wouldn't shut. The handle of the clasp wouldn't turn. It had stuck tight. He must have forced it in some way. He tried for several minutes to get it to close, but it was no use. It was impossible to shut the window.

It was hot in the garden. Too hot to work. He found himself a secluded spot where he could not be overlooked and stripped off his clothes. He stretched out naked in the long grass and closed his eyes. There was just the sound of the crickets in the grass around him.

He lay there for some time thinking. Thinking of a plot. He realized there was no point in sitting down to write until he had something to write about. He had to have a plot. John Dennis had liked his first book. In fact, everybody had. It had been very successful for a first novel. 'A brilliant debut,' the critics had said. 'Here is a new writer to watch.' *The Times* had called it 'Diabolically clever'. Another paper had referred to its 'intricate cunning'. But Tony had never really considered it to be particularly clever. It had just been very simple. Its cleverness had lain in its simplicity. But not many people had realized that.

He had perhaps tried to be too clever with his second book. It had taken much longer to write and it had not come easily. But he had thought that a lot of it was good. It had been a personal book. Perhaps too personal. He had perhaps put too many of his private thoughts into it.

Now he had been told to go back to the style of the first book. In other words, another thriller. But first he had to have a plot. And it mustn't be too personal. He rolled over in the long grass in order to get the sun on his back.

The girl had come into the garden. She had found the gate open and had walked straight in. Her eyes were attracted by the movement in the long grass. She carefully picked her way over the uneven ground towards where Tony was lying, but stopped suddenly when she realized that he was naked. She stood and looked at him for some time before she turned and went quietly back to the gate.

He was aroused by a sound from the road. The girl was approaching the gate. He quickly slipped on his trousers and got up to meet her.

'I came to tell you that you can stay here if you like,' the girl said. Tony noticed that she avoided his eyes and appeared to be blushing. 'My mother said she was sorry for shouting at you. It was rude of her.'

'Don't worry. Thank you for letting me stay.'

The girl appeared reluctant to leave. 'It's very hot,' she said. Tony nodded. 'Yes. I was sunbathing.'

'Yes.' The girl glanced up at him for a moment. 'You'll tell me if there's anything you want. Anything from the village.'

'Thank you. I will.'

'Goodbye.'

'Goodbye.'

She walked slowly back to the gate. Tony watched her pause for a moment in the lane, but she didn't turn round. She hesitated for a moment before walking back towards the village.

She had gone before he remembered that he had not told her about the window.

It got cooler after lunch and he went for a long walk. He always found it easier to think when he was walking. He must have gone a long way. It was nearly seven o'clock when he eventually found himself back at the crossroads. He was just passing the post office when he heard his name being called.

'Monsieur Grainger!' The postmistress had opened one of her windows. 'Monsieur Grainger!'

Tony paused. 'Yes?'

'I am sorry. I have been stupid. I have made a mistake.'

JACKDAW

'Oh?' He walked over to the window. 'What has happened?'

The postmistress shrugged her shoulders helplessly. 'I have been very stupid,' she repeated. 'It was all my fault.'

'What is the matter?'

'There was a letter for you. From England, I think. I forgot that you had moved. I'm sorry. I didn't change the address.'

'You mean it's been delivered to the old house?'

'I'm afraid so. I'm very sorry. Would you like me to go and get it for you?'

'No. It doesn't matter. I can go up there myself.'

'Will you be going up there now?' the postmistress asked.

Tony looked at his watch. 'No, I don't think so. I've just been for quite a long walk. I'll have a meal at the hotel and wander up there after dinner.'

'Then I should go by the main road. There are no lights on the other way, and it can be very dangerous in the dark.'

'All right.'

'I'm very sorry.'

Tony smiled. 'It really doesn't matter,' he repeated. 'Thank you for telling me.'

The postmistress nodded and shut the window. She turned towards her husband who was watching the television. 'I hope I did right,' she said.

Her husband shrugged his shoulders. 'It's no concern of ours,' he replied.

But his wife looked worried. 'I hope I did right,' she repeated.

The hotel dining-room was nearly full and the service was slow. It was almost half past nine before he finally finished his meal. He went into the bar for a coffee. The old man wasn't there and there was a different woman behind the bar. A group of young men were standing around a juke box in the corner. They fed some coins into the machine and the room resounded with the noise of a raucous pop group. Tony quickly drank up his coffee and left.

It was nearly dark and the road was quiet. The young men in the bar had begun to sing. He could hear their voices fading into the distance as he began to walk along the main road. An occasional lorry roared past him on its way to Albi, but apart from that, the road seemed abnormally quiet. He realized that he had drunk rather too much wine. The walk would do him good.

He had just passed the last house of the village when he saw the car. It had suddenly emerged from nowhere and was heading towards him. He was aware of dazzling square headlights approaching. He glanced over his shoulder and saw that there was no traffic behind. The car was approaching far too fast. He stepped over on to the left side of the road in order to avoid it. Suddenly it swerved towards him. He was momentarily aware of the dazzling square headlights and a gold lion mascot as he threw himself out of the way into the rough grass verge. His leg caught the front bumper as he managed to jump clear. The car swerved quickly over to the right side of the road and disappeared through the village. He lay in the rough grass and listened to the roar of the engine fading away into the distance.

It was some time before he realized what had happened. Whoever had been driving the car had clearly intended to kill him. It hadn't been any accident. He lay on the verge and nursed his leg. The blow didn't appear to have broken the skin, but it felt badly bruised. He got up and hobbled towards a wall on the other side of the grass. The combination of the shock and the wine had made him feel sick. He leant over the wall and retched. He was aware of the ground swerving under his feet and the wall reeling in the opposite direction before he passed out.

He must have been unconscious for some time because the next thing he remembered was feeling cold. He could hear lorries thundering past and his head was splitting. He appeared to have been sick. His mouth tasted sour and his shirt smelt of vomit. He tried to stand up but his leg wouldn't support him. He bent down and felt his calf. It was badly swollen.

He looked at his watch. It was nearly half past eleven. He slowly tried to put his weight on to his leg, but the pain was unbearable. He could see the dark mass of the first house a few hundred yards away. He would have to spend the night there. He began to hobble towards it.

It took him nearly a quarter of an hour to reach the house. The key turned stiffly in the lock and the door opened reluctantly. The house felt cold and unwelcoming. He switched on the light. A printed envelope lay on the doormat. It was an invitation for him to join some credit card scheme. He glanced at it for a second before tearing it up. The irony of the situation amused him. He had risked his life for some printed circular.

He rested for a moment on the old settle. The whole thing had been planned. Someone had deliberately attempted to kill him. And what was more, the postmistress must have been involved. She had told him not to go along the back way to the house. She must have known that the car would be waiting for him. It had swung out from the side of the road, but there were no side roads there. Someone had been sitting there, waiting for him to come along. Waiting to kill him.

He shivered and suddenly felt very lonely. He realized that he should ring Elizabeth. Apart from anything else, he hadn't told her that he had moved. He got up and put through a call. The lines were clear and he was connected straight away.

The phone rang for some time before it was finally answered.
'Hallo?'
Tony realized with a sinking feeling that it was Elizabeth's mother who had answered.
'Hallo?' she repeated.
'It's Tony speaking. Is Elizabeth there?'
'Tony?'
'Yes.'
'It's very late to ring. Do you realize what time it is?'
'Yes. I'm sorry. Is Elizabeth there?'
There was a pause before she answered. Her voice was cold and unfriendly. 'No. She's out.'
'Where has she gone?'

'She's gone out to dinner. I'm afraid I don't know who with. I was in bed. Is anything the matter?'

Tony realized that there was no point in trying to explain to her that someone had just tried to kill him. 'No,' he replied. 'I'm sorry to have disturbed you. Could you tell Elizabeth that I will ring her tomorrow evening about seven. Do you think that she will be at home?'

'I have no idea. But I will give her your message.'

He was about to thank her when she put the phone down. He sat thinking for a moment in the dark room before slowly making his way upstairs.

The traffic woke him at about eight o'clock. His leg was stiff and badly bruised. He sat up on the side of the bed and gradually put his weight down on the injured leg. It supported him. No serious harm appeared to have been done. He limped over to the window and opened the shutters. The hot morning sun poured into the room. He leant out of the window relaxing in the warmth on his body. The village lay peaceful and serene on his right. He could see the church spire rising above the conglomeration of roofs. The ugly modern roof of the post office appeared slightly higher than all the rest. He pictured the postmistress attending to her work behind the counter and wondered whether she had given any thought to the English writer who she no doubt thought was lying dead in the ditch by the side of the road.

He hobbled into the bathroom and ran himself a bath. He lay soaking in the relaxing hot water. He could feel it easing the pain in his leg. It was lucky that the blow had not broken the skin. There was just a large angry bruise.

He had left some coffee in the kitchen and half a loaf of bread. It was stale, but the coffee refreshed him. The long soak in the hot bath had relaxed him, and he felt much better when he had eaten. He locked up the house and walked back along the main road to the village.

The car seemed to have come from somewhere on the right. He walked slowly through the long grass at the side of the road.

He hadn't gone far when he found the place. A gate led into a field. There were tyre marks in some soft earth by the gate which had been left open. The marks were deep. The car had obviously been waiting there for some time. The field was empty and totally enclosed. There were no buildings around. Something caught his eye on the ground by the gate. It was a thin cigar butt lying in the long grass. There was another one a few feet away. He bent down and searched amongst the grass. He found five altogether. The driver of the car must have been there for some time, waiting impatiently and smoking his cigars. One butt was much longer than the others. The others had been stubbed out, but this one had been discarded while still alight. The grass had been slightly singed where it had fallen.

Tony smiled to himself. He would give the postmistress a little shock this morning. He would call in on his way home and buy himself some stamps. He wondered how many other people in the village were involved in the plot to kill him. And why? What reason could they possibly have for wanting him out of their way?

He began to walk towards the village. A woman appeared at the door of her house and watched him go past. He was conscious that people glanced at him as he crossed the square. Or was it just his imagination? His presence was bound to arouse some local interest. It wasn't often that a total stranger came to settle in the village.

There was nothing to eat at the house. It was time that he began cooking for himself. He had to get down to work, and couldn't always be running down to the hotel. He went into the small supermarket and bought some food. The people in there smiled at him and wished him good morning. They appeared pleased to see him and asked if he were settling in well. He found it hard to believe that they could have wished him any harm.

But the postmistress was a different matter. He was interested to observe her reaction.

She was busy writing when he entered the post office. Her head was bent down over a mass of papers. He waited patiently at the counter.

Eventually she looked up. Tony could see that she was surprised to see him. He fancied that she looked confused but relieved. After a moment's pause, she smiled at him.

'Thank you very much for telling me about my mail last night,' Tony said. 'But I would be grateful if you could see that it doesn't happen again. It is rather a nuisance having to walk all the way up to that house.'

The postmistress nodded. 'Of course,' she promised. 'I am very sorry. I can assure you that it won't happen again.' And from the tone of her voice, she appeared to mean it.

Tony bought some stamps in order to write to Elizabeth. He was putting them in his wallet when someone behind him spoke.

'Good morning.'

He turned quickly. It was the woman who had come to the house yesterday. She was smiling at him. 'Good morning,' she repeated.

'Good morning.'

'I see that you have been shopping, too.' She was carrying a large bag of groceries.

'You seem to have bought rather more than me,' Tony smiled. 'I'm sorry. I didn't introduce myself to you yesterday. My name is Tony Grainger.'

'And mine is Marie Desroux.' She opened her bag and handed the postmistress some papers, which were stamped and returned to her with some money. Tony was not familiar with the French social services, but it appeared that she was drawing some kind of benefit. She smiled at him again as she moved towards the door.

'Let me carry your bag for you,' Tony offered. 'It looks rather heavy.'

'Yes, it is. Thank you very much.'

They walked together up the lane.

'Why did you come here?' she asked. 'Laurac seems a strange place for a young man like you.'

'I needed peace and quiet, and my wife found an advertisement for a house here. But it was too noisy to work in.'

'Yes. I know that house. The people who own it have had a lot of trouble letting it. Last year it was let to some holiday people, but they were unhappy there. It is a great pity because the house itself is nice. Are you finding that you can work where you are? This side of the village is very quiet and peaceful.'

'Yes. I think this new house will be perfect for me.' He paused for a moment before continuing. 'Did you know Madame Malines?' he asked.

'Yes,' she replied. 'Is your wife not coming out to join you?'

'No. She seems to think I would work better alone. I don't really think Laurac would be quite her scene.'

The woman laughed. 'I can quite understand that,' she said.

'And you live here all the time?' Tony asked.

'Yes.'

'Have you always lived here?'

'No. I used to live in Paris.'

'This must be quite a contrast.'

'Yes, it is.'

They had reached his gate.

'Thank you very much for carrying my bag,' she said. 'I can take it now.'

'Won't you let me carry it home for you?'

She shook her head. 'No, thank you. I don't have far to go. I can easily manage.' She held out her hand. 'Goodbye. I hope your book goes well.'

'Goodbye.' He stood and watched her go. She had a quality of direct simplicity that he found attractive. He turned and walked slowly up the path to his house. The girl was in the kitchen. She looked up quickly as he came in. 'You didn't sleep in your bed last night,' she said.

Tony shook his head. 'No. There was a muddle over some

mail for me. I had to go to that other house. I spent the night there.'

The girl watched him as he crossed the room to put away his groceries. 'You are limping. Have you hurt yourself?'

'Yes. I tripped over something last night in the dark.'

'Let me see.'

'It's nothing.'

'Let me see,' she repeated firmly.

'It's really not worth bothering about.' He pulled up the bottom of his trouser leg. The swelling had almost gone.

'That is a very nasty bruise,' the girl said. 'You should let me put a cold bandage on it for you.'

'No, thank you. It really isn't necessary.' He shook down the trouser leg. 'I must go and work now.'

'I brought you some pâté from the hotel. It is quite nice. I thought you would like it.'

'You shouldn't have done that.'

'Why not? They often give me things.'

'But you mustn't give them to me. What about your mother?'

'I gave her some, too. But I wanted you to have it as well.'

'That was very kind. If you will excuse me, I must go and work.'

'You will be sleeping here tonight?' the girl asked.

'Yes.'

She looked pleased. 'I will bring your breakfast up.'

'Thanks.' Tony smiled at her as he left the room. The girl smiled back at him.

He slowly climbed the stairs to his bedroom. 'What a bloody nuisance,' he thought to himself. 'She's got a crush on me. And I can't think of any woman that could attract me less.' He crossed to the large windows, opened them and went out on to the small balcony.

It was all so peaceful and beautiful. He looked across the field of barley to the house amongst the trees. He pictured Marie Desroux moving about in her kitchen. She must have done all her week's shopping at one go. He had liked her. When she had smiled, she had been almost beautiful. He wondered why she had left Paris to come and live here.

He turned and looked over to his right towards the village. He could just see an occasional roof through the trees. It was hard to believe that anyone there could wish him harm. And yet it was true. Someone in that village wanted him dead. They had already tried to kill him once. He realized that they would no doubt try again.

6

The hotel dining-room had been packed for lunch. The sunshine had attracted the tourists as well as the usual local trade. The girl had been kept busy washing-up and preparing the vegetables and running backwards and forwards between the dining-room and the bar for drinks. It was nearly three o'clock before she had finished her work. She sat exhausted at the large kitchen table drinking a bowl of soup.

'You're late. Have you been busy?'

Her mother stood at the door. She was holding a bag of washing.

'I want you to take these sheets to Mademoiselle Desroux. There's no need to disturb her. She's expecting them. Just leave them outside the door.'

The girl nodded.

'And on your way back, I want you to collect another bundle from the Mairie. They've put up some new curtains there and they want the old ones washed.' She put the bag on the table. 'And don't be long about it. I want to get the curtains done as quickly as possible. It doesn't do to keep the Mayor waiting.'

The girl nodded again.

'Was there anything left over from lunch?'

The girl shook her head. 'I don't think so. We were very

busy. There's a bit of cold turkey left, but they would probably miss it. Everything else got finished.'

The mother shrugged her shoulders. 'Pity,' she muttered. 'We could have done with a bit of that. There's not much at home. Now, don't be long. None of your dawdling.'

The girl watched her mother go before getting slowly to her feet. She picked up the bag and walked to the door of the bar. The patronne and her family were sitting at a table having coffee.

'I'm off now,' the girl said.

No one bothered to look up at her. 'Have you cleared everything up?' the patronne asked.

'Yes.'

'Very well, then. We'll see you tonight.'

The barmaid watched the girl cross the square. 'I don't know why you put up with her,' she said. 'She's always pinching food. How do you know what she's got in that bag she's carrying. It's that mother of hers. She never was any good. I don't mind betting you she took that pâté that disappeared. I don't know why you keep her on.'

The patronne shrugged her shoulders. 'Because she's cheap, that's why. No one else in the village would work for so little money.'

The sun shone fiercely in the cloudless sky. It was fantastically hot. There was no one about. The village was deserted and silent except for the girl's footsteps as she walked towards the crossroads. She felt a sick feeling of longing in her stomach as she turned into the lane that passed the Malines house. Perhaps he would be there again. He obviously liked the sun, because his body was so brown. Every bit of it. He wouldn't be expecting anyone to come past at this time of the afternoon. Everyone would be inside in the cool, behind the closed shutters. But he might be out sunbathing again. Lying naked in the garden. Her pace quickened as she turned the corner.

The garden was deserted. He was nowhere to be seen. The windows of the front bedroom were open. He was probably resting up there. She continued slowly along the lane towards Mademoiselle Desroux's house. As she approached, she walked more slowly than ever. The upstairs windows were shuttered and the house was silent. She put the bundle down on the front doorstep and turned back towards the village.

The Mairie was at the other end of the village past the station. There was a short cut across the fields. There had once been an old footpath that went through the middle of the barley field, but it was seldom used now and had almost disappeared. She had used to wander along it when she was a child. It was ages since she had done so. It would save a great deal of time if it was still there.

It took her quite a while to find the opening in the hedge where the path began. It was obvious that no one used it any longer. The gap in the hedge had almost closed up and the old path was barely discernible between the tall stalks of barley. She edged her way through the hedge and carefully made her way along the narrow path.

It was difficult to walk between the barley. Sometimes the path was totally overgrown. At times the barley was so high, the stalks almost covered her head.

There was a mound in the centre of the field and the path led right over the top of it. She remembered that as a child she used often to lie up there and look down over the village. One morning she had climbed up there very early. It had been a beautiful morning and she had seen Madame Malines open her bedroom shutters. She had been wearing her nightdress and she had stood at the open window for a moment before getting dressed.

The hill was higher than the Malines' house, and the girl had been able to look right down into Madame Malines' bedroom. She could see the bed through the wide open windows. Madame Malines had seen her watching her and had waved angrily at her to go away before slamming the shutters.

But no one would be able to see her now. The field had just been grass in those days, but now she was almost invisible amongst the tall barley. She was nearly out of breath as she made her way up the slope pushing a path for herself between the stalks.

She was exhausted when she reached the top. She paused for a moment to look about her and regain her breath. There was a little natural clearing at the top of the hill where the ground was stony and the barley hadn't grown. She lay down in the hot sun and looked down over the village. It was a peaceful place to be, away from everyone. She could rest there and look at the view. She turned and looked down at the Malines' house directly below her.

The bedroom windows were wide open and the sun was shining straight on to the house. She could see right into the bedroom. He was lying on his back on the bed fast asleep and stark naked. She felt a stab of excitement in her stomach as she gazed at his body. She had never seen a naked man before; never seen anything so exciting and so beautiful.

Tony stirred in his sleep. He had been dreaming about Elizabeth. It had been a strange dream. A disturbing confusion of violence and passion. They had been making love, but there had been blood. They had cried together, sometimes in ecstasy and sometimes in terror. He had taken her, and she had lain underneath him crying with excitement as he had plunged deeper and deeper into her. But there had been this blood. It had been everywhere and she had gone on crying. It was her cries that had woken him up.

The sun was streaming into the room on to the bed. He stretched luxuriously in its warmth and remembered his dream. He wanted Elizabeth there beside him. His body longed to penetrate her softness. He ached with the need to release his strength into her soft darkness. He lay naked in the sunlight and it was some moments before his body quietened.

He had awakened feeling worried. A dull feeling of anxiety was nagging at him. It was some time before he remembered.

He had gone into the study to write. A plot was beginning to emerge in his mind, and he had gone there to draft its outline.

He had left his pens and papers in the centre of the desk, but they had been moved. He had also put some books in one of the drawers. When he had opened it, he had found that they too were in a different place. Someone had been through the desk while he had been away.

There seemed only one person who could have done it, and that was the girl. But why should she search through his things? Somehow he didn't believe that she would have. But then who else could it have been? It had made him feel anxious and uneasy.

He looked at his watch. It was almost five o'clock. He had slept all afternoon. His leg was much less painful and the swelling nearly gone. He got up and dressed.

The outline of an idea was forming in his mind. The long sleep had refreshed him. He felt that a walk through the fields would do him good. He could call in at the other house and telephone Elizabeth.

He went round the house shutting all the windows and locking the doors, taking the keys with him. But he was half-way down the lane before he realized that there had not been much point. Anyone who wanted to get in could simply climb in through the study window. He must remember to get the clasp repaired.

It was a glorious evening and he walked for miles along the river bank. It was past eight o'clock when he finally reached the other house. He was lucky again with the telephone lines and didn't have long to wait. The line was very clear and Elizabeth sounded pleased to hear his voice.

'You don't know how lucky you are,' she said. 'It's pouring with rain here and there seems to be every chance of some engineering strike which will stop all the trains. I really fail to see the point of living in this country any longer. What's it like where you are?'

'Perfect. The weather is glorious and I've found myself another house which suits me much better. I think I've found myself a story, too. The only thing I miss is you.'

Elizabeth laughed.

'Why don't you come out here and join me?' Tony asked. 'I could still work. We wouldn't be in each other's way.'

'It certainly sounds tempting. Mother wants me to go and stay with her for a bit, but I don't particularly want to. Susan's off to the Algarve soon and has asked me to go with her, but I don't really feel like that either. She's having a party on the twentieth before she leaves and I've promised to go to that. Perhaps some time in France might be a good idea. I'll have to think about it.'

'I'll ring you again in a few days.'

'Yes. Do that. Goodbye.'

'Goodbye.' He heard her put down the receiver.

He locked up and set off across the fields to the Malines' house. It would be a change from going through the village and it should also be quicker. But he hadn't gone far before he realized his mistake. The railway line to Albi crossed his path, passing through a deep cutting, so that he had to make a wide detour, causing him to lose his bearings. He had been walking for about half an hour before he saw what seemed to be a familiar landmark. It was the roof of Marie Desroux's house nestling among its trees. He had not recognized it at first because he had approached from the opposite direction. The house was silent with the upper windows shuttered, but the front door was open.

He went up and knocked. There had been something attractive about her. He felt he would like to get to know her better. Perhaps take her out to dinner somewhere.

There was no reply. He knocked again more loudly. There was still no answer. He looked inside. The door led straight into a large living-room with a view right across the valley. It was a gay feminine room, totally different from the pretentious stuffiness of the Malines' house. It seemed to reflect the simple charm of its owner. But the room was empty. Marie Desroux appeared not to be at home, although she surely couldn't be far away with the front door left wide open.

He was just about to leave when something caught his eye.

There was a photograph on a small table by the door. It was of Marie Desroux. She was smiling gaily at the camera and leaning against a car. Her arm lay along the bonnet and her hand was on the lion mascot. There was no mistaking it. He could never have been mistaken about those aggressive square headlights and that gold lion mascot.

7

'Mademoiselle Desroux?' The woman at the supermarket looked up from her till. 'But of course I know her. She is one of our best customers. She comes in nearly every day.'

'Has she been in today?' Tony asked.

'Not yet. She usually comes in the afternoon. She'll certainly be in later because we have a delivery of her favourite kind of biscuits and she likes to buy them fresh.'

'What time do you think she will be here?'

'She usually comes down about three o'clock.'

Tony thanked her and moved to the door. He paused for a moment. 'Does she have a car?' he asked.

The woman shook her head. 'No, monsieur.'

'That's funny,' he said. 'I must have made a mistake. I thought she had a car with a lion mascot on the bonnet.'

It may have been his imagination, but he fancied the woman's face hardened.

'No, monsieur. Mademoiselle Desroux has no car.' She moved to the back of the shop and began to unpack some cases.

'Do you know the car I mean?' Tony asked. 'It also has rather distinctive square headlights.'

The woman went on unpacking. It was some time before she replied.

'No, monsieur. I don't know any car like that,' she finally replied.

Tony thanked her and walked back to the house. It was nearly half past two. Mademoiselle Desroux would be coming past in about half an hour. He brought out a small table and chair and put them in a part of the garden where he would be able to see up the lane. It would look as if he were working when she came past.

She might not own the car that had tried to run him down, but she was certainly familiar with it. One didn't have one's photograph taken leaning against strange cars.

She also appeared to know the Malines' house well. He remembered the morning he had met her. He had heard her footsteps in the shuttered dining-room. The room was full of heavy furniture and it must have been pitch dark in there, but she had walked straight through quite confidently. Surely, anyway, no stranger would enter an unfamiliar house? They might knock at the outside doors, but they wouldn't go in. It was obvious that Marie Desroux knew the house, and knew it well.

One had a good view of the Malines' house from where she lived; he had seen that when he was up there this morning. It was in a slight dip and clearly visible from her windows. She would be aware of all his movements, and could easily see whenever he left the house. She could watch him until he turned the corner towards the village and know that she was free to look for whatever it was that she was searching. It was she who had disturbed Madame Malines' clothes and it was she who had moved his things when he had been sent up to the other house. She had probably arranged it all.

He realized that he would have to get to know Marie Desroux much better.

He didn't have long to wait. He hadn't been sitting there ten minutes before he heard her footsteps approaching. He pretended to be surprised when he saw her.

'Hallo!' He got up and went to the gate.

She stopped and smiled at him. 'Hallo. Are you working? Please don't let me disturb you.'

'Oh, I'm glad of a break. I've already done quite a lot today. I think I've earned myself a rest. Why don't you come in?' He held open the gate for her.

She hesitated for a moment. 'I was on my way down to the village.'

'Surely you can come in for a moment, can't you?' Tony insisted. 'The shops are open until about five.'

She laughed gaily at him. 'Goodness! I can't stay until then.'

'Let me get you something to sit on. I shan't be long.' He went into the house to fetch another chair. He watched her for a moment through the sitting-room window. She had sat down, and was leaning back peacefully enjoying the sun. It was hard to believe that she had been involved in planning his death.

She turned towards him and smiled as he came out of the house. 'Are you settling in all right?' she asked.

'Yes. I'm very comfortable. I've got everything I need.'

'That's good.'

'It's a perfect place to work. Do you know this house well?'

There was a pause before she answered. 'No. Not really.'

Tony glanced at her quickly. Their eyes met for an instant before she looked away. 'You're not a very good liar,' Tony thought to himself.

'What sort of books do you write?' she asked, changing the subject.

'Thrillers.'

'Oh.' She looked vaguely disconcerted. 'I don't read many of them. Perhaps I should. I mostly read the classics. Flaubert and Balzac. Do you know them? I like some English writers. George Eliot for example. I very much enjoyed *Middlemarch*. But I could never read Dickens. I suppose he was too English. I just found him long-winded and boring.'

'I've never read him either,' Tony said. 'Except for an abridged version of *A Tale of Two Cities* when I was at school.'

She smiled. 'I thought every English writer would like Dickens.'

'I'm afraid I'm not that kind of writer. What made you come here after Paris?'

She leant down and began to fiddle with the strap of her shoe. 'I had to. There were some things I had to look after.'

'Do you like it here?'

'I don't mind it. It's rather gloomy in the winter. But I don't mind it.'

'Your house seems pretty.'

She looked up sharply at him. 'But you haven't seen it,' she said.

'I can see it from here. It looks very pretty up among the trees.'

'Oh.' She seemed to relax again. 'You must come up one day. Not at the moment. I'm having it decorated.'

'Another lie,' Tony thought to himself. There were no traces of decorators when he had visited it.

'When I've had it done, you must come and see me. Come and have a meal.'

'I should like that.'

She glanced at her watch. 'I must be going,' she said, getting to her feet. 'It has been nice to talk to you.'

'I've got an idea,' Tony said. 'Decorators can be an awful nuisance. Why don't you let me take you out to dinner tonight?'

She looked uncertain and startled. 'That's very kind. But I couldn't possibly.'

'Why not? Have you got a car?'

She shook her head firmly. 'I couldn't. I really couldn't.'

'Have you got a car?' Tony persisted.

'No.'

'A car came past here a couple of nights ago. I thought it might have been yours.'

She shook her head again. Her eyes were anxious and frightened. 'No,' she replied. 'I have no car. You were very kind to ask me, but I never go out at night. Goodbye.'

JACKDAW

She held out her hand. He took it in both of his.

'My name is Tony,' he said.

She glanced up timidly at him.

'Do I have to call you Mademoiselle Desroux?'

'No,' she replied softly. 'My Christian name is Marie.'

'May I call you that?'

'Yes.'

'Then, goodbye, Marie. I hope one day you will let me take you out to dinner.'

'You are very kind. But I must go. Goodbye.'

He stood at the gate and watched her walk towards the village. He saw her pause uncertainly before turning the corner. She hesitated for an instant and then looked back at him. He smiled at her and waved.

He was still writing when she returned. He put down his pen and went to meet her at the gate.

'I've got some iced tea in the fridge. Would you like some? I know I would.'

'Oh, I'd love some,' she replied. 'But I mustn't stay long.'

'I'll go and bring it out. Sit down and rest. I shan't be long.'

He had had it all prepared. She smiled at him as he put down the tray.

'How well organized you are. I always thought men got into terrible muddles without their wives.'

'Not this one,' Tony replied. 'Anyhow, I've got to get used to that.'

'Why?'

'Elizabeth's mother is ill and can't be left. I have to travel a lot for my work. We have a mutual understanding.'

'It must be difficult for you.'

'I get lonely sometimes,' Tony replied.

She picked up her glass and sipped the tea. 'This is delicious. Thank you.'

'My wife and I love each other very much, but it's hard for us both at present. However, we understand each other. I hope you don't mind my talking to you like this.'

'Of course not. Why should I?'

'You're very attractive.'

Marie glanced up quickly at him and blushed. 'I'm almost twice your age,' she replied.

'We must both be in our thirties.'

She leant back in her chair and laughed. 'What nonsense you do talk! But it's nice nonsense. I haven't been paid a compliment like that for ages.'

'You're not married?' Tony asked.

'No.'

'You're very attractive,' he repeated.

She laughed again and lightly touched his arm. 'You shouldn't tease older women,' she said, getting to her feet. 'And now I really must go, and you must get on with your book. Thank you for the tea.'

'We need a car,' Tony said. 'You must show me the countryside. We can't stay in Laurac all the time. Do you think I can hire one in the village?'

'No. The nearest place is Albi. I'm sure you will be able to hire one there.'

'Can I get there by train?'

'Yes. There are several. There's a fast one in the morning at half past eight.'

'Will you come out with me then?' he asked.

She smiled shyly at him. 'I should like that,' she replied. 'Goodbye.'

'You've forgotten something.'

She began to look about her. 'What?'

'My name is Tony.'

'Of course. I'm sorry. Goodbye, Tony.'

'Goodbye, Marie.'

He held open the gate for her and watched her until she was out of sight. He was smiling as he walked back to the house.

He got up early next morning and was in the kitchen finishing his breakfast when the girl arrived. She looked surprised and reproachful to see him up.

'I'm going into Albi,' he explained.

The girl nodded and went upstairs to make his bed.

He arrived at the station just as the train was pulling in. There were only two coaches. A group of students were climbing into the first coach, pushing and shoving to get through the doors. He saw them running through the coach shouting at their friends who were already in the train. A window was pushed down and one of them stuck his head out and yelled something to his friends who were still climbing aboard. Tony caught sight of a woman's face in the carriage glaring disapprovingly at the youngsters. He could see that she was going to be in for a noisy journey.

He walked along to the other coach. An elderly lady was about to climb up into the train. She was struggling with a suitcase which Tony could see was too heavy for her.

'Let me help you,' he said, taking it from her and lifting it up on to the floor of the coach.

She turned round quickly and smiled at him. 'Thank you. It is rather heavy.' She waited for him to get in. 'Shall I put it up on the rack for you?' he asked.

'That would be very kind.'

There were two empty seats by the window. They sat down opposite each other. The old lady smiled at him again.

'You must be a visitor,' she said. 'I don't think I've seen you before.'

Tony nodded. 'Yes. I've taken a house in the village. I'm a writer.'

'Oh?' The old lady appeared to be interested. 'My husband was a writer. He was the schoolmaster here a long time ago. But he didn't really like teaching. He wanted to write. I was a teacher as well, so we got married. I used to teach and he used to write.' She chuckled to herself. 'I really think that was why he married me. So as to be free to do his writing.'

'What did he write?' Tony asked.

'Rather bad historical novels. One or two were published. He used to get very cross with me because I wouldn't read them. But, you know, I just didn't think they were very good. And there's nothing worse than reading a bad book. I was devoted to him, but I didn't much like the books he wrote.'

Tony laughed.

'And what about you?' the old lady asked. 'What do you write?'

'Thrillers.'

'My goodness! And what brought you to Laurac?'

'Its peace and quiet really. I find London very noisy.'

The old lady nodded. 'Where are you living in Laurac?'

'The Malines' house.'

She looked up sharply. 'You're living there?'

'Yes. Do you know it?'

'But of course I know it. I know it well.'

'Did you know Madame Malines?'

'Naturally.'

'She was murdered, I believe.'

'Yes. It would make a good story for one of your thrillers.'

'What happened?' Tony asked. 'What sort of person was she?'

'I never liked Mathilde. That was her name. She was a most unattractive person. I don't think anyone liked her. She was certainly most unpopular in the village. I was a great friend of her sister. She came to live in the village after Mathilde was widowed. You know, I never understood how Angèle and Mathilde could have been sisters. They were so unlike. I missed Angèle so much when she died.'

'Tell me about Madame Malines. How was she murdered?'

The old lady shuddered. 'Oh, that was a terrible thing. She was stabbed. Over and over again. It was dreadful. But, you know, I think it was partly her own fault. She talked too much. She was boastful and greedy, and she talked too much in the village.'

'What did she talk about?'

'The jewels. Angèle had been given a lot of jewellery. When she was young, she had been in the household of the Empress of Mexico. But I don't expect that you have ever heard of her.'

'Yes, I have. She was married to Maximilian, Franz Josef's

brother, wasn't she? He was created Emperor of Mexico and got himself shot. I remember an old film about it.'

'Very likely. I didn't know there had been a film. The Empress returned to Europe and became insane. She lived in Belgium and didn't finally die until nineteen twenty-seven. Angèle had been a member of her household, and the Empress became very fond of her. When she had to leave, the Empress gave her a great deal of her jewellery.

'Mathilde used always to boast about this. She used to go around the village telling everyone about her wealthy sister. She was so jealous of Angèle. They gave her a nickname in the village. Jackdaw. That's what they called her. Just Jackdaw. Because she always wanted what belonged to other people. She wanted those jewels. And I believe she got her hands on them too, because they were never found when Angèle died.

'When Mathilde was widowed, she made a great fuss about being lonely and on her own. She wrote to Angèle and pleaded with her to come and live with her. If you ask me, it was just so that she could get her hands on those jewels. She had never cared anything for her husband, poor man. She had made his life hell for him. But when he finally died, she made this great display of grief and persuaded Angèle to sell her old home in Belgium and come down here to live with her.'

'In that house?' Tony asked.

The old lady nodded. 'To begin with, yes. But that didn't last long. They had some kind of a row. I don't know what it was about. Angèle would never discuss her affairs with anyone. Anyhow, she bought herself a house nearby and lived there until she died about eighteen months ago. She was one of my dearest friends. I missed her so much when she died. Everyone loved her. They adored her in the village. They only tolerated Mathilde because of Angèle.'

'And she left Mathilde all the jewellery?'

'I don't know what happened. I never saw the will. It was said there was no mention of any jewellery. I don't know who she left it to. I just don't know. What I do know is that no sooner was Angèle dead, but her house was completely ransacked. Turned upside down it was. Before the body was even cold. Mathilde knew that her sister was dying and she wouldn't let anyone go anywhere near her. I remember when I went up to say goodbye, Mathilde refused to leave the room. She sat there in a corner the entire time. Then, when Angèle finally died, a woman from the village went up to prepare the body and she told me that the room had been turned upside down. The mattress had even been unstitched.'

'So Mathilde got all the jewels.'

The old lady nodded again. 'But it didn't do her much good, did it? Everyone knew how much she hated banks. It was one of her pet subjects. Going on about how much money banks made and how much interest they charged. Nothing would ever persuade her to put her money in a bank, she always said. So she kept everything hidden in the house. And that's why she was killed. I know it sounds terrible, but in a way she asked for what happened. She caused her own death by talking too much.'

'And they never found out who did it?'

'No. There was no one who cared enough to pursue the matter. The police made some routine enquiries, and then blamed it on the young hippies who were passing through. It seemed the easiest way out. I suppose it would all make a good thriller for you.'

'Yes, I think it might,' Tony replied.

'You should go and talk to Monsieur Perroton,' the old lady said.

'Who is he?'

'He was a great friend of Angèle's, and he knew Mathilde as well. He lives in Albi. He has a senior job at the Palais de la Berbie, the art gallery there. He could tell you so much more than I could. Angèle never spoke to me about her family, but Monsieur Perroton would know a great deal.' She looked out of the window. 'Here we are. This is Albi. It has been a most interesting journey. I have enjoyed talking to you very much. I hope your book goes well.'

The train came to a halt at the station. Tony helped the old lady with her luggage.

'Can I get you a taxi?' he asked.

'No, thank you. My daughter will be meeting me. There she is waiting by the barrier.'

A woman waved and came towards them. Tony handed her the old lady's suitcase and said goodbye. He watched them get into a car and drive off. He had brought a Michelin Guide with him and had a list of the principal garages. He was able to hire a car very easily. The old lady had told him that this Monsieur Perroton worked at the Palais de la Berbie. It was clearly marked on the map of Albi in the Michelin. He parked the car in a side street by the Place Sainte-Cécile, and walked to the Palais.

An attendant was standing in the entrance. Tony asked if he could have a word with Monsieur Perroton. The man disappeared for some time and eventually came back to say that Monsieur Perroton was busy and couldn't be disturbed.

'Is it important?' the man asked. 'He will be busy all day. Some art experts down from Paris. I can make an appointment for you to see him later in the week.'

Tony shook his head. 'No, it doesn't matter. It's not all that important. I only just wanted to see him for a moment. Do you happen to know his address?'

The man looked uncertain. 'No, I don't,' he replied. 'But if you only wanted a short talk, he always takes his lunch at a restaurant in the Place Sainte-Cécile. It's just a small place, but you can't miss it. It's next door to the Syndicat d'Initiative.'

'What time does he have lunch?' Tony asked.

'Usually about one o'clock,' the man replied.

Tony thanked him and walked across to the restaurant. He booked a table for one o'clock. There was nearly an hour to wait. He wandered across the square to look at the cathedral. The organ was playing as he went in. He sat down at the end of the nave and listened to the music until it was time to go.

The waiter showed him to his table and presented the menu.

He ordered trout and a half bottle of white wine. The restaurant was almost full. It was obviously a popular place to eat. There were several men sitting on their own. The waiter came back with his wine.

'Is Monsieur Perroton here?' he asked.

The waiter pointed to an elderly man sitting by himself in the far corner. 'Do you wish to speak to him?'

Tony shook his head. 'No, thank you. He was a friend of my father's. He wouldn't know me.'

'He is a fine old gentleman,' the waiter said. 'One of our best clients. He always eats here. He is very generous.'

Tony watched him as he ate. Monsieur Perroton looked as if he was in his seventies; a large handsome old man with snow-white hair and a trimmed goatee beard. He looked rather sad and lonely and his clothes were in need of attention. Tony noticed that his suit was old and the cuffs were frayed. The waiters tended to hover around him, making sure that he had everything he wanted. They clearly regarded him as a special customer. He frequently spoke to them, and it was obvious that they were fond of him.

Tony finished his meal and called for the bill.

He walked back to the car. He wasn't quite sure of the way back to Laurac. He needed to find the main road out of Albi to Toulouse. But the streets around the Place Sainte-Cécile were a maze of narrow one-way alleys. It wasn't long before he was completely lost. He was just about to edge his way out of a narrow medieval street into something that gave the appearance of being a main road when his path was suddenly blocked by a large car emerging from a blind alley on his right. He had to slam on his brakes to avoid a collision.

'Bloody arrogant bastard!' Tony swore at the man driving. The car turned quickly into the main road and then swerved off into a side street on the left.

The sun glistened for an instant on the gold lion mascot before the car disappeared down the dark side road.

8

Tony made a quick left turn, just managing to avoid an oncoming lorry. There was a great deal of outraged tooting from the cars behind as he swung out suddenly into the road. It was a narrow one-way street that curved its way between tall medieval buildings on either side. He could just see the car vanishing round the corner ahead of him. An old man emerged from a shop and began to shuffle across the road. He hadn't even looked to see if there was traffic approaching. Tony braked and the old man stopped and stared at him for a moment before continuing across the road.

'For Christ's sake, hurry up,' Tony muttered. The old man finally reached the other side. Tony quickly accelerated and turned the corner. The road lay straight ahead of him for some way, and there were no side turnings, yet the car had disappeared.

He slowed down and looked around him. The old man had not delayed him long enough for the car to have reached the end of the street. The narrow road stretched straight ahead of him, walled in by the unbroken line of tall buildings on either side. 'There must be some way out,' Tony thought. 'Cars don't just vanish.' He slowed down to a crawl, looking carefully at both sides of the narrow street.

He hadn't gone far before he saw the archway on his right with a notice above it. 'Hostelrie Saint-Antoine. Garage.' A narrow lane led into the yard. He drove up the tiny alley-way. The car was parked in a corner of the yard. It was empty. The driver had presumably gone into the hotel. Tony parked in an opposite corner. He took a piece of paper and a pen out of his pocket and made a note of the car's registration number before entering the hotel. The foyer was deserted except for the clerk at the reception desk. He looked up and smiled as Tony approached.

'Good morning, sir. Can I help you?'

'Yes,' Tony replied. 'I'm afraid I've had a slight accident with my car. I was trying to park in a restricted space and I grazed the car in front of me. I made a note of its number. I don't think I did much damage, but I feel that I should apologize to the owner. Do you happen to know if it belongs to anyone here?' He passed across the paper with the registration number.

The clerk looked at it for a moment and then checked it against one of his ledgers.

'Yes. It belongs to one of our regular clients. Would you like me to ring his room?'

Tony shook his head. 'No, thank you. I'm in rather a hurry at the moment. The damage was only very slight. I think I would prefer to write him a note. What is his name?'

'Monsieur Devine.'

'Is he staying long?'

'He is leaving today. He has already paid his bill. But he will be returning as usual next weekend.'

'He stays here a lot, does he?'

'Every weekend.'

'Where does he live? Do you have his address?'

'He lives in Bordeaux. But I am afraid I cannot give you his address. We never disclose our clients' addresses without permission.'

'I quite understand. It's just that I wanted to write him a note of apology.'

'You could leave it with me,' the clerk suggested.

'I haven't got time at present. I'll post it to him. You say he will be back here at the weekend?'

The clerk nodded. 'He has booked the room for next Friday as usual. He always comes every Friday night and leaves on the following Monday morning. This week has been unusual. He has stayed on much longer.'

'He sounds like a man of habit,' Tony said.

'Yes, he is. He always insists on the same room, and gets most distressed if anything is changed. He always has Number Eleven.'

'Does he work here then?'

'I don't know. We don't know very much about him. He seldom eats in the hotel. He leaves quite early after breakfast and usually returns about ten in the evening.'

'How long has he been coming for?'

'Since about the beginning of the year. January or February. Something like that.'

A couple had come into the hotel. The man approached the desk carrying two suitcases. 'You have a reservation for us. Monsieur and Madame Bertrand.'

'Thank you very much,' Tony said. 'I'll write Monsieur Devine a note.'

'Very well.' The clerk nodded and turned his attention to the new arrivals.

A small page-boy had emerged from a cloakroom by the main entrance. The clerk had rung for him to take the luggage upstairs. Tony stopped him as he was crossing the hall.

'Can you tell me the name of the receptionist on duty?'

'Monsieur Vincent,' the boy replied.

Tony pressed five francs into the boy's hand. 'Thanks,' he said. 'Don't tell him I asked. It's just that he has been very helpful to me, and I wanted to know his name.'

The boy nodded and pocketed the coin.

'Is there by any chance a public library here?' Tony asked.

'There's one almost in the centre of the town.' He fetched a map and gave Tony the directions. It wasn't far from the hotel. But it turned out to be very small and contained mainly fiction.

'Can I help you?' a librarian asked. 'You seem to be having difficulty in finding what you want. Did you want anything in particular?'

'Yes. I wanted to do some research about the Emperor and

Empress of Mexico. You don't happen to have anything about them, do you?'

'Not here, I'm afraid. There's not much demand for that sort of thing. I wish there were. It would make my job much more interesting. We can order special books for you, but if you are in a hurry, you would do better to go to Toulouse. They have an excellent Reference Library there.'

Tony thanked him and walked back to the car. The car park was empty. Monsieur Devine had apparently returned to Bordeaux.

He spent the next day in Toulouse. The librarian at Albi had been right. It was a magnificent library. He explained that he was a writer and needed to do some research on the ill-fated Mexican Empire. He was particularly interested in the Empress, he explained. She had apparently lived on in Belgium until nineteen twenty-seven.

They were very helpful and produced several books about the unfortunate imperial couple. He became completely engrossed in their extraordinary story.

The Empress Carlotta of Mexico had been born Princess Charlotte of Belgium, daughter of King Leopold the First. She married the Hapsburg Archduke Maximilian, brother of the Emperor Franz Josef, in 1857 when she was barely seventeen. The early years of their marriage were spent mainly in Northern Italy where Maximilian had been appointed Governor-General of Lombardy and Venetia by his brother. He built himself a castle called Miramar near Trieste.

In 1862, Maximilian was invited by Louis Napoleon, Emperor of the French, to become Emperor of Mexico. Louis Napoleon and his wife, the Empress Eugénie, were attempting to colonize Mexico as a French satellite, and were intent upon defeating the Mexican liberal leader, President Juarez. Under intense pressure from his wife and the Empress, Maximilian agreed to become Emperor, dependent upon support from Louis Napoleon, and Charlotte changed her name to Carlotta as a gesture towards her newly adopted country.

They left Miramar for Mexico City on 14 April 1864.

It became apparent after two years that the venture was doomed to failure. Louis Napoleon, realizing the hopelessness of the situation, begged Maximilian to abdicate, but Carlotta refused to entertain such an idea. The French troops were withdrawn, and the country swung towards the rebel Juarista troops of the President. Maximilian was continually advised to return to Europe, but both he and Carlotta remained determined to fight for their Empire. Eventually, the position became desperate, and Carlotta agreed to return to Europe to beg for support from Louis Napoleon.

She left for Paris in July, 1866 but had the greatest difficulty in persuading Louis Napoleon to see her. She was under tremendous nervous stress and there had been signs that her mind was giving way. Unsuccessful with Louis Napoleon, she left France for Italy, where she attempted to persuade the Pope to support her cause. It was in Rome that her sanity finally collapsed.

She was brought back to Belgium by her brother, who was now King Leopold the Second, and she spent the rest of her long life, a virtual prisoner, in the ancient medieval fortress of Bouchout, just outside Brussels.

Maximilian was finally captured by the Juarista troops and was shot on 19 June 1867. The Empress never regained her sanity. She finally died of pneumonia in January 1927.

Tony had been completely engrossed. He looked at his watch. It was nearly five o'clock. The library would be closing at any minute. The librarian was watching him anxiously. He was the only person there. He copied something down hastily on a piece of paper, before getting up and carrying the books across to the librarian's desk.

'Thank you very much,' he said.

'Were you able to find anything of interest?' the librarian asked.

Tony nodded. 'Yes. Quite a lot.'

'Enough to write your book?'

'Enough for two or three,' Tony replied.

It was late when he got back to Laurac. He poured himself some wine and went upstairs to have a shower. He kept on thinking about the unfortunate Empress shut up in her medieval castle for almost sixty years. Almost an entire lifetime. It was like some fairy story. He turned off the shower and crossed the landing into the bedroom. He didn't bother to dry himself. It was a warm night. He would dry naturally. His wet feet made marks on the carpet as he crossed to open the window. The light was on by the bed behind him. He picked up his glass of wine and sat naked on a chair on the balcony, his feet up on the ornate balustrade.

It was a glorious night. The sky was like soft black velvet interspersed with tiny diamonds. The country was silent except for the continual chirruping of the crickets and an occasional distant bark from a dog in the village. A soft breeze ruffled the barley in the field opposite. It looked as if there was an animal up on the hillside in the middle of the field. He fancied he could see the stalks waving as something moved amongst them. Probably a fox. He got up to pour himself some more wine.

He wanted a woman. He was unaccustomed to a life of celibacy. His body ached with the need to make love. If only Elizabeth were here with him, everything would be perfect. He pictured her lying naked on the bed waiting for him, her legs parted, her eyes taunting, her mouth slightly open. His need was almost unbearable. He realized it wasn't just Elizabeth he wanted. Any woman would do. He looked across at the house amongst the trees. He could see there was a light on upstairs. The shutters had been left open. Marie would be alone there in bed. He could go to her and take her in his arms. He would kiss her mouth and her breasts, and his body would sink itself in hers and he would be content.

But it was not like that. He remembered her smiling and leaning against the car. The car that had been used to try to kill him. The car that belonged to Monsieur Devine. Who was he, and what was her connection with him? He would have to find out, and he couldn't relax until he did. He must get to know her better. He sensed that she was attracted to him. He would take her out for a meal and begin to make love to her. She was considerably older than he was, but she was by no means unattractive.

He shivered in the night air. It was beginning to get chilly. He closed the window and got into bed. He would go down to Marie's house tomorrow and take her out. He might even ask her about the photograph and see what she said.

He looked up at the old wedding picture above the bed. God, the woman was ugly! He shivered as he remembered that he was lying where she had been murdered. She had lain dead in that bed for a week before anyone had come anywhere near her. The woman that no one had liked. That they had called Jackdaw because of her greed. They had all hated her, so no one had cared when she was murdered.

He remembered something the postmistress had said to him. 'Laurac is a small village,' she had said. 'Everyone knows everyone's business.' It would be hard to have secrets in a place like that. Madame Malines had secrets, and she had gone around the place boasting of them. And her greed had been her downfall. So no one in the village had cared. They hadn't minded that she had been stabbed to death. But nevertheless they didn't like to talk about it. The woman at the hotel had been angry with the old man for gossiping. Why should they be so reluctant to talk, he wondered. The girl's mother had abused him for asking questions. Why? There could only be one reason. They knew who the killer was. They all knew.

He knelt on the bed and looked at the old photograph. It was incredible to think that the woman's sister had known the Empress of Mexico. He got up and crossed to where he had left his wallet on the dressing table and took out a piece of paper. He had copied something down from the last letter that the Empress had written to her husband. He took it over to the bedside lamp to read it.

'The moment one assumes responsibility for one's destiny,

one does it at one's own risk, at one's own danger, and one is never free to give it up.'

It appealed to him a great deal. She must have written it just before going out of her mind.

He switched off the light and got into bed. It was no time before he dropped off to sleep.

He dreamt about the old woman lying murdered in her bed. He was standing in the room looking at her body. There were people laughing. He looked round and saw that everyone in the village was also there. They were all looking at the body on the bed and laughing. They were pointing at the places where she had been stabbed, and telling him to look.

He turned back towards the bed. But this time the body was naked. A chill of horror passed through him when he saw whose it was.

9

He slept badly that night. The terrifying image of the all too familiar body lying naked and mutilated on the bed kept recurring. He was unable to get it out of his mind. He tossed and turned in the large double bed until the morning light began to filter through the chinks in the shutters. He could hear the village church faintly chiming in the distance. He put out his hand and looked at his watch. It was seven o'clock.

He knew that he wouldn't be able to sleep and he didn't want to read. His mind was active. It was always like this when he was planning something. He had been fascinated by the story of the Empress Carlotta, and he was certain that there were more things that he needed to know. What were these jewels that everyone talked about? Why should the Empress have given them to Madame Malines' sister? How many jewels were there? Or was it just rumour that had got exaggerated out of all proportion by jealous village women? He needed to find out. But first he needed to talk to Elizabeth.

He got up and opened the shutters. It was another perfect morning. He would go over to the other house and telephone her. He desperately needed to hear her voice, and the lines to London should be almost clear at this time of the morning. She might be a bit fed up about being woken up so early, but it would be nearly eight o'clock, and she was usually awake by then.

He turned on the radio and listened to the World Service of the BBC while he dressed. England appeared to be in rather a bad way. There had been freak storms all over the Home Counties, and as if that were not enough, a national train strike had been declared. The roads in and out of London were totally blocked by mile-long queues of traffic. It all sounded perfectly bloody. He felt sorry for Elizabeth having to be there. But that was nonsense. She didn't have to be in London. She could easily come out here. Laurac might not be stimulating, but it was peaceful and the weather was perfect. She could lie and sunbathe in the garden while he worked, and then in the afternoons they could drive around exploring the countryside. It would be much better for her than being cooped up in London while it poured with rain.

He took the short road to the house and put through a call. He was right. The lines were free. He was connected almost straight away. He listened to the phone ringing in the flat. She must be asleep or in the bathroom. It went on ringing for about ten minutes before he was prepared to accept that she was not at home. He looked at his watch. Not yet eight o'clock. And today's date was the twenty-first. She had promised to go to Susan's party on the twentieth. She would never have missed that. It was possible that she might have gone down to stay with her mother, but he thought it unlikely. She never liked going there, and would always find some excuse if she could. She might be ill, Tony realized. But then someone would have sent him a telegram. He had given her his new address. He paused for a moment and then rang Susan.

The phone rang for some time before it was finally answered, Susan's voice was bleary with sleep. He had obviously woken her up.

'Susan?'

'Yes?'

'It's Tony. Tony Grainger.'

'For Chris'sakes! Where are you ringing from? I thought you were in France.'

'So I am.'

'You're ringing from France?' She sounded incredulous. But much more wide awake. 'What's the matter? Has something happened?'

'I believe you had a party last night.'

'That's right. So what?'

'Was Elizabeth there?'

There was silence at the other end of the line. It was quite some time before she replied.

'Yes. Why?'

'She doesn't appear to be at home. I've rung the flat and there's no answer. I thought she might have gone down to her mother's.'

'She might have,' Susan replied. But her voice sounded unconvincing.

'Do you know where she is?' Tony asked.

'No idea.'

It was some time before either of them spoke.

'Well, thanks, Susan. Sorry to have woken you. If you do happen to see her, ask her to get in touch with me, will you. A letter only takes about a couple of days.'

'Yes, of course I will.'

'Was it a good party?'

'Not bad.'

'Did Elizabeth enjoy it?'

'I think so.'

'Good. Well, goodbye Susan. Sorry to have troubled you. Hope you have a lovely holiday. It's the Algarve, isn't it?'

'That's right.'
'Goodbye.'
' 'Bye, darling.'

He crossed to the window and stood for several minutes looking out at the flat fields before closing up the house and walking back to the village. He walked slowly, unaware of his surroundings. It took him nearly half an hour to reach the cross-roads. He turned down the lane towards the Malines' house.

But he couldn't face going in. The girl would be there, simpering reproachfully at him because he hadn't had his breakfast. There was something about her plain vacant face that irritated him enormously.

She would be creeping around the house now. She always wore a soft pair of slippers and had an infuriating habit of suddenly appearing in front of him when he least expected it. He could sometimes hear her padding about upstairs when he was working in the study. He had often wondered what she was doing up there. Poking about in the upstairs rooms and attics. Was she looking for something? Something like the jewellery that had belonged to the Empress of Mexico? Was it she who had been searching through Madame Malines' drawers and cupboards?

He walked past the house and continued on up the lane. He was deep in thought when he heard his name being called.

'Tony!'

He paused and looked up. Marie was at one of her upstairs windows.

'Tony!' she repeated. 'I've called at you twice, but you didn't hear me. You were lost to this world. Good morning.'

'Good morning. I'm sorry.'

'You must have been thinking about your book. Is it going well?'

'Not bad,' he replied. 'I'm getting quite a few ideas.'

'How exciting it all must be. Have you had breakfast?'

He shook his head. 'No, not yet. I've been ringing up Elizabeth.'

'How is she?'

'Her mother is much worse. They seem to think she could die at any time.'

'Oh dear, I am sorry. Let me make you some coffee. Wait there. I'll be down in a moment.'

She disappeared from the window. Tony stood and waited outside the house. It was some time before she opened the door. She stood aside to let him in.

He stepped into the room and looked about him. There was nothing on the small table by the door. The photograph had been removed.

'Sit down.' Marie pointed to a large comfortable chair by the fireplace. 'I'll go and make some coffee. I shan't be long. Would you like something to eat?'

'No, thank you.'

She went into the kitchen next door and began to lay a tray.

'Have the decorators gone?' Tony asked.

There was no reply. He heard her shut a cupboard door. Eventually she came back into the room.

'I'm sorry. What did you say?'

'I asked if the decorators had gone.'

It was some time before she answered. 'Yes. They've gone.'

'This room hasn't been done, has it?'

She shook her head. 'No. They had to do a room upstairs.' There was the sound of a kettle boiling in the kitchen. 'Excuse me, will you?' she said. 'I must make the coffee.'

He looked around the room when she had gone. The walls were hung with old prints and photographs. There were two gaps on the opposite wall. He got up and crossed the room. His suspicions were confirmed. Two pictures had recently been taken down. He could see their marks clearly on the coloured wallpaper. There were also the holes in the wall where the nails had been. He had not noticed any gaps there when he had last been in the room. He was certain of that, because it was the sort of thing that would have immediately attracted his attention. He remembered that she had taken some time to open the door. She must have removed the pictures then. But why? he wondered.

Marie came in carrying a tray which she put down on a table.

'Do you like milk?'

'Thank you.'

She poured out the coffee and took it across to him.

'I'm so sorry to hear about your wife,' she said. 'It must be miserable for you.'

'I miss her a lot,' Tony replied. He looked around the room. 'This is charming. How long have you lived here?'

'Nearly two years now.'

'What made you come to live in Laurac? Didn't you say that you used to live in Paris?'

'That's right. I had to come here. I have some relatives. They are all on their own. I have to look after them.'

'Do you like it here?'

She smiled sadly. 'I don't think I would exactly choose it, but sometimes one has no choice. One misses the stimulus of Paris. And the excitement.'

'There appears to be no lack of excitement here,' Tony said.

'Oh? What do you mean?'

He shrugged his shoulders. 'Well, there was the Malines' murder.'

She looked at him intently for a moment before replying. 'Oh that. That's over and done with.'

'How long ago did it happen?'

'I've really no idea. I can't remember.'

'Did you know her?'

'Who?'

'Madame Malines.'

'Yes. I knew her. Would you like some more coffee?'

'No, thank you. What was she like?'

'Why are you so interested in her? All that is finished with now. Can't we talk about something else? Something interesting. Like your book. Tell me how it's going. Or would you prefer not to talk about it?'

'I don't mind,' Tony replied.

'What is it about? Or shouldn't I ask?'

'Have you ever heard of the Empress Carlotta of Mexico?'

Marie got up and put her cup back on the tray. 'Are you sure that you won't have another cup?' she asked.

'Positive. Thank you.'

'Then I'll put them back in the kitchen.'

He sat and waited until she returned.

'Well, have you?'

'Have I what?'

'Have you heard of the Empress Carlotta of Mexico?' Tony repeated.

She went and stood by the window with her back to him. 'Yes. I've heard of her,' she replied. 'Is that what your book is about?'

'I think so.'

'Is that why you came here?'

'No. Why should it be? What possible connection could there be between Laurac and the Empress of Mexico?'

She suddenly turned and faced him. 'Don't you know?' she asked.

Tony shook his head. 'Is there any?' he asked.

She turned away from him again and looked out of the window. He could see the Malines' house clearly. From upstairs one could probably see right into the front bedroom. 'Do you want us to be friends?' Marie asked.

'Yes, of course. Don't you.'

She nodded.

'Well, then. Why did you ask?'

'Because I don't want you to ask me any more questions, that's why. I just want us to be friends. I don't want all these questions.'

'I'm sorry.' He moved behind her and held her gently by the elbows. He felt her body stiffen at his touch.

'Please,' she whispered. 'Don't.'

'I like you, Marie. I like you very much.'

She kept her body rigid. 'I like you, too,' she replied softly. 'But you mustn't. Your wife. You're married.'

'She knows and understands,' Tony murmured. 'I've told you about her. And she knows about you. About how much I like you. She was glad. She knows that I'm lonely.'

He felt her body relax a little. 'Did she really say that?'

Tony nodded. 'She said she would have liked to have met you. She was glad that we could be happy together.'

'She really said that?' Marie asked.

He gently moved his hands and covered her breasts. 'Yes,' he whispered. He held her close to him and could feel her resistance weakening. Her body was limp in his arms. 'You're very beautiful,' he murmured.

She shook her head. 'I'm not beautiful. Really I'm not.'

'I want you.'

She gave a little whimper. 'No,' she whispered. 'No.'

'Why not? I want to kiss you. Want to love you.'

'No,' she repeated, struggling slightly in his arms.

He gently began to kiss her neck. His tongue flickered inside her ear. 'Let's go upstairs,' he whispered.

'No!' She broke away from him and leant against the wall. 'No. We mustn't. It wouldn't be right. There's your wife. And apart from that, it wouldn't be right.'

'Why not? I've told you Elizabeth understands.'

She shook her head. 'It isn't only that. It would be wrong.'

'But why? What can possibly be wrong in a man and a woman making love? I've told you, I like you very much. And I want you.'

'It isn't possible. You don't know me. And I'm much older than you.'

'What possible difference does a few years make?'

She turned and smiled at him. 'A great deal, Tony, I'm afraid.'

He moved forward and took her in his arms. This time she didn't resist. He kissed her over and over again. 'I want you,' he persisted.

She shook her head. 'No. Not yet,' she whispered. 'Please don't ask me again. Not yet.'

'Why not?'

She sighed and broke away from him. 'Don't ask me.'

'Why not? Is there someone else?'

She shook her head. 'Oh, no,' she replied. 'No. There's no one else.' She gave a little ironic laugh.

'Well, then?'

'Please, Tony. We must wait. Don't ask me any more questions. Please trust me, and wait.'

'I don't understand. What is it that we have to wait for?'

She looked up at him, her face grave and sad. 'Please, no more questions,' she pleaded. 'Please. If you care for me at all, don't ask me questions, because I can't answer them. I can only ask you to trust me and wait.'

'What for?' Tony wondered. 'Very well,' he replied. 'No more questions.' He moved to take her in his arms again, but she slipped away.

'I have to go down to the village,' she said. 'There are some things I have to get.'

'May I come with you?'

She looked up quickly and smiled. 'I'm afraid it wouldn't be very interesting for you.'

'I would enjoy your company. Anyway, I've got a car now. We could go for a drive somewhere. Let me take you out to lunch.'

She looked uncertain. 'I don't think I can do that. I would love to, but I don't think I should.'

'For God's sake!' Tony said impatiently, but she interrupted him.

'Please don't be cross. I asked you to be patient. Please, Tony, don't be cross with me. I couldn't bear that. Things are difficult for me at present, and I can't explain. You could take me to lunch here. I should like that so much.'

'At the hotel here?'

She nodded. 'I really would enjoy that. You've no idea what a treat it would be for me.'

'Oh, very well,' he agreed. 'It's not very good food, you know.'

'Maybe not. But it would be good company. That's what counts. The food would be much less important.' She looked at her watch. 'There's no need to bore you with all my shopping. I can do that on my own. I'll meet you at the hotel at about half past twelve. Will that be all right?'

'That will be fine. I'll book a table.'

'Thank you.' She reached up and kissed his cheek. 'Now, you must go. I've got some housework to do. I'll see you at half past twelve.' She went and held the front door open. 'You've no idea what a treat this will be. To have a meal cooked for me. A real luxury.'

She waited until he had turned the corner of the lane before going upstairs.

The girl was just leaving the Malines' house. She stopped when she saw him coming and waited for him. He cursed her under his breath. He would have missed her if he had been a few minutes later. He forced himself to smile.

'Good morning.'

The girl didn't reply. She stood there looking reproachfully at him. 'Have you had breakfast?' she asked.

'Yes, thanks. Will you be going to the hotel?'

'Later on.'

'Can you book me a table for lunch?'

'For yourself?'

'A table for two. At half past twelve. And ask them to put a bottle of champagne on the ice. You won't forget, will you?'

The girl looked down at the ground and shook her head. 'No, I won't forget,' she promised. 'Is there anything else you want?'

'No, thanks.'

'Then I'll be going,' she said.

Tony nodded and went into the house.

The girl walked slowly down the lane towards the crossroads. Her mother was just finishing the washing when the girl got home.

'You're late,' she said. 'Whatever have you been doing? And you've been crying.'

The girl's eyes were red.

'What's the matter with you?'

'I had to go to the hotel. He wanted a table booked for his lunch. He wasn't in his bed this morning. He wasn't there when I took up his breakfast. He was up with Mademoiselle Desroux. And now he's taking her out to lunch and giving her champagne.' She leant against the wall and began to sob.

Her mother shook her head sternly. 'Don't be so stupid,' she said. 'I don't know what you bother about him for. He's got nothing to do with you. You're making a complete fool of yourself over him. Do you honestly think that a man like that could possibly have any interest in you? For goodness' sake, be sensible. Now, I want you to deliver this washing for me. You won't have time to do it all this afternoon, but you can take the rest round when you've finished at the hotel tonight. And no hanging about either. You may think I'm stupid, but I'm quite aware of what time you've been coming in at nights, and it's got to stop. I don't know what you've been getting up to, but I do know that it's not good. I can tell that by the guilty way you creep in. You don't fool me, my girl. I'm not having that sort of a daughter in my house. If you want to get up to those tricks, you don't do them under my roof. Do you understand?'

The girl left the room, slamming the door behind her.

'Dirty little bitch!' the mother muttered.

The girl walked slowly through the village towards the hotel. When she got to the square, she saw Tony approaching from the direction of the crossroads. He turned suddenly when he noticed her and walked into the church. A sudden blaze of anguish flared up inside her as she realized that he had gone in there purposely to avoid her.

JACKDAW

Tony arrived early at the hotel. He checked that the table had been booked and that the wine was on the ice.

There was a large pile of shopping in the hall. The patronne glanced at it as she came out of the bar.

'Someone's been buying a lot,' Tony said.

The patronne nodded. 'Madamoiselle Desroux,' she said. 'She asked to leave it while she did some errands. She said she would be back at half past twelve. I believe she's having lunch with you?'

'That's right,' Tony nodded. It might have been his imagination, but he fancied the patronne was looking closely at him. She walked past him into the back of the hotel.

He went into the bar for a drink. It was almost empty. A few men who looked like representatives and the old man sitting by himself in a corner. He looked up and waved his stick at Tony.

'Good morning,' he called. 'Are you settling down well in Laurac?'

'Yes, thanks. Can I get you a drink? What are you having?'

The old man nodded enthusiastically. 'I'll have an Eau-de-vie with you.'

Tony ordered the drinks and took them across.

The old man raised his glass. 'They tell me you're a writer,' he said. 'Well, you'll have plenty to write about here.'

'How do you mean?'

The old man chuckled to himself. 'Oh, you'll no doubt find out. You could fill up a dozen books with what's been going on here.'

'Such as?' Tony asked.

The old man shook his head. 'You find out for yourself. It's always best. They all tell me I'm just a foolish old gossip. "Hold your tongue," my daughter says to me. "You talk far too much. And most of it's nonsense." That's the trouble when you're old. No one listens to you. And when they do, they only do it as a duty. You can tell that by the bored looks on their faces.'

'You don't bore me,' Tony assured him.

The old man looked at him closely. 'Maybe not,' he finally said.

Tony took a sip of his drink. 'When was Madame Malines murdered?' he asked casually.

The old man chuckled to himself. 'About the beginning of the year it was. Around the end of January.'

'Monsieur Grainger!' The patronne appeared at the door of the bar. 'Mademoiselle Desroux has arrived. She's waiting in the dining-room. Your table is ready.' She gave the old man a disapproving look.

Tony thanked her and crossed the hall into the dining-room. Marie was sitting at a table by the window. There was a small shopping bag at her feet.

He glanced back at the hall. The large pile of shopping had disappeared. He joined her at the table.

'Were you able to get everything you wanted?' he asked.

She picked up the shopping bag. 'There we are,' she said smiling.

'Is that all you bought?'

'That's all,' she assured him.

The patronne came over with the wine.

'Champagne!' Marie exclaimed. 'Oh, Tony, you shouldn't! What an extravagance! I can't remember when I last had champagne.' She clapped her hands with delight.

Tony handed her the menu. 'What would you like to eat?' he asked. He watched her closely as she studied it. She seemed so open and uncomplicated. And yet she was continually trying to deceive him. And deceive him about such ridiculously unimportant things.

Why should she pretend that she hadn't done a lot of shopping? And it was surely a lie about having had decorators in the house. And why had she removed the two pictures from the wall? And the photograph of her leaning against Monsieur Devine's car?

She glanced up at him and smiled. 'It's so difficult to choose,' she said. 'There are so many delicious things.'

'Take your time,' Tony said. 'There's no hurry.'

He kept on hearing the old man's voice. 'You could fill up a dozen books with what's been going on here.' The old man had said that Madame Malines had been murdered around the end of January.

That was the time that Monsieur Devine had started coming to Albi.

10

He turned off the shower and crossed the landing into the bedroom. It had been a good lunch, and they had both eaten and drunk a bit too much. He had bought another half bottle of champagne and had persuaded Marie to drink quite a lot of it. He had asked her several questions, but had always got the same reply.

'You must trust me and wait.'

It was so hot that his body had dried almost immediately. Perhaps he should close the windows. He realized that quite possibly Marie could see into the room from the upstairs of her house. But so what? All men looked the same. Only some looked better than others. And he had always been told that he was one of the better ones. If Marie objected to the sight of his body, she had only to look away. The room was stuffy and airless with the windows shut.

He lay down on the bed and thought.

'You could fill up a dozen books with what's been going on here.'

Then again, John Dennis's Etonian drawl. 'The first book was so good. It had an excellent quality of ruthlessness. Try for that hard ruthless quality. That's what we want.'

Tony knew the quality only too well. He had been thinking about it a lot during the morning. A germ of an idea was beginning to formulate in his mind, but he needed to know much more. There were still a great deal of things that he had to find out about.

There was a pretentious plaster moulding of flowers around the centre light just above the bed. He stared at it as he thought. Marie had continually lied to him. Silly little lies that he couldn't understand. But whenever he asked her a question, she smiled enigmatically and told him to wait. What was he supposed to wait for? What was going to happen?

The old man knew much more than he was prepared to say. Or did he? Was he just a senile old village gossip? 'Find out for yourself,' he had said. It was precisely what Tony intended to do. But he realized that he wouldn't be able to do it here. No one in Laurac would tell him anything. They were all like the woman in the bar. 'Some things are better left forgotten,' she had said. He would have to go elsewhere. But where? Where else but Laurac? He remembered the old lady in the train. 'Monsieur Perroton would know a great deal,' she had said. Tony realized that he would have to get to know this Monsieur Perroton. But he would have to go carefully. It wouldn't do for the old man to see what Tony was up to.

He had bought himself a guide to Albi when he was there. He looked up the Palais de la Berbie. It was open every afternoon until five o'clock. He got up and dressed quickly.

It was about half past four when he got into Albi.

The attendant at the entrance remembered him. 'We close in about half an hour,' he said.

Tony nodded. 'I know. I just wanted to look at a couple of pictures. I'm writing a book about the Belle Époque, and I need to do some research.'

'Will you be coming in often, then?' the man asked.

'Very probably.'

'Then I should get a student's ticket. Tell the man at the cash desk that you are doing research and he'll probably let you have one. Then you can come back whenever you like.'

Tony thanked him and walked to the desk. He had no difficulty in getting the ticket.

The attendant followed him into the first gallery. 'Wasn't it you who wanted to see Monsieur Perroton?' he asked. 'Would you like me to see if he is free?'

Tony looked uncertain. 'I may have made a mistake,' he said. 'I'm not quite sure whether he is the Monsieur Perroton that we used to know. Is he rather short and dark, with a waxed moustache?'

The attendant shook his head. 'No. Monsieur Perroton has white hair and a beard.'

'It was a long time ago that we knew him,' Tony explained. 'His hair could have gone white. Actually, I hardly remember him. He was a great friend of my father's. Does he have an office here? I might recognize him if I saw him.'

'His office is at the end of the Toulouse Lautrec Gallery. You can't miss it. His name is on the door.' The attendant looked at his watch. 'He usually goes home at around a quarter to five. If you are in the gallery then, you will be able to see him.'

Tony thanked him. He looked at his watch. He would only have a few minutes to wait. He made his way quickly to the Toulouse Lautrec Gallery. The office was at the far end. There were a series of daguerreotypes of the Toulouse Lautrec family by the door. Tony wandered over and appeared to study them.

It wasn't long before the door opened and Monsieur Perroton appeared. He was carrying a shabby brown leather brief-case and had wrapped a long woollen scarf around his throat. He gave Tony a cursory glance as he went past. Tony appeared to take no notice, but watched him intently in the glass of the picture. An attendant got up from his chair as the old man walked past. Tony could hear them wishing each other good evening. He waited for a few moments before leaving.

'Well? Did you see him?' The attendant at the door asked.

'Yes,' Tony replied.

'Was he the Monsieur Perroton you used to know?'

Tony shook his head. 'No. I don't think he was. But I need

to take another look. I'm not quite sure. What time does he get to his office in the morning?'

'Usually around ten,' the attendant replied. 'Sometimes later, but never before.'

Tony thanked him and tipped him five francs. 'Don't mention me to him, will you?' he asked. 'I really don't think he is the same man. Goodbye.'

The attendant touched his cap before closing the doors.

Tony took to going into Albi every day. He would arrive at the Palais at about a quarter to ten and be outside Monsieur Perroton's office when he arrived. He would then book himself a table at the restaurant as near as possible to the table where Monsieur Perroton ate. He would be back in the Toulouse Lautrec Gallery when the old man left his office for lunch, and would go into the restaurant about a quarter of an hour later.

He always tried to give the impression of working during lunch, spreading his books on the table and making notes. He was conscious that the old man had become aware of him. Occasionally he would look up and catch Monsieur Perroton watching him. He would return to the gallery at about half past four, and would be working there when the old man left.

The waiters in the restaurant began to get to know him too. He told them he was writing a book about the Second Empire, and was expanding it to include certain personalities like Toulouse Lautrec. He explained that he usually worked during lunch and needed a quiet table in the far corner of the room.

'Perhaps I could always have the one next to the old gentleman's?' he asked.

'I think Monsieur Giraud is away at present,' the waiter replied.

'Who is Monsieur Giraud?'

'He is a prominent local business man. But I think he is in Paris at the moment. He always likes to have that table when he is here.'

'So I can have it?' Tony asked.

'Certainly,' the waiter replied. 'We will keep it for you.'

Tony worked solidly for the next week. He made friends with most of the attendants in the Palais, and told them all about the book that he was writing. He was aware that Monsieur Perroton had become interested in him, no doubt the attendants had told him what he was doing. The old man didn't speak to him, but he had taken to nodding when they passed in the gallery. Tony felt that it was time to make a move.

He left the gallery early, went into a phone box in the Place Sainte-Cécile and rang up the restaurant.

'I'm speaking on behalf of Monsieur Giraud,' he said, disguising his voice. 'He would like to book his usual table for lunch today.'

There was a pause at the other end of the line. He could sense the waiter's confusion. 'I'm afraid the table has been booked,' he said hesitantly. 'I can offer another table. A very nice one, by the window.'

Tony made his voice sharpen. 'I'm afraid that won't do,' he said firmly. 'Monsieur Giraud asked specifically for his usual table.'

'But I'm afraid it has been booked,' the waiter replied uncertainly.

'Booked? That's impossible. You know Monsieur Giraud always has the same table. Who has booked it?'

'A young gentleman. He is writing a book.'

'Does he live in Albi?'

'No. I don't think so.'

'He's just here for a short time?'

'Yes.'

Tony made his voice sound annoyed. 'And you are prepared to inconvenience a regular client like Monsieur Giraud for the sake of some passing tourist. Very well. I will tell Monsieur Giraud that he can no longer have his table. He will no doubt be able to find another restaurant quite easily. Goodbye.'

'Monsieur! Please don't do that! Of course Monsieur Giraud must have his usual table. We will have it all ready for him.'

'No,' Tony replied. 'He won't want you to lose your tourist

trade. Have you no other tables to offer this young man?'

'He can have one by the door. I'm sure he won't mind.'

'Monsieur Giraud can easily go elsewhere,' Tony said. 'There are several good restaurants in Albi.'

'No, no, no. Monsieur Giraud will have his usual table. It will be all ready for him.'

'Thank you,' Tony replied and rang off.

He was in the gallery when Monsieur Perroton left for lunch. He waited for about a quarter of an hour before going across to the restaurant.

The waiters were all busy when he arrived. He went and sat at the table. He had purposely arrived late, and all the other tables were occupied.

A waiter came out of the kitchen. He saw Tony and hurried to whisper something to the head waiter who was serving by the door. Tony could see them having a consultation together. He helped himself to some bread and began to spread his papers over the table.

The head waiter approached. 'I'm sorry,' he said. 'This table has been booked.'

Tony smiled up at him. 'That's right,' he said. 'By me. I come here regularly.'

The waiter shook his head. 'I'm afraid it has been booked by one of our other clients. A Monsieur Giraud. He has been coming here for many years. I'm sorry.'

'But I booked this table myself,' Tony said loud enough for Monsieur Perroton to hear. 'I've been here every day for the past week.'

The waiter shrugged his shoulders. 'If you would like to wait. There should be a table free in about ten minutes.'

'Ten minutes! I can't possibly wait as long as that. I'm in the middle of working.'

'I'm sorry,' the waiter insisted. 'But you can't have this table. It is booked.'

Tony shrugged his shoulders and slowly began to gather his papers together. 'Where can I eat then? I've been working all morning and I'm hungry. Is there another restaurant nearby?'

'There are several in the centre of the town.'

'But that's miles away! I'm working at the Palais de la Berbie. I can't go right into the town.'

'I'm sorry,' the waiter repeated.

Tony slowly gathered up his things.

'Perhaps Monsieur would care to share my table?'

The waiter turned thankfully towards Monsieur Perroton. He looked enquiringly at Tony.

'Oh, no. I couldn't possibly disturb you,' Tony replied, smiling at the old man. 'It is most kind of you, but I couldn't disturb you.'

'It would be a pleasure,' Monsieur Perroton assured him. 'I would enjoy your company. I think I've seen you in the Palais. I believe you are preparing a book.'

Tony nodded and moved to the old man's table. 'May I sit down?' he asked. 'This really is very good of you. I'm so sorry for putting you to this inconvenience.'

'I can assure you that it is no inconvenience. It will be nice to have someone to talk to.'

Tony sat down. The waiter came and took his order. He ordered an expensive bottle of wine. He had noticed that the old man had nearly finished his small carafe. When the waiter brought the wine, Tony invited Monsieur Perroton to share it with him.

The old man's face beamed with pleasure. 'Château-Laffitte!' he exclaimed. 'You're a very extravagant young man.'

'I'm celebrating,' Tony explained. 'I've been doing some research, and I'm nearly finished.'

'What is your book about?'

'Famous personalities of the Second Empire and later. The Belle Époque.'

'Ah!' Monsieur Perroton savoured the wine carefully. 'It's a long time since I've had a wine like this.'

'It's a period of history that fascinates me,' Tony said.

The old man nodded.

'My grandmother used to know the Empress Eugénie,' Tony continued. 'It was when she was in exile in England. My grandmother had a house near the Empress at Farnborough. They used to go for drives together.'

'Really? How interesting.'

'The Empress used to talk a great deal to my grandmother. She told her many stories about the famous people she had known.'

'Indeed.' The old man continued to sip his wine.

'It was through talking to my grandmother that I became fascinated by the Second Empire. People like Mérimée, Plon Plon, Bazaine.' He watched the old man intently. 'It was a time when so much was happening. Like the fiasco of the Mexican Empire.'

The old man nodded.

'I think it was that that interested me mainly. It is a fascinating story.'

Monsieur Perroton broke off a piece of bread. 'It was a tragedy,' he said quietly. 'A tragedy because of its inevitability. There are great lessons to be learnt from it.'

'Such as?'

The old man looked up at Tony. 'Greed,' he said. 'The Second Empire was a time of great superficiality. Louis Napoleon was a greedy man. And badly advised. The Mexican Empire was based on Greed, and Greed is evil. Maximilian was idealistic and a fatalist. A terrible combination. He was a weak man who allowed himself to be dominated by his wife. The Empress was strong-willed and ambitious. It was all bound to lead to tragedy. In many ways, you know, it was a situation remarkably like that of the last Tsar of Russia. The couples were very similar. And look what happened to them. History is full of these inevitable tragedies. This really is a most delightful wine. I must be grateful to the gentleman who booked your table. I notice though that he hasn't arrived yet.'

Tony didn't bother to turn round. 'You seem to know a lot about history,' he said.

The old man nodded. 'Yes. It interests me. Are you staying here for long?'

'I've taken a house in a village not far from here. You may know it. It's called Laurac.'

Monsieur Perroton raised his eyebrows. 'Yes. I know it very well,' he said.

'It suits me for my writing,' Tony continued. 'I have been lucky and found myself a quiet house. You probably wouldn't know it. I believe it used to belong to a Madame Malines.'

'I know the house well,' the old man said quietly.

'Did you know Madame Malines?'

'Yes.'

'What was she like?'

'A rather unattractive lady,' Monsieur Perroton replied.

'Unattractive to look at?'

'Unattractive in every way.'

'How do you mean?'

The old man shook his head. 'I would really rather not discuss her. She was not a person I cared for.'

'They tell me she was murdered.'

'Please,' Monsieur Perroton said firmly. 'I really do not wish to discuss her.'

Tony refilled the old man's glass. He could see that the wine was beginning to take effect. The old man's eyes were slightly glazed. Tony ordered another bottle.

'There seems to be some extraordinary story in the village about jewellery,' he said. 'I can't make head or tail of it. But it seems to have something to do with Madame Malines.'

The waiter came and presented the wine. Tony took the bottle and waved the man away. Monsieur Perroton had nearly finished his glass. Tony reached across and filled it up. The old man didn't seem to notice.

'Didn't she have a sister?' Tony continued.

Monsieur Perroton nodded. 'Yes. She had a sister.'

'What was her name? Did you know her?'

'Yes. I knew her. Her name was Angèle.' He sat there for a

moment sipping his wine. 'It seems strange your living in that house. How did you find it?'

Tony told him. Monsieur Perroton listened intently.

'So Mathilde left the house to someone in the village,' the old man remarked. 'She always was a spiteful woman.'

It was the second time that someone had said that. The girl had used virtually the same words. He had thought it odd at the time. What could be spiteful about leaving one's house to someone?'

'How do you mean?' he asked.

The old man looked up at him. 'You've given me too much wine,' he said. 'I'm not used to as much as that. I think some fresh air would do me good. You have been very kind, but you shouldn't have given me so much wine.' He looked around the restaurant. They were the only people there. All the other tables had been cleared. The waiters were standing in a group by the wall watching them.

'I think we should go,' Monsieur Perroton said. 'We must have been talking a long time.' He slowly got to his feet. 'I have enjoyed your company very much. It is a great pleasure to talk to someone. I lead rather a lonely life, you understand. My wife died about a year ago.'

'I'm sorry,' Tony murmured. The waiter presented him with his bill. Tony looked at his usual table which was still laid. 'So much for your Monsieur Giraud,' he said.

The waiter looked embarrassed. 'I can't understand it,' he said. 'It is not like Monsieur Giraud to let us down. I am very sorry.'

Tony shrugged his shoulders. 'I suppose these things happen,' he said.

Monsieur Perroton was making his way to the door. He paused outside and waited for Tony.

'I don't feel like going back to my office,' he said. 'Would you care to join me for some coffee? I live just across the square.'

'I would like to very much,' Tony replied. He followed the old man towards a tall medieval building opposite the cathedral.

'I have a flat at the top here,' Monsieur Perroton explained. 'I was lucky enough to find it after my wife died. It isn't big, but it suits me quite well. The only trouble is the stairs. I find it rather tiring going up and down. I take them slowly, I'm afraid. You will just have to be patient with me.'

'Take your time,' Tony said.

The old man led the way into a dark empty hallway which smelt of drains. A horribly deformed young boy was sitting on a wooden chair at the foot of the stairs. He had a huge head and his tongue lolled out of his mouth. He made a sort of gurgling noise in his throat as they went past.

'That's the concierge's boy,' Monsieur Perroton remarked. 'Such a pity. There's a lot of that sort of thing around here.' He slowly led the way up the winding stone stairs.

They paused for breath at the second landing. The old man leant against the elegant iron balustrade. The landings were dark and cold, and the plaster was peeling off the walls.

'It's a pity they don't do anything about the staircase,' Monsieur Perroton said while he regained his breath. 'But the flats are not bad, once one is inside.' He led the way up the last two flights to the top landing.

'This is beautiful,' Tony exclaimed. The landing was in the roof with a tiny dormer window level with the cathedral tower. There was a magnificent view across the clustered medieval roofs and out over the surrounding countryside.

Monsieur Perroton unlocked a door on his right. He led the way into an attic room that was simply but charmingly furnished.

'Take a seat,' he said. 'I'll make some coffee.'

'Let me help you,' Tony offered.

The old man shook his head. 'I know where everything is. I'm quite experienced at looking after myself these days. I shan't be long. Would you like to wash?'

'No, thank you.'

The old man opened a door into a tiny kitchen under the roof.

'It's a delightful flat,' Tony said. 'How many rooms do you have?'

'It's not big. Apart from this, there's just my bedroom and a small bathroom. But it's all I need. The concierge is very good. She keeps it clean for me.' He came back carrying a tray with a coffee pot and two elegant cups. 'It's only this instant stuff,' he apologized. 'I tend not to bother with the other.'

'That's perfect,' Tony assured him.

'Can I offer you some Cognac?'

'No, thank you. But please have some yourself.'

The old man chuckled to himself. 'I don't think I'd better. You gave me far too much wine. It's a long time since I've felt like this.' He poured out the coffee and handed a cup to Tony.

'It's strange your living in that house,' he said. 'Especially as you're a writer and interested in the Empress Carlotta.'

'Why is that?' Tony asked.

'There's quite a strong connection. You mentioned the name of Angèle, Madame Malines' sister.'

'Yes.'

'She became a good friend to the Empress before the old lady died.'

'Really?'

'She was appointed to her household in the Castle of Bouchout, and remained there until a few weeks before the Empress died.'

'But what was all this about jewels?'

'The Empress was a very wealthy woman. She had brought a lot of treasures back with her when she left Mexico. I think she probably brought the Sunburst with her.'

'What is that?'

'Part of the coronation regalia of the Aztec Kings. It was an ancient shield, made entirely of gold. It had originally belonged to Montezuma. There are several old drawings which show him holding it. It was an object of great veneration amongst the Ancient Mexicans. It was known to be in existence before the Emperor Maximilian came to the throne. There is a record of two American explorers having seen it in the cathedral of Mexico City in the middle of the last century. But it disappeared during Maximilian's reign. When President Juarez assumed power, he searched everywhere for it. It was one of the great symbols of the country. But it was never found. It was said that it had been stolen by the Empress and brought to Europe.'

'Why?'

'Because she desperately needed money, and Maximilian was not a wealthy man. His brother, the Emperor of Austria, had made him renounce all his Hapsburg revenues when he assumed the throne of Mexico. When he left Europe he was totally dependent financially on the whims of Louis Napoleon. His treasury was maintained by the French.

'When they withdrew their support, his source of income dried up. The Empress was an extravagant woman, determined to maintain the outward trappings of royalty. She spent great sums on their castle at Chapultepec and held continual audiences rivalling the splendour of her brother-in-law's court at Schönbrunn. All this needed a great deal of money and it had to come from somewhere.'

'But why do you think she stole the Sunburst?' Tony asked. 'What proof do you have?'

'There are records in existence of several journeys made by the Empress to the great Aztec and Mayan temples. In eighteen sixty-five, when her husband's treasury was virtually bankrupt, she visited the sites of Yucatan. One can still see her signature displayed in the visiting book of the hotel there. Again, just before her final departure from Mexico, she spent several days at the temples of Uxmal and Chichen Itza. An odd pastime for a young woman with no great interest in antiquities. She made these visits accompanied only by her husband's private secretary, and a series of confidential letters were dispatched to the Emperor 'for his eyes alone'. After the Empress's visits, further visit was made to each site by a member of the Emperor's most trusted staff. The sites were mostly in very isolated places, hidden deep in thick forests, far from any kind of human habitation.'

'But there was no proof that she took the treasures,' Tony remarked.

'There was some circumstantial evidence,' Monsieur Perroton replied. 'These ancient sites were temples to the Gods, and burial places of Aztec and Mayan kings and nobles. In nineteen fifty-two, an archaeological expedition investigating the sites discovered that relatively recent entries had been made in the floors of several pyramids containing the remains of Inca noblemen. The usual burial treasures were found to be missing. It was calculated that these entries had been made about a hundred years before. The robbers were not just local thieves because the entries had been carefully made and equally carefully concealed. Tomb robbers are notorious for their carelessness. They are so keen to get away with their loot that they never repair the damage they have done. And apart from that, no Mexican would pillage the temples of their ancient Gods. Aztec religious art continually stresses the strong influence of the Gods, and their power over human life. The Mexicans are obsessed by the cult of Death. Anyone stealing from the dead would be cursed for the rest of their life. There is a legend in Mexico that such a person will die violently or be cursed for the remainder of his life.'

'Like the Emperor Maximilian,' Tony said.

The old man nodded. 'And the Empress, too,' He finished drinking his coffee. 'There is an old saying in Mexico that Greed breeds destruction. The Second Empire was based on Greed. And so was the Mexican Empire. And they were both destroyed. As indeed most Empires are. Because most Empires are built on Greed.'

'And Madame Malines was a greedy woman,' Tony said. 'Or so everyone says. And she died violently. You think it was because of the jewels? That she was cursed by the Ancient Gods? Surely not!'

'Stranger things have happened,' the old man replied quietly.

'But it was her sister who actually had the jewellery. Did she die violently, too?'

Monsieur Perroton shook his head. 'Angèle never cared about the jewellery. It was of no interest to her. She died peacefully in her bed.'

'And you knew her?'

'Yes.'

'Did you ever see the jewellery?'

'No. We never discussed it.' The old man smothered a yawn.

Tony glanced at his watch. It was past four o'clock. He could see that Monsieur Perroton was tired. It was time for him to go. He got up and thanked the old man. 'I'm sorry to have taken up so much of your time,' he said. 'It has been most interesting. You seem to have made quite a study of Mexico.'

The old man smiled. 'Yes. It's a fascinating country. I have enjoyed talking to you very much. I hope you will come and visit me again. Do you mind if I don't get up? Can you find your own way down?'

'Yes, of course,' Tony replied, moving to the door. He paused as he opened it. It was a long shot, but it might be worth trying.

'You wouldn't by any chance know a Monsieur Devine, would you?'

The old man looked up sharply. 'You mean Auguste?'

'I don't know his Christian name. He has a large car with a rather unusual gold lion mascot.'

Monsieur Perroton nodded. 'Auguste,' he said.

'Who is he?'

'He was a cousin of the Thibauds.'

'Who are they?'

'Angèle was a Mademoiselle Thibaud. It was her family name. Auguste was her cousin. His mother was their aunt. She was a sister of Madame Thibaud's, and married very well. Auguste's father was a wealthy industrialist in Bordeaux. He's dead now, so Auguste will be well off. Not that it can do him much good. Why do you ask? Do you know him?'

'He tried to run me down once in his car.'

'He is a reckless man. He was unfortunate enough to inherit some of the family's instability. There was a streak of insanity in some members of the Thibaud family. It must have been on the mother's side. He used to have to have periodic treatment. There's a psychiatric hospital here in Albi. He must be having more treatment there.'

'Do you know his address?' Tony asked.

'He used to have a house in the Rue de la Course in Bordeaux.' The old man yawned. 'But it's a long time since I've seen him. I've lost touch. I never really liked him much.'

'Understandable,' Tony thought to himself. He opened the door. Then he thought of something else. The old man had known the Thibaud family and Auguste. He might know the connection between Auguste and Marie Desroux.

'Do you also know Mademoiselle Desroux?' he asked.

But there was no reply. Monsieur Perroton was asleep. Tony tiptoed out of the room and shut the door.

He drove slowly back to Laurac. So Auguste Devine was Madame Malines' cousin. He would know all about the jewellery. He had started coming to Albi just after her death. Tony didn't believe that he came for psychiatric treatment. One didn't have that at weekends. He came to search for the jewels and Marie Desroux was helping him.

He suddenly understood why the girl had said that Madame Malines had left her mother the house out of spite. Normally it would have been left to Auguste. But Madame Malines had been a mean and spiteful person. She had not wanted Auguste to have it. So she had left it to some woman in the village.

But Auguste and Marie knew about the jewels. Marie had virtually admitted this. She had clearly indicated that she knew the connection between the Empress Carlotta and Laurac.

She had given up living in Paris to come to Laurac. And there could be only one reason. She was helping Auguste to find the jewels. She had moved to that house so that she could watch everything that happened at the Malines' house. She would have an uninterrupted view of it from the upstairs windows. It must have been a considerable blow to them when they discovered that it had been let to an English writer. He had found Mademoiselle Desroux searching the house. She had obviously been doing it frequently. He remembered how she had known her way about the dark cluttered dining-room. She could always watch until he went out before continuing her search. Only she had failed to replace his things in their proper places. He had become a nuisance to them, so she had sent for Auguste late one night. Together they had planned to kill him because he was in their way. He remembered that she had been in the post office the following morning; no doubt asking whether the English writer had gone up to the other house. It must have been a shock to her when he had walked in. But she had concealed it well.

He realized that he was dealing with two ruthless people who would stop at nothing to have him out of the way. But they didn't really know him. And they neither of them knew that he had discovered about the jewels. If they were hidden in the house, and they obviously were, he wanted them every bit as much as they did. And he had an advantage. He could look for them without being interrupted.

Marie Desroux was cunning. She had given the impression of being an affectionate unsophisticated woman, and had responded readily to his advances. But she had not been quite clever enough. She hadn't known that he had been in her house before, and had seen the photograph of her against Auguste's car. And she would never realize that he had discovered who Auguste was, and what he was after.

She would not know that he now had the advantage. It was going to be quite a duel. Perhaps even a duel to the death.

11

He was woken up by the girl coming into the room. She put the tray down by the bed and stood for a moment looking at him. He opened his eyes and stretched.

'Good morning.'

The girl smiled shyly at him. 'Good morning,' she replied. 'I'm sorry if I woke you.'

He sat up in the bed and poured out the coffee. 'I'm glad you did,' he said. 'I've got quite a lot to do today.'

'You must have been working hard. You haven't been at home much recently.'

Tony nodded. 'I've had to do some research in Albi. But I think I've finished that now.' He sipped the hot coffee. The girl turned to go.

'Don't go just yet,' he said. 'I want to ask you something.'

'Yes?'

'Do you know Monsieur Devine?'

The girl looked frightened. It was some time before she replied. 'Yes,' she murmured.

'Monsieur Auguste Devine?'

'I think his name is Auguste. Why?'

'Someone mentioned his name to me yesterday. He tried to run me down in his car.'

The girl looked pale. 'I'm not surprised,' she said. 'He is a dangerous man. And violent, too.'

'Who is he?' Tony asked.

'He was Madame Malines' cousin. Her nearest relative. He expected to be left this house. He was very angry when it was given to my mother. He came to our house and made a terrible scene. He was like a madman. He screamed and shouted and we were terrified that he was going to attack us. He made us promise never to live in the house and never to sell it. He paid us a small amount of money on condition that the house should remain empty. Nothing had to be touched. Everything had to be left exactly as it was when the old woman died.'

'I wonder why?' Tony asked.

The girl shook her head. 'I don't know,' she said.

Tony laughed. 'Perhaps it was because of these wild stories about jewellery hidden here,' he said.

The girl shook her head. 'That is all nonsense,' she replied. 'Just local gossip. Why should Madame Malines have all that jewellery? I don't believe it.'

'Did you search the house?'

'Not really. We never believed it.'

'The old man at the hotel said that she got the jewels from her sister.'

The girl laughed scornfully. 'Him! You don't want to believe a word he says. He doesn't know anything. He's just a silly old gossip. Worse than a woman he is. He makes up stories in order to get drinks out of strangers. You don't want to listen to him.'

'He said Madame Malines' sister had worked for some queen. And she had been given her jewellery.'

'A likely story! Why should Mademoiselle Thibaud be given jewellery? Whatever for? And what would she have done with it? She wasn't that sort of person. She wouldn't have been interested in it at all. She was a nice lady. She wouldn't have jewellery hidden away. We never believed all those stories about this mad old queen. It was just some fairy story. Queens aren't mad, and they don't give jewellery away. It's all nonsense. Mademoiselle Thibaud was just an ordinary woman. Why should she have been a friend of some queen?'

'I really have no idea,' Tony admitted.

'There you are, then,' the girl said as she left the room.

Tony slowly poured himself another cup of coffee. It had always seemed odd to him that the Empress should have given her jewellery to Mademoiselle Thibaud. Still, she had been insane, and mad old women do strange things. There must have been some reason for Madame Malines to have gone around the village boasting about her wealthy sister. And Auguste Devine was probably no fool, either. He wouldn't travel to Albi every weekend unless he had a good reason. Nor would Marie Desroux have moved down from Paris without one.

There was no doubt about it. The jewellery was hidden somewhere in the house, and he intended to find it.

He waited until the girl had gone, and then he began to look. He searched every corner of the house, going through all Madame Malines' drawers and cupboards and making a thorough inspection of the two attics. There was a large room over the front bedroom, and a further small one over the bedroom at the back of the house. But both were empty and had obviously never been used.

There was certainly nothing hidden in the house. He searched the floors for any loose boards, but there were none. The only possible place was the garden, and that would be an impossible task. It was large and completely overgrown. He walked round it carefully, looking for any likely hiding places. But he had to be careful. Marie Desroux would no doubt be watching him. He mustn't appear to be doing anything more than just wandering about casually through the long grass.

He found nothing. Madame Malines would have had to hide the jewellery herself. She would never have entrusted the job to anyone else. She was not a big woman. Her wedding picture showed that she was slight and rather delicate-looking. She would not have been capable of digging big holes in the ground. But where could she have hidden everything? Tony realized that it was not going to be an easy job. Auguste was also obviously finding it difficult.

He spent the rest of the day pacing the large garden, but found nothing. Apart from digging the place up, there was nothing more that he could do. It was getting dark when he finally gave up.

He was tired and hungry, and there was nothing to eat in the house. He carefully locked all the doors and windows and walked down to the hotel. On his way he stopped at the supermarket and bought a reel of cotton and some chewing gum. It was a long time since he had spoken to Elizabeth. He booked a call while he was having dinner.

It came through about half an hour later.

'How are you?' he asked.

'All right. It's a long time since you rang. I'd begun to think you'd forgotten all about me.'

'No chance of that,' Tony assured her. 'I've been busy doing some research.'

'For the book?'

'What else?'

'You've got a plot, then?'

'I think I'm getting one. But there's still more work to be done. I may have to go away for a few days.'

'Oh? Where?'

'Bordeaux.'

'Whatever for? What's the book about?'

'I'll tell you when I see you. Why don't you come over for a few days?'

'It certainly would be nice. It's bloody awful here. I really am sick of this country.'

'Then let's have a few days together before I go.'

Elizabeth hesitated before replying. 'I would like to. But I don't think I can leave at such short notice. Perhaps later, when you've finished. When are you going to Bordeaux?'

'Probably tomorrow, if you won't come out. I'll ring you when I get back.'

'Yes, do that. I'd probably like to come later. Goodbye.'

But this time it was Tony who put the receiver down first.

There was a pile of telephone directories on a ledge at his side. He was in luck. There was one for Bordeaux. He found the name quite easily. Auguste Thibaud lived at Number Seventy-two, Rue de la Course.

The patronne was at her desk in the hall.

'How does one get to Bordeaux?' he asked. 'It's probably too far to drive, isn't it?'

'I should go by train from Toulouse,' she replied. 'I've got a time-table here.'

There was a train that left Toulouse at about ten in the morning. He would be in Bordeaux during the afternoon.

He thanked her and went back into the dining-room to finish his dinner. He noticed the girl come in to collect some dishes. He smiled at her and called her over to his table.

'I've got to go away for a few days on business,' he said. 'I shan't be away long, but I'll lock the house up and take the key with me. Don't bother to go up there until I get back.'

The girl nodded. But he noticed that she looked disappointed.

He got up early next morning and went around the house making sure that the windows and doors were all shut, sealing them with the cotton and securing it with the chewing gum. If anyone tried to get in while he was away, he would know. He locked the doors and put the key in his pocket.

It was late afternoon when he arrived at the Gare Saint Jean in Bordeaux. He bought himself a map of the city at the station bookstall.

The Rue de la Course was in the centre of the town. It ran along one side of the Jardin Public and continued down to the Cours de Verdun. He walked into the street in front of the station. He noticed a tram standing outside with a queue of people pushing their way on and saw that it was going to the Place de Tourny. He checked on his map. The Cours de Verdun was one of the many roads that led out of the Place de Tourny. He took his place at the end of the queue and asked the driver to give a shout when they arrived.

He opened his Michelin during the short journey and studied the list of hotels. He wanted somewhere comfortable to sleep because he might have a lot of standing around to do. He noticed that there were several in the Allée de Tourny, just a few minutes' walk from the Rue de la Course. The driver turned and shouted.

'Place de Tourny.'

Tony thanked him. The Allée de Tourny was a wide gracious street leading away at an oblique angle from the Cours de Verdun. There were several hotels on the far side. He went into the first one and asked for a room. He was lucky, the receptionist told him, they had had a cancellation. How long would he be needing the room for?

'It's rather hard for me to say,' Tony replied. 'I'm here to meet a friend who is motoring down from England. I don't really know when he will get here. But it will certainly be for a few days.'

He went up to his room to wash and unpack. It was quiet and comfortable. Exactly what he wanted.

He strolled across to the Rue de la Course. Number Seventy-two was a large house facing on to the Jardin Public. It would be very easy to watch. There was a small children's playground almost directly opposite the house. It was obviously a popular place for people to sit. He noticed a couple of young men reading their papers in the last of the evening sun. He wouldn't be conspicuous there. There were several places where he could sit and watch the house without being noticed.

But he must be careful. He doubted whether Auguste would have had time to study his face that night on the road, and he certainly hadn't been aware that he was being followed in Albi, but Marie would no doubt have told him what the English writer looked like. He must have had some idea before attempting to kill him that night. Tony realized that he would need to take great care. But he must watch the house, and somehow or other find out what he could about Auguste Devine.

He hadn't been there long when the car drove up and parked outside the house. He watched Auguste get out and lock the car door. He ran up the steps and went into the house. Tony glanced at his watch. It was about a quarter to six. Probably the time that Auguste usually got home from his office.

The sun had gone in, and it had begun to get cooler. Tony

realized that he would be conspicuous if he remained there any longer. Auguste might look out of a window at any time and see him. The little playground was almost deserted. There was just a young hippie stretched out asleep on another bench. He had been reading. The book had fallen from his hand and was lying on the ground.

Tony got up. He passed the young man's bench and glanced down at the book as he went by. It was a paperback copy of *The Idiot*. Tony looked at the man's face, or what could be seen of it between the mass of long dank hair and a huge untrimmed beard. He stooped and picked up the book. It was in English. A name was written on the fly-leaf. 'Andrew Langton. Kent University.' Tony remembered that Kent was a university in America. The one where they had had that bit of trouble. He put the book down on the bench beside the boy, and walked away. How predictable the young were. It was always Dostoevsky. And usually *The Idiot*.

He didn't sleep well that night. He realized that it would be hard to watch the Devine house without himself being clearly visible. He had noticed that all the windows had net curtains. It would be the simplest thing for someone in the house to watch him continually, and he would be none the wiser. The job was not going to be as simple as he had imagined.

He walked back to the park after breakfast. It was obviously a favourite meeting place for people with children. Nearly every seat was taken by women enjoying the sun and watching their children play in the little playground. They occupied every seat except one, the one occupied by Andrew Langton. He was still there, but this time he was awake. He lay sprawled along the bench reading *The Idiot*.

Tony walked to the other side of an ornamental lake in the centre of the gardens. He could still see Andrew Langton, but he was out of sight of the Devine house. He slowly wandered up and down as an idea formed in his mind.

A park attendant came along the path picking up litter and putting the waste paper in a bag. He was about fifty with a cross, discontented face, the sort of man who would take a great dislike to young unshaven American layabouts lolling about in his park.

Tony nodded at him as he approached. 'Good morning,' he said.

The attendant looked Tony up and down. 'Good morning,' he replied.

'These are lovely gardens you have here,' Tony continued. 'You certainly keep them beautifully. You must be very proud.'

The man stopped and put down his bag. 'They are nice,' he said.

'How long have you been looking after them?'

'Nearly five years now.'

'It's so peaceful.' Tony looked about him. 'That young man over there has certainly made himself very comfortable.'

The attendant snorted. 'I've no time for him. He's nothing but a nuisance.'

'Oh? Why?'

'He spends the whole day there. Sprawled out all the time on that seat. He's there waiting in the morning when I open the gate, and he stays there until I throw him out at night.'

'Always on that same bench?' Tony asked. It commanded an excellent view of the Devine house.

The attendant nodded. 'You'd think he would have something better to do with his life. He should be out working like everyone else.'

'He's not French, is he?'

'American, I think.' The man picked up his bag. 'Well, I'd better be getting along. The gardens don't look after themselves, you know.'

Tony nodded and went to sit on a nearby bench. He sat there for nearly an hour watching Andrew Langton and the women sitting by the little playground.

He consulted the map of Bordeaux he had bought. He saw that the Municipal Library was nearby on the other side of the

Place de Tourny. He got up and strolled out of the gardens.

The librarian thought for a moment. 'Yes. I think I can find something about that for you. But it may take a little time. We're short staffed at the moment. Holiday time, you know.'

Tony nodded. 'That's quite all right. I'm not in any great hurry. Perhaps I could call back in a day or so.'

'That will suit me very well,' the librarian replied. 'I will have it ready for you.'

Tony was feeling pleased with himself as he came out of the library. He had started the day feeling worried, but it seemed that things could be slipping into place. He treated himself to a good lunch at a restaurant in the Cours de Verdun and then went to a nearby cinema. He had noticed that the Jardin Public closed at eight o'clock. He had nothing to do until then.

He got to the gardens at about ten to eight. Andrew Langton was fast asleep on the bench. Tony stood by the railings and waited. He could see the attendant locking the gates into the Cours de Verdun. There was another gate into the Rue de la Course. Tony watched the attendant approach. He went and shook the young man roughly. Andrew Langton nodded and slowly got up. Tony watched him amble across to the gate; his face was pale under the long hair and his eyes were sunken with exhaustion. He looked as though he could do with a good meal.

The attendant almost pushed him through the gates and locked them behind him. The young man hesitated for a moment and then came slowly down the street towards Tony.

'Excuse me.'

Andrew Langton stopped and stared at Tony.

'I'm sorry to trouble you,' Tony continued. 'But you're English, aren't you?'

Andrew Langton shook his head. 'American,' he replied.

'It doesn't matter,' Tony said. 'It's the same language. I

hope you'll excuse my speaking to you, but I'm here on business and I don't speak a word of French. It's such a relief to talk to someone. I hope you don't mind.'

'No. I don't mind,' Andrew replied.

'Are you on holiday?' Tony asked.

'I guess so.'

'Where are you staying?'

Andrew laughed. 'I spend my nights in a waiting room at the Gare Saint Jean.'

'How long are you here for?'

'I don't know. I haven't given much thought to it.'

'You're a student?'

'I was. I guess you'd probably call me a drop-out.'

'What brought you here?'

'To Bordeaux, you mean?'

Tony nodded.

'Well, it all came about by accident. I got a boat here from South America.'

'Travelling your way around.'

'I guess so.'

'I hope you don't mind my talking to you like this,' Tony repeated. 'But you've no idea what a luxury it is to speak to someone in English. To be understood for a change.'

'Yeah,' Andrew nodded.

'Would you think it impertinent if I asked you to have a drink with me?' Tony asked. 'And perhaps a meal, if you've got the time.'

'I wouldn't consider it impertinent of anyone to offer me some food.'

They went to a nearby restaurant. One that catered for foreigners. It took Tony all his time to remember not to speak in French. He sat and watched Andrew eat an enormous meal. When he'd finished, they sat and talked over coffee. It was the usual story.

Andrew Langton was the son of a wealthy bank president in Kansas City. He had enrolled at Kent University and had been there when the trouble had occurred. One of his best friends had been shot.

'Paul was one of the greatest guys you could have imagined,' Andrew said softly. 'He was so alive and so pure. And those bastards shot him down. He died in my arms with his head in my lap. And those bastards stood over us with their guns. I remember one of them was grinning. He was grinning as Paul died. Christ, how I hated those bastards! I didn't know how to hate until then. It's a terrible thing to hate. I guess you wouldn't know what it feels like.'

'Yes. I think I do,' Tony replied.

Andrew had walked out of the university and left America in disgust. He had worked his way south, doing several jobs until he had turned up in Rio. There had been the chance of a trip to Europe. A job was going on a ship bound for Le Havre. He had gradually hitched his way down. Until he had run out of money in Bordeaux.

'I guess I've got to earn myself a bit of money,' he said. 'Then I can get down to the south. Where the girls are.'

Tony looked at him. He could hardly imagine many girls being interested in him in his present state. 'Do you really want to earn some money?' he asked.

Andrew looked uncertain. 'I guess so,' he replied. 'Do you know anyone who would give me a job?'

'Yes.'

'Who?'

'Me.'

'You?'

Tony smiled and nodded. 'That's right,' he said.

'What would I have to do?'

'Pretty well what you're doing now, but you'd have to stay awake. It might also offend your idealistic principles.'

'A guy will do most anything when he's hungry,' Andrew replied.

Tony realized that the idealism was wearing thin. He explained what he wanted done. 'You must watch the house for the next few days. Make a note of everything that happens. I want a description of everyone who comes and goes. We can meet here in the evening for dinner.'

'What's it for?'

'Does it matter?' Tony asked. 'Would it really make any difference?'

Andrew shrugged his shoulders. 'I guess not,' he agreed.

'Then, let's not waste time. You'll do it?'

'Sure, I'll do it. How much do I get?'

'A hundred francs a day and a bloody good meal in the evening.'

'Then I guess we're in business,' Andrew grinned.

They agreed to meet at the restaurant at eight o'clock the next evening.

Tony slowly walked back to his hotel. He had a feeling that he would sleep well that night.

He was at the library early in the morning. The librarian had found several books for him. There was one that was especially interesting, a pictorial record of ancient Aztec jewellery. Several of the plates were in colour. He slowly turned the pages, marvelling at the superb gold necklaces and the fantastic jewels. There was a separate section on Montezuma with a picture of him holding the Sunburst. It was not large, a round shield, probably no more than two feet in diameter, but magnificently engraved with a design of the blazing sun.

There was a detailed description of the shield written by the two Americans. They had seen it in 1855 in the cathedral where it was guarded as a sacred relic. The article related that the shield had mysteriously disappeared without trace during the short reign of the Emperor Maximilian.

The librarian came over to where Tony was sitting. 'It's beautiful, isn't it?' he said, pointing to the picture of the Sunburst.

'Yes,' Tony agreed.

'We have someone who is always coming in to look at it,' the man continued. 'He comes in and studies it for hours. He often takes the book home with him.'

'Oh? What's his name?'

'Monsieur Devine.'

Tony remained silent.

'He seems to be planning some kind of an expedition. I see that that particular shield has been lost. I wonder if he could be trying to find it?'

Tony nodded. 'Could be,' he replied.

12

Andrew took a piece of paper out of his pocket. 'I've got it all written down,' he said. 'Just like you wanted. I'd better read it to you. My writing's not that good.'

He peered at some pencilled scribbles.

'I guess there's a family living there. The guy looks about sixty. Kind of a sour face he has.'

'Does he have a car?' Tony asked.

'He sure does. A super one. I've noticed it before. He always leaves it parked outside the house at nights. You should see its mascot. A bloody great gold lion. He must have had it specially done. You should see it.'

'I have,' Tony replied dryly.

Andrew looked up and smiled. 'Isn't it great? Jesus! It'd be great to have one of those.'

Tony smiled to himself. He could sense that Andrew's days as a drop-out were numbered. At any moment he would be ready to hurl himself into the fast stream of American materialism. He might even make bank president yet.

'Well, go on,' Tony urged.

'Oh, sorry. Well, this guy goes off at about nine thirty in the car and gets back around five. Goes to work, I guess. Then nothing much happened. A sad-faced sort of woman came out at about eleven and came back around twelve. There's a young girl turned up at ten and left after lunch. She doesn't look like a member of the family. She doesn't dress so good. I guess she works there. They look as though they'd have some kind of staff. And then there's a woman lives next door. She comes and goes quite a lot. She's about fifty, and dresses quite smart. She went in and out of the house quite a few times.'

'And that was all?' Tony asked. 'There was no one else?'

'No. Except for the butcher. He called at about twelve and delivered some meat. The girl answered the door.'

'What was she like?'

'Not bad.'

'Would you fancy her?' Tony asked.

'Me? Christ! I'd fancy just about anything, I can tell you. It seems like ages since I laid someone.'

'You'll have to smarten yourself up a bit. Get rid of all that beard.'

'I'd get rid of anything to get a girl under me.'

Tony grinned. He had been lucky in finding Andrew Langton. The boy had excellent possibilities. Eminently malleable. He was sure that in time he would make an excellent president of the bank.

'Thank you, Andrew,' he said. 'I want you to do the same for me tomorrow. But I think we should perhaps meet for dinner at a different restaurant. I don't want us to become conspicuous. There's a place in the Cours Clemenceau on the other side of the Place de Tourny. We'll meet there at eight tomorrow evening.' He handed Andrew a hundred francs note. 'How's *The Idiot?*' he asked.

Andrew looked confused for a moment. Then he laughed.

'It's *The Brothers Karamazov* now,' he replied.

Tony nodded. That figured, he thought to himself. A predictable laddie, our Andrew.

They met again the next evening. Andrew produced another scrumpled piece of paper. 'It was all just the same as yesterday,' he said. 'Except for the woman next door. She came and sat in the park in the afternoon. She had a little girl with her. Looked like a granddaughter. They were in the park for about an hour. Apart from that, everything was the same.'

'Did the girl still turn up?'

Andrew nodded. 'She came and sat in the park too for a bit. She left when the other woman turned up.'

'Are you any good with women?' Tony asked.

'How do you mean?'

'Can you chat them up? You're not queer or anything, are you?'

Andrew looked affronted. 'Hell, no!' he replied.

'Then I want you to get yourself cleaned up. Get your hair cut and your beard trimmed. Buy yourself some decent clothes. I want you to get talking to this girl. Find out all you can about that family. Everything you can, do you understand? I'll meet you here the same time tomorrow.' He took a five hundred franc note out of his wallet and handed it to Andrew. 'And make yourself look good. Get a bath. And for Christ's sake buy some deodorant.'

When Tony got to the restaurant that evening, Andrew had not arrived. He went and sat at a secluded table at the back of the room and waited. But Andrew didn't turn up. Tony ordered an apéritif and looked at his watch. It was nearly twenty past eight. Something must have delayed Andrew. Tony sat and watched the few people in the restaurant.

There was a middle-aged couple at a table nearby, and a young man sitting by himself on the other side of the room. An elderly man got up and paid his bill. A young couple stood outside for some time studying the menu. They discussed it for some time before hesitantly entering the room. A young man entered, but it wasn't Andrew. Tony looked at his watch again. It was almost half past. Something must have gone wrong.

Tony noticed that the young man on the other side of the room was grinning at him. There was something about him that was vaguely familiar. He was smartly and expensively dressed and was grinning broadly at Tony. Somehow, he didn't really look French. Possibly German or Dutch. Or even American. Tony took another look. And then he realized. It was Andrew. He waved at Tony.

'Hi!' He got up and came over to Tony's table. 'I guess you didn't recognize me. Do I look that different?'

'You look like the son of a bank president.'

Andrew laughed. 'Well, you've got yourself to thank for that.'

'How did you get on?' Tony asked.

'Great! But I can't give you too much time. I'm meeting Michelle at half past nine.'

'Who's Michelle?'

'She works for your friend Auguste Devine. I'm taking her to a late movie.'

Tony smiled. 'You work fast,' he said.

'Got to make up for lost time,' Andrew replied. 'Do you want to know how I got on?'

'Very much. But let's order something to eat. We've already wasted half an hour, thanks to your highly developed sense of humour.'

Andrew grinned. 'Sorry about that. But you looked so comic staring around and peering at your watch.'

'I dare say,' Tony replied dryly. He ordered a quick meal from the waiter. 'Well?' he asked.

'The house belongs to this Devine guy. He sounds a bit of a bastard. Michelle loathes him. She only stays there because of Madame Devine. She's sorry for her. And the money's good. Monsieur Devine has a factory out near the airport here. I gather he's got quite a lot of dough. He leaves the house each morning at around nine thirty and gets back about five in the afternoon. His wife and he don't get on too good. Michelle says they hardly talk to each other. Then every weekend he goes away.'

'Where to?'

'A place called Albi.'

'Does he take his wife with him?'

Andrew shook his head. 'No. Never. According to Michelle, he used to be off his head. He became very violent and had to be restrained. I gather he nearly killed his wife. He was sent to Albi for treatment. There's a psychiatric hospital there.'

'When was this?' Tony asked.

'About a couple of years ago.'

'And he's still going to this hospital after two years? You don't have psychiatric treatment at weekends.'

'That's right. That's what I said to Michelle. She reckons he's got a girl down there. He and his wife don't sleep together. They have separate rooms. Michelle reckons he's got some woman down in Albi.'

Tony nodded. 'Yes. He has,' he replied.

'Madame Devine is friends with the woman who lives next door. A Madame Marty. They see quite a lot of each other. Madame Marty has her young granddaughter staying with her at the moment. They go and spend a couple of hours in the playground during the afternoons.'

'I suppose you wouldn't know whether this Madame Marty is a friend of Monsieur Devine's?' Tony asked.

'She loathes his guts,' Andrew replied. 'Won't go into the house when he's there. Michelle has twice heard her trying to persuade Madame Devine to leave him.'

'I see,' Tony murmured. 'Thanks, Andrew. You've done a grand job. I'm very grateful. Now, I won't delay you. You mustn't keep this Michelle waiting. It's nearly nine thirty.'

'What do you want me to do tomorrow?'

'Nothing for me. The job's finished.' He took three hundred francs out of his wallet and handed them to Andrew. 'Thanks,' he grinned. 'Give Michelle a good time.'

'What was it all in aid of?' Andrew asked.

Tony shrugged his shoulders. 'Monsieur Devine and I might be doing a job together,' he explained. 'I just wanted to find out what sort of a man he is.'

'He doesn't sound too nice,' Andrew remarked. 'I guess you should be careful.'

'No. I don't think he is,' Tony replied. 'I shall take great care, I promise you.'

Andrew got up and extended his hand to Tony. 'Then I guess this is goodbye,' he said. 'Thanks a lot. I enjoyed working for you.'

'Goodbye, Andrew. You've been a great help. What are your plans now?'

'I thought I'd stick around with Michelle for a bit. We might go down south together. We'll see how we get on. Then I guess I'll go back home. It'd be kind of nice to see my parents.'

They shook hands.

'So you'll still be doing that job with this Devine guy?' Andrew asked.

'Oh, I think so,' Tony replied. 'But I shall be careful.'

He watched Andrew cross the street. A girl was waiting outside a cinema two blocks away. She smiled when she saw Andrew approaching.

He spent the next morning at the library. There was a different librarian on duty. 'I'm a writer,' he explained. 'I need to do some research on mental illnesses. Can you help me?'

The librarian was away for some time. He returned carrying a huge pile of books. Tony settled down to a morning's read. He was still reading at half past one. He had learnt a great deal, some of it very disturbing. He felt distressed and insecure as he came out into the sunshine. He only had time for a quick snack before taking up his place in the park. He noticed that Andrew was nowhere to be seen. The bench looked quite forlorn without him. He took a Simenon out of his pocket and began to read.

He hadn't been there long before the door of Madame Marty's house opened and she came out holding a little girl by the hand. They crossed the road and came into the park. The girl ran ahead into the little playground, and began to play on the swings. Madame Marty watched her for a moment before going to sit on a bench nearby.

Tony watched the little girl carefully. She was about five years old. The child was swinging backwards and forwards. Madame Marty sat and watched.

After a time, the little girl became bored and went to play on a slide that faced where Tony was sitting. He took a doll out of his pocket and put it on the bench beside him so that it could not be seen from where Madame Marty was sitting. He caught the child's eye and smiled.

The child looked away confused. She had obviously been told not to have anything to do with strange men. Tony took no further notice of her, but went on reading his book.

The child stood at the top of the slide and stared at the doll. Madame Marty's eyes were closing. Tony saw her head jerk forward in sleep. She started and looked about her. The child was standing still on the top of the slide. She looked at her grandmother and waved. Madame Marty smiled and waved back before closing her eyes again. Tony picked up the doll and put it down again beside him.

The child smiled shyly at him. He smiled back. She slid slowly down the slide and stood hesitantly at the bottom. Madame Marty's eyes remained closed. The child began to walk towards Tony.

'Hallo,' he said.

The child smiled.

'What's your name?' he asked.

'Françoise,' she replied softly.

'That's a very pretty name,' Tony said.

The child nodded. She put out her hand and took the doll.

'Do you like it?' Tony asked. The girl nodded again.

Madame Marty opened her eyes. She looked around for the child. 'Françoise?' she called. 'Where are you?'

The child snatched the doll and ran over to her grandmother. Tony could see Madame Marty asking her where she had got the doll. Some argument appeared to be going on. He got up and walked across.

'I'm sorry,' he said. 'Your little girl has taken something of mine.'

Madame Marty had the doll in her hand. The child was sobbing on the bench. Madame Marty looked at Tony with a puzzled expression on her face. 'This is yours?' she asked.

Tony laughed. 'Perhaps I'd better explain,' he said. 'I've just bought it for a god-daughter of mine. I've come here to visit her family.'

'Ah!' Madame Marty's face relaxed. She handed Tony the doll. 'I'm so sorry,' she said. 'I must apologize for my grand-daughter.'

'Perhaps she would like to keep it. It was very cheap. I can easily get another.'

'Certainly not!' Madame Marty replied.

'It is sad,' Tony continued. 'My god-daughter's father is a great friend of mine, but he has just had a complete nervous breakdown. He has even become violent, and he used to be such a gentle man. It is tragic. The strain on his wife is enormous. I've come to try and help, but one doesn't really know quite what to do. One feels so helpless.'

Madame Marty looked sympathetic.

'I'm so sorry for talking to you like this,' Tony muttered. 'Please forgive me. But the past few days have been most upsetting.' He explained his friend's symptoms. 'But I mustn't bore you with other people's problems. It's just a relief to talk to someone about it. One feels so helpless when one is faced with something like this. He has become a completely different person. One just doesn't understand.'

Madame Marty moved up to make room for him on the bench. 'I know how you feel,' she said. 'I have a friend with a similar problem. Her husband has attacks just like that. Insanity is a terrible thing.'

'Can he not be cured?' Tony asked.

Madame Marty shook her head. 'He won't take treatment. It's in his family.'

'How awful for his wife.'

'Yes. I've frequently tried to persuade her to leave him. She lives in continual fear of him. He's sometimes so violent, he's quite uncontrollable.'

'Has he never been in hospital?' Tony asked.

'Oh yes. Twice. But he won't go back. He's frightened, you see. When that sort of thing is in the family, it's very difficult. A lot of the time he behaves quite reasonably. One would think he was perfectly normal. Then stress or worry brings on one of these attacks. And they're usually aimed at his poor wife. It's a terrible thing.' Madame Marty shook her head in desperation at her friend's situation.

'What form do these attacks take?'

'Oh, they're dreadful. The last time he went for her with a knife. She had to send for the police. It was all hushed up, but he was in hospital for several weeks. It was touch and go whether they would let him out.'

Tony made some sort of sympathetic noise. 'I suppose if he were to have another attack – '

A hard look flashed across Madame Marty's face. 'Then there would be no question,' she said firmly. 'He would have to be put away. And he knows it, too.'

Tony glanced at his watch. 'You must excuse me,' he said. 'I must go and visit my friend. He's in a hospital here, and I'm meeting his wife at three.'

'I hope he will get better,' Madame Marty said. 'Perhaps I've made you feel rather depressed. But it really is a terrible thing.'

'No, you haven't made me feel at all depressed,' Tony assured her. 'But it must all be a great strain on your friend.'

'She leads an awful life. And as if that were not enough, her maid has just walked out on her. She came in this morning as bold as brass and announced that she's off to the Côte d'Azur with some young man she's met. Really, the young are heartless.'

'Yes,' Tony agreed. 'They are.'

He said goodbye to Madame Marty and walked back to his hotel.

'I shall be leaving in the morning,' he announced to the man behind the desk. 'I think I need some relaxation and a few pretty girls. Do you know what I mean? Can you give me some addresses?'

The man grinned. 'I may be able to help,' he replied.

13

'Mademoiselle Desroux has been asking a lot of questions about you. She wanted to know where you'd gone, and how long you were likely to be away. She even came down twice to the hotel to ask about you. I told her I didn't know.'

'What did she want?' Tony asked.

The girl shook her head. 'I don't know. She wouldn't say. I told her I didn't know where you were. But I guessed. You went to Bordeaux, didn't you? You were asking the patronne about trains.'

'Did Mademoiselle Desroux talk to the patronne?'

'I don't think so. The patronne hasn't been well for the past few days. She's been upstairs in her room. Are you going away again?'

'No. I don't think so. Not just yet at any rate.'

The girl smiled shyly. 'That's good,' she said. 'I missed you.'

Tony absent-mindedly put his arm around her. She immediately pressed her meagre little bird-like body against him. 'She's like a sparrow,' he thought, quickly releasing her. He had never been attracted to thin women. If anything, they repelled him. The girl gave him a bewildered, reproachful glance before leaving the room. Tony went into the study. He sat down at the desk and took out the drawings he had made of the Sunburst.

It could be buried anywhere in the garden. He sat and stared out of the window at the overgrown mass of weeds and long grass. It was hard to visualize it as a cultivated garden, but no doubt it had been in reasonable order during Madame Malines' lifetime.

He heard the girl moving about in the passage outside, and opened the door. 'The garden's pretty overgrown,' he said. 'Perhaps I should do something about it?'

The girl shrugged her shoulders. She was still looking reproachful.

'Did Madame Malines keep it looking nice?' he asked.

'She used to do a bit,' the girl replied.

'Did she do it herself?'

The girl nodded. 'Yes. She was funny that way. She wouldn't let anyone help her. She was too mean to pay them. She even used to do the heavy work herself. I often saw her digging when I used to go past.'

Tony felt a thrill of excitement. 'Where was she digging?' he asked.

The girl pointed to a series of mounds in the long grass. 'She began to make a rockery over there. It was just after her sister died. I often saw her digging there. But she stopped doing it after a time. I suppose the work was too heavy for her. It's all overgrown now.'

'I quite like gardening,' Tony said. 'I might go and do some work there.'

'As you wish,' the girl replied. 'I'll be off now, then. See you tomorrow. Goodbye.'

'Goodbye.'

He waited until the girl had gone before he went to investigate the site. He could see that the ground had been disturbed, but the grass and weeds had since taken over. No one would have realized that the ground had ever been dug up unless they had known exactly where to look. He stood and stared at the bumps in the ground for some time, a look of triumph on his face. Unfortunately, the spot was in a clear line of vision from

Marie Desroux's house. He would have to be careful not to attract her attention.

She had been asking questions about him in the village, and trying to find out where he had gone. But she had not tried to get into the house. None of his seals had been disturbed.

He went back into the study to examine his drawing. It really was a magnificent thing. It would be worth a fortune. He sat and looked at it for some time. It was incredible to think that it was lying there in the garden where the old woman had hidden it. And only he had discovered the spot. He would be rich and independent for life. He would never have anything further to worry about again.

Suddenly, Marie Desroux was standing at the window. She was staring at the drawing of the Sunburst. He had no idea how long she had been there. He quickly put some papers on top of his drawing.

'Tony!' she said. 'You've been away. When did you get back? I saw you in the garden. Where have you been?'

'I had to go and do some research.'

'Where?'

'Oh, several places.'

'I've missed you. You should have told me that you were going away.'

'I'm sorry,' Tony replied.

'Would you like to come and have some lunch with me?' Marie asked. 'Or are you too busy? Perhaps I shouldn't have disturbed you. I can see that you are working.'

'No. I'd very much like to come.'

Marie was looking at the papers on his desk. 'What are you doing?' she asked. 'You have been making drawings.'

'That's right.'

'For your book?'

'Yes.'

Marie smiled at him. 'Aren't you clever?' she said. 'Then I'll look forward to seeing you at about half past twelve.'

'That'll be very nice,' Tony replied. He sat and waited until she had gone.

She had seen the Sunburst. And she must also have seen him examining the ground where Madame Malines had begun her rockery. He would have to distract her attention by digging in some other part of the garden. He would have to work elsewhere during the day, and only dig up the rockery after it had got dark. It was going to mean a great deal of extra work, but there was no other way around it.

He looked at his watch. It was getting on for half past eleven. He put away his papers and walked down to the village to do some shopping. There was no food in the house. And he also needed a spade.

It was nearly half past twelve when he got back. He put his parcels in the hall and walked on up the lane. Marie Desroux was standing in her garden. Tony fancied that she was looking worried, but she smiled when she saw him coming. She led the way inside the house. Tony glanced around the room. The three pictures were still missing.

'I expect you would like a drink,' she said. There seemed to be something different about her. She looked pale and her hands were shaking as she poured him a glass of wine. He could see that she had something on her mind.

He tried to make some kind of conversation, but it was obvious that she wasn't listening to a word he was saying. Twice he asked her questions which she didn't answer. She just sat looking at him with a tense preoccupied expression on her face.

Tony knew what had made her change her attitude. She had seen the drawings of the Sunburst, and she had probably also realized where it was buried. She had seen him looking at the mounds in the garden. She, like him, was wondering what move to make next. There could be no other explanation.

She got up and stood hesitantly in the centre of the room. 'I must get something for us to eat,' she said finally. 'What would you like?'

'I don't mind. Whatever's convenient,' he replied.

She nodded vaguely and seemed to look intently at him before going into the kitchen. Tony got up and walked to the window. He looked down at the Malines' house. The rockery was clearly visible.

He was standing at the window when he heard the screams. There was a thud above his head and then the screams. Hideous screams. He had never heard anything like them before.

He could hear Marie run upstairs. A door slammed, partially muffling the sound. Her footsteps were moving overhead and he could hear her talking to someone, begging them to stop. But the screams continued for several minutes, until they died down to a sort of agonized wailing. He went and stood at the bottom of the staircase.

A door opened upstairs and Marie appeared at the top of the staircase. Tony noticed that she was crying, and her dress was torn. The wailing had stopped except for an occasional moan. He stood at the foot of the stairs, looking up at her.

For a moment neither spoke. They stood staring at each other. Then Tony slowly began to climb the stairs.

'No!' Marie shouted at him. 'No!' She put out her hand to stop him. 'No! You mustn't come up.'

'What is it?' Tony asked.

Marie shook her head. 'You mustn't come up,' she said. 'Please go.'

'What is it?' he repeated.

'You must go,' she said again. 'Don't ask me to explain. Just go.'

'But let me help.'

Marie shook her head. 'You can't. There's nothing to be done. It'll all be over soon. Nothing can be done.'

'But – '

'Please,' she insisted. 'Please go.' The moans had ceased. The house was silent. They stood facing each other on the stairs. 'There's really nothing you can do for me.'

'Are you sure?'

'Yes,' she nodded. 'I'm quite sure. It's all over now. I'm sorry this has happened. You must go home.'

'Very well.' He left the house, and looked up at the windows of the room upstairs. They were firmly shuttered as usual. He turned and walked back down the lane.

There was a letter for him lying on the hall floor. It was from the library in Albi. He had reserved a book there about the Aztecs. It had arrived and was being kept for him. The letter had taken a long time to reach him. The book had to be picked up that afternoon.

He realized that he was feeling hungry, and he didn't feel like cooking anything himself. He might as well drive straight into Albi, have a late lunch at the restaurant and pick up the book afterwards.

They were pleased to see him. The head waiter welcomed him and escorted him to Monsieur Perroton's table.

'Has Monsieur Perroton already had lunch?' Tony asked.

The waiter shook his head sadly. 'He is very ill,' he replied. 'He hasn't been in for several days.'

'I'm sorry. What is the matter?'

'He has a lot of trouble with his chest. And his heart is not strong, either. We have been so worried for him. At one time the doctor was afraid that he might not get better. I believe now that he's over the worst, but it's left him very weak.'

'I am sorry,' Tony repeated. 'Perhaps I should go and see him. Do you think he would like that?'

'Yes, I think he would,' the waiter replied. 'I know he gets lonely. He likes to talk to people.'

'I'll go this afternoon,' Tony promised.

He collected the book after lunch and then crossed the square to the old man's flat. The concierge was sweeping out the main hall.

'I've come to see Monsieur Perroton,' he explained. 'I hear he hasn't been well.'

The woman nodded. 'He'll be glad of someone to talk to,' she said. 'I'll come up and let you in. He's still not allowed to get out of bed.'

Tony followed her up the stairs and waited while she unlocked the old man's door.

'A visitor for you,' she called, standing back to let Tony in. 'Go right in,' she said. 'The bedroom door is open.'

Monsieur Perroton was sitting up in bed with a rug around his shoulders. His eyes lit up when he saw Tony. 'Come in,' he called. 'It's nice of you to come and see me.'

The concierge smiled at Tony and closed the door behind him. The bedroom door was half open and the old man beckoned to him to come in.

Tony pushed open the door. The bedroom was small and simply furnished. The old man motioned to Tony to pull up a chair.

'Get the one from by the window,' he said. 'It's the most comfortable.'

Tony crossed the room. The chair was in front of a small desk in a recess made by the dormer window. There were two photographs on the desk. They were both of women. Very much alike. The elder one was in her sixties. Tony was aware of the gentle quality of her face and the radiance of her smile. The other photograph was of Marie Desroux.

'She tells me that you have been very good to her.'

'Who?'

'Marie.'

'You know her?' Tony asked.

'But of course,' the old man replied. 'She's my daughter.'

14

Tony picked up Marie's picture. 'Your daughter?' he asked.

Monsieur Perroton smiled and nodded. 'And that is her mother.' He pointed to the other photograph.

'She has a very beautiful smile,' Tony said.

'She was a very beautiful person.'

'What was her name?'

'Angèle Thibaud.'

'You were married to Angèle?'

The old man shook his head sadly. 'Alas, no,' he said quietly. 'Her parents forbade it. They didn't consider that I was good enough. In a way, they were right, but not in the sense they meant. No one was good enough for Angèle. She was, quite literally, a saint, and most men are just ordinary mortals. But her parents didn't consider that I was good enough to marry into their family because I had no money and no prospects. My parents were poor, you see. My father was killed in a train accident when I was a boy, and my mother had to take a book-keeping job in order to keep us. She worked for a large concern in Brussels. But I was always keen on art. My father had wanted me to be a painter. So my mother saved every penny in order to send me for lessons. And it was there that I met Angèle. Her parents had also sent her to art classes. It was considered the right thing for young ladies to do in those days. But I remember that she was not allowed to attend the life classes. She had to leave the studio when we were drawing the nude.'

Tony laughed.

'We fell very much in love,' the old man continued, 'and Angèle became pregnant. I shall always remember how proud and humble we both felt when we knew. I wanted to rush and tell her parents. I'd never met them, you see. She had never wanted to take me to her home, and I could never understand why not. But I soon did. She insisted on telling them alone. I never saw her again until after her parents' death.'

'Why ever not?' Tony asked.

'They forbade her ever to see me again. She was sent away from home. Their family doctor obtained a post for her in the household of the Empress Carlotta.'

'So that was when she met the Empress,' Tony muttered. 'Rather a peculiar job for a young pregnant girl, wasn't it?'

Monsieur Perroton shook his head. 'Not really. Not when one understands the Thibaud family's dilemma.'

'What was that?'

'They had three daughters. Angèle was the eldest. Then there was Mathilde, who married Monsieur Malines, and lastly, there was Thérèse.'

'Thérèse?'

'Yes. She was the youngest. She had always been a delicate child, but with tremendous nervous energy. As she got older, she became subject to periodic fits of violence. She was mentally quite unbalanced, you see. Then, just after Angèle became pregnant, Thérèse had some kind of attack. I never really found out quite what happened, but it had something to do with Mathilde leaving home. I think Thérèse became jealous, and there was some kind of a scene. Angèle was the only member of the family willing to look after Thérèse, but her parents would not allow her to remain at home. So she was found this position with the Empress, and Thérèse was placed in some institution.

'Angèle remained with the Empress until just before Marie was born. We had lost touch with each other. She had been made to promise not to write to me. As far as I was concerned, she had totally disappeared. I went several times to her parents' house, but they always refused to see me. I had no idea where Angèle was. And then my mother was offered a much better job in Paris. So we moved there. I discovered later that Angèle had tried to write to me when Marie was born, but I never got the letter.

'The Empress became devoted to Angèle, and so did the Baroness of Roeselare, the Empress's lady-in-waiting. She found a home for Marie. It was very difficult for a girl of Angèle's age and class to have an illegitimate baby in those days. So Marie was adopted by a family called Desroux, friends of the Baroness. The Empress died just before Marie was born, so Angèle devoted her life to looking after Thérèse. She had become almost totally irrational with occasional bouts of extreme violence, and no one else would accept responsibility for her. Angèle was the only person who could handle her.

'By then, I was becoming successful in the Paris art world. I set up my own studio and held occasional exhibitions. Angèle must have read about me in some paper, because she wrote to me. I had never forgotten her, you know. A day never went by without my kissing her picture, and I never touched another woman. I only used to go with prostitutes because they were unimportant.

'But she never mentioned the baby, so I assumed that it was dead. Then her parents died. First, her mother, and then her father a few months later. I begged her to marry me, but she refused. There was insanity in her family. Her cousin Auguste was also subject to these fits, and she refused to marry me because of this. I had my studio in Paris, and she wouldn't leave Thérèse.

'And so I met my wife. Her father was a great art patron, and had been very good to me. I frequently used to visit his house in the Bois de Boulogne. Claude, his daughter, was beautiful, and I think she liked me. And I imagined that I was in love with her. So we got married. Claude was a good wife, and I tried to be a good husband. But I don't think that we ever really loved one another. It was a marriage of convenience. And like so many of those marriages, it was quite successful. She died about four years ago. Of cancer.'

'I'm sorry,' Tony said.

'I had read about Monsieur Thibaud's death in a paper, and I wrote to Angèle. She had been left her parents' house near Brussels and she lived there with Thérèse. But my wife was jealous. She knew that it was Angèle I loved, and not her. I think it was her jealousy that caused her illness. Cancer can be a psychological disease.

'Angèle had established contact with Marie who had inherited my interest in art. She sent her to me to ask for a job. I had no idea who she was, but I immediately liked her and took her on in my studio. You know, it was a funny thing, but I think Claude always knew who Marie was. She was dying then, although I didn't realize it. She hid it from me until it was too late to do anything. And then she told me. She also asked me to look after Marie. She died a month later.

'Angèle had moved down here to Laurac. Mathilde's husband had died, and she had persuaded Angèle to sell the family house and move in with her. Thérèse was kept in one of the upstairs attics. But they didn't get on. There was a quarrel over Thérèse. Mathilde refused to have her in the house. She said she must be put into a mental home, and Angèle refused. There were other upsets as well. Mathilde was always asking about money and other things. So Angèle left. She bought the house at the end of the lane, where Marie is living. It was a quiet house. She could live there with Thérèse without disturbing anyone. But she hadn't been there long before she became ill. She had devoted her life to looking after Thérèse, and the strain had been too much. She was too tired to go on.

'She wrote to me and told me about everything. She begged me to forgive her for deceiving me over Marie. But she had done it for the sake of my wife, and she wanted Marie and I to be friends. I was fortunate to get this job down here. It isn't really a job. I have some friends in high places, and they pulled a few strings. The post was created for me. So I came to live in Albi. Angèle knew she was going to die, and she still refused to marry me. She didn't think it was fair that I should have to live with Thérèse.

'And then she died. Suddenly. It was Mathilde who told me, but not until after Angèle had been dead for two days. She said it had all happened very quickly, and she had wanted to spare me distress. She pretended not to realize how close Angèle and I had been. When I did go to the house, all Angèle's things had been removed, even her clothes. Mathilde had taken everything. She was a dreadful woman. Greedy. Jackdaw was the right name for her.'

'So what happened to Thérèse?' Tony asked.

'Mathilde refused to have anything to do with her. When I got to the house, Thérèse had been lying in her bed without food ever since Angèle's death. She had been lying there in her own dirt for days. The smell was appalling. I think Mathilde and Thérèse had always disliked one another. Mathilde was determined to put her in the asylum here in Albi, but I fought her over it. Angèle had written a last letter to Marie begging her to come and look after Thérèse. She had seen a doctor just before she died and he had assured her that Thérèse would not live much longer. Every attack weakened her considerably, and the attacks were becoming more frequent. She had become very violent and dangerous.

'I realized later that this was why Angèle refused to marry me. She wouldn't leave Thérèse. And Thérèse hated to see other people happy. When she saw two people happy together, she would fly into the most violent rage and could do terrible things. Angèle realized that Thérèse would have been jealous of me, and she wasn't prepared to risk anything happening. She was afraid that Thérèse might even attack me, and she could do terrible harm. Although she is a frail woman, it is as if she were possessed of the devil during these attacks, and she has astonishing strength.'

'Did she kill Mathilde?' Tony asked.

The old man shrugged his shoulders. 'God knows, but I think so,' he replied. 'She certainly hated her. Marie was out of the house at the time. She had had to go down to the village. She had left Thérèse apparently asleep in bed, but when she came back, she found Thérèse lying unconscious in the lane. She managed to get her home and put her to bed. The idea that Thérèse might have attacked Mathilde never occurred to her, and she never visited her aunt. She disliked her far too much to do that. It was only later, when Mathilde's body was found, that Marie wondered. Thank goodness, no one else had seen anything. I'm sure people in the village suspected what had happened, but everyone disliked Mathilde so much that nothing was done.'

'So that was why Marie left Paris to come and live in Laurac?'

'Yes. That was why. It was her mother's dying wish. But I don't think it will be for much longer. Thérèse is weakening, and her attacks are becoming much more frequent.'

'I think she had one today,' Tony said. 'I was to have had lunch with Marie, but there was this awful screaming, and Marie made me go. She wouldn't let me help her.'

'I know. She is far too independent. Just like her mother. She telephoned me after you left and told me what had happened.'

'But isn't she in danger?' Tony asked.

'Not really. The doctor has given her a strong sedative for Thérèse that immediately quietens her down. She just falls into a deep coma. But Marie has to give it to her in time. That is why she doesn't like to leave the house. If Thérèse didn't have those pills she would become violent, and then Marie would be in danger. Except, of course, that Thérèse has become fond of her. But she could get very jealous if Marie were to be with you. That is why Marie was worried about becoming too friendly with you.'

'So that was why she said we would have to wait. She must have meant until after Thérèse had died.'

Monsieur Perroton nodded. 'Very likely,' he said, looking intently at Tony. 'The doctor has said that Thérèse cannot live for much longer. She could go at any time. Marie is reluctant to leave her at the moment. It's bad luck.'

'But surely it will be better when Thérèse is dead, won't it?' Tony asked.

The old man smiled sadly. 'You misunderstood me,' he said. 'It is bad luck that I am ill just now. It means that Marie is not able to visit me, and it is my birthday the weekend after next. We have always spent my birthdays together. Last year I went down to Laurac, but I won't be able to do that this time. It's a great disappointment to us both. The first time that we have separated for I don't know how many years. Things like that count as one gets older. One never really knows how many birthdays one has left.'

Tony nodded sympathetically.

'We'd both been looking forward to it for so long,' Monsieur Perroton said. 'It really is bad luck.'

'But perhaps you'll be better by then.'

The old man shook his head. 'The doctor says there's to be no question of my getting up for at least two weeks,' he replied.

Tony looked at the old man for a moment. 'Where is your telephone?' he asked.

'In the entrance hall. It's a nuisance at the moment, but I can just about manage the stairs. The concierge is very good and carries messages if I am not feeling well.'

'We've been talking a long time.' Tony said, getting to his feet. 'I think you should have a rest.'

Monsieur Perroton nodded. 'Perhaps you're right. But please come and see me again before too long. I enjoy talking to you very much.'

'Yes, I will,' Tony promised.

He walked downstairs slowly. He nearly bumped into a man at the corner of one of the landings, but took no notice. He was not even aware of him.

The concierge's boy was sitting in the sun downstairs. The telephone was on the wall by the door. Tony looked up the number he wanted and dialled. 'Hostelrie Saint-Antoine?' he asked.

A man's voice answered.

'Is that Monsieur Vincent?'

'No. I'm afraid he's not on duty at the moment. He will be in this evening.'

'Never mind,' Tony said quickly. 'Perhaps you can help me. I wanted to know whether Monsieur Devine has booked in for the next two weekends.'

'Yes. He will be here as usual on Friday night.'

'And the weekend after?'

'Yes. He will be here from the Friday night until the Monday morning.'

'There's no doubt about that then?' Tony asked. 'He will be there the weekend after next.'

'None at all,' the man replied.

'What time does he usually arrive?'

'Around four o'clock in the afternoon.'

'Thank you.' Tony replaced the receiver. He was glad that Monsieur Vincent had not been on duty. He might have recognized his voice.

He turned to see the idiot boy grinning at him. A chill of fear passed through his body. He went up to the boy and spoke to him. The boy just grinned and made obscene noises in his throat.

The concierge came out of her room. 'There's no point in talking to him,' she explained. 'He's completely deaf. He can't hear a thing.'

Tony sighed with relief. 'What a pity!' he said. He bounded up the stairs two at a time and burst into Monsieur Perroton's bedroom.

'I've got an idea!' he exclaimed excitedly. 'You and Marie can spend your birthday together after all.'

'But how?' the old man asked.

'She can come here. She can sleep on the couch in the sitting-room.'

Monsieur Perroton sighed patiently. 'But she has to look after Thérèse.'

Tony smiled and shook his head. 'No, she doesn't,' he said. 'She can spend the weekend with you.'

'But, Thérèse?'

'Thérèse will be all right. You and Marie can be together.'

'You are talking nonsense,' the old man said.

'No, I'm not,' Tony assured him. 'You will have your birthday as usual with Marie.'

'And who will look after Thérèse?'

Tony leant against the door and grinned. 'I will,' he replied.

15

'He should never have told you,' Marie said.

'Why not?'

'Because it's nothing to do with you. They are family matters. He had no business to involve you. It was very wrong of him. He talks far too much.'

'I wanted to help,' Tony explained.

Marie smiled at him. 'You are very kind. But things like these are best kept in the family. It doesn't do to involve outsiders.'

'I'm sorry that you look upon me as an outsider,' Tony said. He noticed that the two pictures had been replaced on the wall. They were photographs of her parents.

She shyly put her hand on his arm. 'Don't make things difficult for me,' she pleaded. 'I never wanted you to know about Thérèse. It isn't a thing one likes to talk about.'

'But it's nothing to be ashamed of,' Tony replied. 'It can happen in all families. I know that only too well. My grandfather died in some institution. But I'm not ashamed. Why should I be? It's just a fact of life. Your father is sick, and he wants you to spend his birthday with him. It would mean a great deal to him. I think you should go. You've said yourself that your aunt's condition can be controlled by drugs. Very well, then. There's no problem, is there? Nothing whatever can happen. If by any chance there is trouble, I can always telephone you. I will, anyhow, to put your mind at rest.'

Marie hesitated.

'Please,' Tony urged. 'Please let me help you. Surely you want to be with your father, don't you? It would do you good to get out of this house. It isn't natural the life you're leading.'

'Oh, you don't have to tell me that.'

'Very well then. You have all the necessary drugs?'

'Yes.'

'Then there's nothing more to be said. The matter's settled. I'll drive you to Albi myself on the Friday morning.'

Marie shook her head. 'But that's just it. You see, you don't understand. Thérèse can never be left. You would have to stay with her all the time. It is too much to ask of you.'

'I'm sorry. I forgot. Of course I'll stay with her. It was stupid of me to forget. Marie?'

'Yes?'

'May I see Thérèse?'

Marie looked uncertain.

'Please,' Tony urged. 'It's important that I see her. I'll have to sooner or later, won't I?'

'I suppose so,' Marie replied. 'Follow me.' She led the way upstairs and paused outside a door on the landing. Tony noticed that the key was in the lock. 'She has the best room. It's directly over the salon so that I can hear if she becomes upset. She's very thin and old now, but they say that she used to be quite pretty.'

She slowly turned the key and opened the door.

The room was dark and shuttered. It was some time before Tony's eyes became accustomed to the gloom. And then he saw the bed. A large brass double bed that at first appeared to be empty. He looked more closely. He could just see the woman's head against the mass of pillows. A frail hand clutched at the sheet. The wrist was thin, like a dead twig. Tony noticed that the woman was tiny. Her body made barely any impression under the bedding. It was almost as if the bed were empty.

There was just the small emaciated head against the pillows, and the claw-like hand that clutched at the sheet. If it hadn't been for a convulsive twitch of the hand, Tony would have sworn that it was a corpse lying there.

'She looks as if she is dead,' he whispered.

Marie nodded.

Tony crossed to the shuttered windows that were on three sides of the room. 'Do these have to be closed?' he asked.

'Yes. All the time. The light has a bad effect on her.' She bent over the bed and adjusted her aunt's pillows. Tony opened one of the shutters a crack. It was just as he thought. The room commanded a view of the whole valley. He could see the Malines' house perfectly, right into the main bedroom. He quietly closed the shutters. Marie was standing by the bed. He went over and joined her.

'Is she drugged now?' he asked.

Marie nodded. 'The whole time. I keep the tablets downstairs. She has to have six a day. As long as she has those, she can come to no great harm.'

'But she still has fits,' Tony said. 'Like the time when I was here.'

'Yes. She can get upset. It tends to go in cycles. She has periods when she is difficult. We have just been through a bad time. But they don't last long, and she can always be controlled. That last time was partly my fault. It's just that I hate to see her lying there like a vegetable all the time. I hadn't given her enough drugs.'

'Can she hear anything?' Tony asked.

'Yes. She has very acute hearing. But she seems to be asleep just now. There are some things of hers downstairs that I must get. I shan't be long. You can stay with her if you like.'

Tony stood and stared intently at Thérèse. She lay there inert and helpless in the bed. It was exactly like looking at a corpse.

Until she opened her eyes. Suddenly, she sat up in the bed and stared at Tony. Her eyes were dark and terrifying. He had never seen such an expression of hatred before. She remained like that for several minutes before she groaned and fell back against the pillows. Her hand fluttered for a moment, but her eyes remained open, staring malevolently at Tony.

He heard Marie coming upstairs. Thérèse's eyes flickered for a moment and then closed. She was lying peacefully when Marie entered.

'I think she's asleep,' she whispered. 'We'd better leave her.'

Tony picked up the photograph that was beside the bed. 'This is a good picture of you,' he said.

Marie nodded. 'It was taken by Auguste. He came and took Thérèse and me for a drive. She likes to have it beside her bed. But she broke it recently. She threw it across the room, and I had to get it mended. I have to take it away from her when she gets violent.'

'I see,' Tony said as he followed Marie out of the room.

'She didn't wake up?' she asked when then they were on the landing.

Tony shook his head. 'I thought once that she smiled at me. But it could have been my imagination.'

'You are very kind,' Marie said.

'Then you will let me help you. You will go to your father for that weekend?'

'Yes.'

'You needn't worry,' he assured her. 'I shall look after Thérèse.'

'Yes, I know you will. I shan't worry, I promise you.'

'And now I must go,' he said. 'I have a lot of work to do.' He felt in his pockets. 'I think I must have left something in the bedroom.'

Marie waited while he went back into the bedroom. There was an electric point by the bed.

'Did you find what you were looking for?' she asked.

'Yes,' Tony nodded.

He kissed her goodbye, walked through the village to the old house, and put through a call to Elizabeth. He was lucky. She was at home.

'Where have you been?' she asked. 'It's ages since you've rung. I was beginning to think that you'd forgotten all about me.'

'Far from it,' he assured her. 'I've just been extremely busy. I think I've got a bloody good plot. But I have to go away again to do some final research.'

'Oh? Where?'

'Bordeaux, most probably.'

'What's it about?'

'I'll tell you when I've got it all finally sorted out. It's a bit complicated. What's it like in England?'

'Bloody awful. It hasn't stopped raining for the past two weeks.'

'It's beautiful here. Why don't you come over and spend a few days here? You can have the house while I'm away. It seems a pity not to use it. I shall be leaving on Friday week. You can fly out to Toulouse, hire a car at the airport, and drive down. I'll be back about a week later, and we can have some days together. Would you like that?'

'I might.'

'It would be wonderful to see you. You could stay as long as you like. There's plenty of room here.'

'I shall have to think about it,' Elizabeth said.

'Well, do that. But I must know soon. I needn't pay the rent if you don't want the house.'

'You say you'll be away for a week?'

'Yes.'

'When do you need to know?'

'I really should give a week's notice, and tomorrow's Friday. Can't you make up your mind now? What's the problem?'

'Nothing really. It certainly would be nice.'

'Then you'll come?'

Elizabeth paused. 'Let me ring you back,' she said. 'I've got to make some phone calls, and I'll ring you back. I won't be long. It's just that I've got seats for a couple of theatres, and I'll have to see if I can get rid of them.'

'Fair enough,' Tony replied. 'I'll wait for you to ring me back.'

He replaced the receiver and unpacked the food that he had bought in the village. He had anticipated that this might happen, so he had come prepared. It was rather a special meal. Pâté de foie gras and champagne.

He didn't have to wait long. Elizabeth rang back about an hour later. 'I'm coming,' she said. 'You did say that one can get a car at the airport, didn't you?'

'Yes. I'll send you all the necessary directions tomorrow. I think you'll be very happy here. You won't be bored while I'm away?'

'I'll try not to be. When did you say you'll be back?'

'The following Friday, I expect. Anyhow, I'll write and let you know. I shan't just turn up.'

'All right. I'm quite looking forward to it now.'

'I just hope that you won't find it too isolated,' Tony said. 'There aren't any houses nearby, you know. And one can't get domestic help. Does that matter?'

'No. I don't expect that I will make it all that dirty.'

'Fine. Well, I'd better ring off. I've got quite a few things to do. I'll send you the directions. You must come on Friday week. There's a plane gets in at about one in the afternoon. You would be out here by half past two at the latest. I'll get in some food for you, and drop you a line when I'm coming back. I hope you like it here.'

'I'm sure I shall.'

'I'll ring you again on Thursday night, just to make sure that you're coming.'

'All right. Goodbye.'

'Goodbye.'

Tony picked up the champagne bottle. It was almost empty. He should have bought himself another one.

16

There was a bookshop almost directly opposite the Hostelrie Saint-Antoine. If he stood in the corner by the window, he could just see the reception desk through the large glass doors. He looked at his watch. It was half past four.

The proprietor was giving him curious glances. Tony realized that he had been standing there for quite a long time. He took down a book from the shelves and added it to the pile that he had accumulated.

Suddenly he noticed some activity at the reception desk. Someone had arrived by the back entrance from the car park. Monsieur Vincent was on duty. Tony could see him get up and signal to the page-boy.

Auguste Devine walked up to the desk. Tony watched as he filled in the visitors' form. Then he picked up the pile of books and turned to the proprietor.

'I would like to take these,' he said. 'But I'll pick them up later. I haven't got my car with me now.'

'Very well,' the man said, as he took the money.

Tony was just about to leave the shop when the hotel doors opened and Auguste came out. He stopped for a moment on the pavement before walking towards the centre of the town. Tony followed him, keeping at a reasonable distance.

Auguste walked quickly along the main street towards the river. The pavement was crowded with shoppers. He appeared to be in a hurry. Twice he pushed his way through groups of people who were in his way.

He turned right into the Rue de la République. The street was almost deserted. Tony bent down and pretended to adjust his shoe buckle. Auguste had turned into a block of flats farther up the street.

He crossed to the other side of the road, and slowly walked past the building. It was a small block of modern flats. He glanced casually up at the windows. One was open on the first floor. Tony could just see into the room. A woman came to the window and looked out for a moment. She had long red hair and was wearing a green housecoat. Auguste came and stood behind her. He put his arms around her and kissed the back of her neck. She smiled tolerantly and went on looking out on to the street. Tony was aware that she had seen him. Then he heard the window being closed.

He waited for some time before he went into the flats. It was a new building and there was no concierge's office. He walked up the stairs to the first floor. There were only two flats on each level. The woman's door was closed. There was a name plate on the door. Suzanne Declair. The door of the flat opposite opened and a couple of young men came out. They gave Tony an amused look as they passed. One of them said something in a low voice, and the other laughed. He turned and grinned at Tony.

'You want Suzy?' he asked.

'Do you know her?'

'Of course. But you're out of luck just now. She has a regular guy at weekends. She won't be free until Monday.'

'Who is he? Do you know?'

The young man shook his head. 'Some bloke from Bordeaux. Comes every weekend. You can try her on Monday if you're still around.'

'Thanks,' Tony replied. He waited until the two men had left the building. So Auguste had a mistress. A prostitute called Suzanne Declair. He wondered how long he would have to wait.

He had passed a bar at the corner of the street. He could wait in there until Auguste came out. He thought it unlikely that they would spend the night together.

He had to wait nearly an hour. There was a mirror at the back of the bar. Tony got up and ordered another drink while he watched Auguste turn the corner into the main street. He finished his drink and slowly wandered back to the flats.

The woman opened the door. She smiled when she saw Tony.

'Suzy?' he asked.

'Well, hallo,' she replied. 'I saw you before, didn't I? You were down in the street. Thanks for waiting. Come on in.' She stood aside to let him enter.

He walked into a tiny hall. There were two doors leading off, and both were open. He could see into a kitchen and a large bed-sitting-room. The air was thick with acrid cigar fumes and the bed was unmade.

'Have I come at the wrong time?' Tony asked.

Suzy shrugged her shoulders. 'I wasn't expecting you.' She went and opened the window. 'Let's have some fresh air.'

There was an ash-tray by the bed. It was full of cigar butts. The same that he had found by the roadside.

'He smokes a lot,' Tony said.

'Yes.'

He went and took her in his arms. The green housecoat fell to the floor.

She undid the buttons of his shirt. 'Come to bed,' she whispered. 'I liked you the moment I saw you.' Her hands were cold against his skin as she loosened his belt.

It was quiet in the room. She had been asleep for about half an hour. He had lain there for some time before he got up and went to the door. He glanced back at her before leaving the room. She was still fast asleep. He tiptoed into the kitchen and looked around him.

She stirred and turned over in the empty bed. It was cold. She shivered and opened her eyes.

He was standing at the door, fully dressed. He came over and kissed her. 'I must go,' he said.

'Will you come back?'

He shrugged his shoulders. 'Who knows?' he replied.

She yawned and reached out for the housecoat. 'I'll come and see you out.'

'Don't bother.' He bent down and put some money by the bed. She watched him go. He turned as he shut the front door. She was still in bed, smiling at him.

He walked quickly down the street and turned into the main road. There was a telephone box about two blocks down

'Hostelrie Saint-Antoine.'

'May I speak to Monsieur Devine?'

'Hold on. I'll connect you to his room.'

Tony had to wait several minutes before Auguste answered. He must have been asleep. His voice was blurred and tired.

'Is that Monsieur Devine?'

'Yes.'

'My name is Grainger. Tony Grainger.'

'Who?'

'Tony Grainger. I've taken your cousin's house at Laurac.'

'Oh yes. You're the English writer.' Auguste's voice had changed. The tiredness had disappeared.

'I want to talk to you,' Tony said. 'But I would rather not do it over the telephone. Can we meet somewhere?'

'What is it about?'

'It's to do with the house. I've found something. Something valuable.'

'What is it?'

'I don't quite know. I've never seen anything like it before. It looks like part of an old necklace. I think it's gold.'

'Where did you find it?'

'In the garden. I was doing some digging and I found it.'

'Where are you ringing from?'

'A call-box on the Laurac-Albi road. I can be in Albi in about a quarter of an hour. Could we meet outside the bar of the Chiffre? I think it best that we don't meet in your hotel.'

'Very well. I'll see you there in a quarter of an hour.'

'Fine. Goodbye.' Tony grinned as he put down the receiver. He had a quarter of an hour to wait. Plenty of time to go back to the car.

He was waiting outside the bar when Auguste appeared.

He stood hesitantly by the door and looked around him. Tony realized that Auguste had no idea what he looked like. He introduced himself.

'There's a quiet corner over there where we can talk.' He pointed to a bench under some trees.

'Well?' Auguste asked impatiently. 'What is all this about? What have you found? Let me see it.'

Tony shook his head. 'I haven't got it with me. I didn't want to bring it. I may be wrong, but it looks very old.'

'What is it like?'

Tony described one of the pieces of Aztec jewellery that he had read about in Bordeaux. 'But it probably isn't of much value,' he said casually.

Auguste could scarcely contain his impatience. 'You must show it to me,' he said.

Tony shook his head again. 'Hang on,' he said. 'I don't think we should be too hasty. I've got a feeling that there may be some more things buried there.'

'Why did you telephone me?' Auguste asked.

'Because I thought you might know what it is. They could be things that belonged to your family.'

'That's right. They are. They were my cousin's. She was given them. They are mine now.'

'Hold on,' Tony said. 'You're saying they belonged to Madame Malines?'

Auguste nodded. 'Yes. She was my cousin.'

'But she left all her property to this woman in the village. That's why we have to be careful. These things should really all belong to her. And it's her daughter who looks after the house for me. She's cleaning it this weekend. She mustn't realize that I've found this. I must continue looking without her realizing. Don't you understand?'

Auguste remained silent.

'I shall have to work there alone in the evenings,' Tony explained. 'I will let you know if I find anything.'

'Why have you told me this?' Auguste asked.

'Because I agree with you. These things are logically yours. And I have a feeling that you have been looking for them for some time. Am I right?'

'Yes,' Auguste nodded.

'You searched the house while I was away, didn't you? And you used to drive past late at night to see if I was there?'

'Yes. It should have been my house.'

'I want a cut,' Tony continued. 'You won't be able to find these things without my help. And they would probably be difficult for me to get rid of. Now, do you understand?'

'I understand.'

'Then, do you think that we can work together? If not, I can probably manage alone.'

There was a pause before Auguste answered. 'Very well,' he replied finally.

'So let's shake hands on it,' Tony said.

Auguste reluctantly extended his hand.

'Good.' Tony grinned at Auguste. 'I shall go on searching all next week. If you can be back here on Friday, I will give you a ring during the evening and tell you whether I've found anything else. If I have, then I suggest that you come out to the house and take a look. If not, then there's just this necklace. We can discuss what we do with that when I ring you. Do you agree?'

Auguste nodded.

'Excellent. I'd better be getting back. I don't much like leaving the place when that girl is around.'

'How did you know I was here?' Auguste asked.

'There's a lot of gossip in the village. They say you come here every weekend to look for the jewels. They even say that you have been seen searching the house. That's why you should keep away. It doesn't belong to you now, you know. You're trespassing. So you could be prosecuted. It's essential that you don't go anywhere near the place until I send for you. Do you understand?'

'Yes.'

'Good. I'll ring you at your hotel next Friday evening. Let's hope I've been successful.'

'Let's hope so.'

'Oh, I nearly forgot. There's just one other tiny point,' Tony said. 'The small matter of my commission. I would suggest we split fifty-fifty.'

'But – '

'Well, if you don't like that,' Tony continued, 'I can easily go elsewhere. I'm not entirely without contacts of my own in London. And you must agree that it's me that is doing all the work. And, of course, with me living in the house, there's not really much else that you can do about it, is there?'

'Very well,' Auguste agreed.

'Fifty-fifty, then?'

'Yes.'

'Fine. I'll ring you on Friday. Goodbye.'

'Goodbye.'

He watched Auguste leave before he entered the bar of the Chiffre. 'Bring me a half bottle of champagne, will you?' he said to the barman. 'And do you know a good stereo equipment shop?'

'There's one in the Avenue Gambetta.'

'Thanks.'

He sat and waited for the champagne. There were quite a few things he needed to get. He watched as the barman poured out the champagne. He had always loved champagne, but never been able to afford it. He smiled to himself as he sipped the wine. Perhaps soon he might be able to afford more of it. He might even be able to have as much as he wanted.

17

The girl came slowly along the lane. She had washed some shirts for him, and was bringing them back. He never seemed to notice that she did all his washing for him. He took it for granted that there should always be clean shirts in his drawers. Perhaps all men were like that, she wondered. But it would have been nice if he could have thanked her just once. If just once he could have taken some notice of her as a person, instead of continually treating her as a servant.

She could see that he was in the garden again. He had spent the whole week digging up that old rockery. She paused for a moment to watch him. He was just wearing a brief pair of shorts. She watched the muscles of his back as he dug deeper and deeper into the ground.

He hadn't seen her. But she was used to that. He never saw her. She might just as well not have existed so far as he was concerned. There were times when she almost hated him for the way that he ignored her.

She entered the house and went upstairs. She was just about to go into the bedroom when she noticed that the door up to the attics had been left open. She put down the shirts and crossed the landing. A shaft of sunlight fell across the steep staircase which led up to the attics. One of the shutters must have swung open up there. She went to investigate.

But someone had been up there recently. The place had been tidied up. There had used to be a lot of junk and old packing cases belonging to Madame Malines. But they had all been moved and stacked neatly against the wall.

She stumbled and tripped over a loose floorboard. Her shoe was caught in a hole in the floor. She bent down to pull it free. The board had been prised loose and a hole had been made in the ceiling. She could see right down into the main bedroom below. The hole was directly over the bed.

She got up slowly and walked to the door of the other attic. It had always been stiff. The hinges were rusty and squeaked when they were moved. But they had recently been oiled. The door now opened without a sound. She stood and stared at the little room, an expression of bewilderment on her face.

It was some time before she came downstairs. She paused on the landing and looked down on the garden. He was still digging. She was just about to go down the stairs when she realized that she had forgotten to put his shirts away. She picked them up and went into the bedroom.

She looked up at the ceiling. It was impossible to see the hole. It had been cunningly made in the ornate plaster moulding around the light, and was completely invisible amongst the design of leaves and flowers. She crossed to the chest of drawers. They were almost full of parcels. He must have been shopping. There was no room for the shirts. She opened another drawer. He had put more things in there, too. She moved them aside in order to make a place for the shirts, and felt something hard under some loose clothes. She picked the clothes up and stared with horror at the thing lying at the bottom of the drawer.

She walked slowly out of the house. Tony was still digging in the garden. He glanced up and saw her at the gate.

'Hallo, there!' he called.

She stopped and looked at him.

'Are you all right?' Tony asked. 'You look pale.'

'Yes. I'm all right,' the girl replied.

'I've got to go away again,' he said. 'The day after tomorrow. There's no need for you to come up. You can have a holiday. It'll do you good. I'll come and let you know when I'm back.'

The girl nodded.

'Are you sure you're all right?' he asked again. 'You're terribly pale. A holiday will do you good.'

'Yes, I expect it will. So you don't want me to come up here while you're away?'

'No,' he replied.

She nodded. 'Very well. You'll tell me when you get back?'

'Yes.'

She walked slowly back to the village and crossed the square towards the hotel. The patronne was at her desk in the hall. She looked up as the girl entered. 'You're early,' she said.

The girl nodded. 'You owe me a week's holiday. I want to take it.'

The patronne sighed. 'Oh, very well,' she agreed. 'When do you want to go.'

'The day after tomorrow.'

'That's Friday,' the patronne said.

'Yes. That's right,' the girl replied.

18

The taxi was waiting outside to take Marie to Albi.

'Are you sure you will be all right?' she fussed.

'Yes. Of course I will,' Tony assured her for about the tenth time.

'I've put out everything that you could possibly need. Now, you do understand about the tablets, don't you? They're absolutely essential. You do understand that?'

'Marie! For God's sake! Of course I understand.'

She handed him a piece of paper. 'I've written everything down.'

'Thank you. Now you really must go. The taxi's been waiting for ages.'

Marie nodded. 'Very well. Tony, it is so good of you to do this for me. You really are very kind. But I still don't think I should leave you like this.'

'What nonsense! It isn't as if it's for very long. You'll be back on Monday.'

'Yes, I know. But it's not much fun for you.'

'Rubbish! I can just as easily work here as at my own house. It's a good opportunity to get on with some writing.' He led the way firmly out to the taxi, and opened the door.

Marie paused for a moment. 'I hope I've left you enough to eat.'

'I'm sure you have.' He gave the directions to the driver. 'Goodbye. See you some time on Monday morning. Don't hurry back. And give my regards to your father. Wish him many happy returns of the day for me.'

Marie smiled and nodded. 'You'll ring me, won't you?'

'Of course. Goodbye.'

'Goodbye, Tony.'

He stood and waved until the taxi was out of sight. He glanced up at the shuttered windows of Thérèse's room. She was fast asleep. Marie had given her a couple of tablets before she had left. She would sleep now for the rest of the morning, until it was time for her to have another dose at midday. He walked down the lane to the Malines' house. He didn't need to be there long. He had got everything ready earlier in the day.

He drove back to Marie's house and carried the things upstairs. Thérèse was lying asleep on the bed. He crossed to the windows and threw open the shutters. The strong sunlight poured into the room.

Thérèse stirred and opened her eyes. She struggled helplessly to avoid the light which shone directly on to the bed. Her eyes blinked and her head tossed wildly from side to side.

Tony stood at the foot of the bed and laughed. 'I've come to give you a bit of a concert,' he said. 'But first, we must make you comfortable.' He picked up some strong straps, passed them over Thérèse's thin body and fastened her securely to the bed.

'We can't have you getting up just yet,' he said. 'I've got to go out. So you must be a good girl and wait patiently until I get back. I've brought you some music to listen to while I'm away. I didn't want you getting bored.' He unpacked a tape-recorder and ear-phones and plugged it into the point by the bed. 'Do you like Wagner?' he asked. 'I've had a tape made especially for you. The *Liebestod* from *Tristan und Isolde.* They were great lovers, you know. And the music describes their feelings. Does it quite well, I think. It's fairly hot stuff. Wagner was good at that sort of thing. And I put another piece of music on the tape as well. The *Venusberg* music from *Tannhäuser.* That's pretty sexy stuff, too. I'm sure you'll like it. Sex is a lot of fun, you know. There's nothing nicer than lying around with a beautiful woman in one's arms. There's no better feeling in the whole world. But, you've been rather unlucky with all that, haven't you? Mathilde and Angèle both had their men, but you seem to have missed out. That was bad luck. I don't blame you for feeling sore about it. Even Marie gets it, you know. That's where she's gone now. She couldn't bear to stay here any longer. And why should she? It isn't natural. Everyone needs love. You just as much as anyone else. That's why I've brought you this music. I think you'll like it. Anyhow, see what you think.'

He attached the ear-phones to the old woman's head and turned the tape on full. Her eyes opened in terror as the blast of music rang through her head.

Tony could see Thérèse's face contort with agony as the climax of the music approached. The tape was a long one. It would play the music over and over again for about an hour and a half. He had recorded it himself, breaking up the phrases and repeating them over and over again. It had nearly driven him insane, and he could well imagine the effect it would have on someone who was already deranged. And he had occasionally spoken on the tape himself. He had whispered things about Mathilde. Private, secret things. Things that one didn't usually talk about.

He could see Thérèse wince. The noise in her ears must have been almost deafening. And yet he couldn't hear a sound.

He ran downstairs and telephoned Blagnac Airport at Toulouse. Elizabeth's plane was due in about three quarters of an hour. He had rung her the previous evening to confirm that she was coming.

'I'm looking forward to it,' she had said. 'What a pity that you won't be there.'

'I'll try and get back around the middle of next week,' he had promised. 'We can have as long as we like together after that.'

'Yes.'

'Oh, there's quite a good restaurant nearby if you can't be bothered to cook. They do a good dinner in the evening, and their wines are excellent.'

'What's it called?'

'La Maison du Vigneron. It's at Gaillac. About ten kilometres from Laurac on the Toulouse road. It's worth going to one evening.'

'Thanks,' Elizabeth had said. 'I'll make a note of the name.'

Tony grinned to himself as he started the car. He looked up at the open windows of Thérèse's room. He couldn't hear a sound.

He got to Blagnac ten minutes before the plane was due. He parked the car in an inconspicuous corner of the car park and entered the terminal building.

Elizabeth's plane was posted on the arrival indicator. There had been no delays. A group of people were already assembling around the barrier. He climbed the stairs up to the terrace and sat down in a secluded corner.

The terrace was almost deserted. A group of small children were playing by the railings at the far end. Suddenly, one of them gave a cry and pointed at the sky.

There was a roar of engines, and the plane suddenly emerged through the heat haze. Tony watched as it made a perfect landing and slowly taxied to a halt. There was a pause as the steps were wheeled up and the doors eventually opened.

Tony moved into the shadow of the wall. He watched as the passengers began to emerge from the plane. They all paused and blinked in the strong sunlight before descending the steps.

And then he saw Elizabeth. She was looking beautiful in an apricot trouser suit that he had never seen before. She paused at the top of the steps and looked around her. Then she turned and spoke to someone behind her in the plane. He could see her laughing.

A man stepped out of the plane behind her. His face was in shadow but Tony could see that he had his hand on Elizabeth's shoulder. He glanced up as he stepped into the sun. A surge of hatred passed through Tony's brain as he recognized Julian Harbord. He watched as they crossed the tarmac together. They were talking and laughing together. Tony could hear Elizabeth's laugh as they disappeared into the terminal building.

It would take them a few minutes to pass through the customs. Then they would have to collect their car. He waited a few minutes before he moved to the staircase and looked down into the terminal. Julian was standing at the Avis car desk. Tony could see Elizabeth at the bookstall. Julian turned towards her and together they walked out of the building.

He went back on to the terrace and watched them in the car park below. An attendant opened the doors of a car and handed Julian the keys. Tony could hear the engine starting as he ran down the stairs.

He reached the car park as they drove off. They were turning the corner as he reached his car. There was little traffic on the road. Tony let them get quite a long way ahead as he followed them to Laurac.

He waited at the crossroads for several minutes in order to give them time to get into the house, and then drove quickly past up the lane.

He could hear Thérèse moaning as he parked the car. He ran upstairs. The tape had ceased. She turned her head quickly as he entered, and for a moment he felt a shiver of panic at the look of hatred in her eyes.

'Filth!' she spat at him. It was the first time that he had heard her speak. Her voice was surprisingly young. 'Filth!'

'Didn't you like the music?' he asked. 'What a pity! Perhaps you couldn't quite understand it. I'll play it all again for you.'

'Dirty filthy scum! Who are you? Why are you here?'
'I'm looking after you.'
'Where's Marie?'
'I've told you.'
'She's with some man?'
'That's right,' Tony nodded.
'She's gone to some man?'
'Yes.'

Thérèse began to shake her head violently from side to side. 'She's with some man,' she repeated over and over and over again. 'She's with some man.'

'It's time for you to have your medicine.' He bent down and took a bottle of whisky out of a suitcase. 'This'll do you good,' he said, pouring the neat liquid into a glass. 'Drink it up. It'll do you the world of good. Put some hairs on your chest.' He supported the old woman's head and forced the whisky down her throat. She shook her head suddenly, spilling the liquid all over the bed.

'Careless bitch!' Tony muttered. 'Can't you be more careful?'

'Who are you?' she repeated. 'Why are you here?'

'We've got a little job to do together,' Tony replied softly.

The old woman stared at him malevolently. 'You're evil,' she said.

Tony nodded. 'That's right, darling. Evil and single-minded. But not many people have realized it.'

'Where's Marie? I want her.'

'I've told you you can't have her. She's with this man.'

'She's happy with some man?'

'Very happy,' Tony replied.

'Everyone's happy,' Thérèse muttered. 'They're all happy. Except for me. I've never been happy.'

Tony crossed to the window. 'You poor old thing,' he said. 'Never mind. We'll try and make each other happy. We'll try and do each other a good turn.' He looked down towards the Malines' house.

They were standing together on the balcony. Julian had taken off his shirt.

'Let's go to bed,' he suggested. 'It's too hot to do anything else.'

Elizabeth was looking at the view. 'It's beautiful, isn't it?' She stared up at the field in front of the house. 'I wonder what that stuff is?'

Julian put his arms around her and kissed her neck. 'Barley, I think.'

'It's very high.'

'Yes.' He moved his hands over her breasts. 'I want you,' he murmured.

'Can't you wait until tonight?'

'No. Not possibly.'

Elizabeth smiled and turned to him. 'Then perhaps we'd better go inside. We can't make love out here.' She moved into the room and began to undress. Julian was already naked, lying on the bed waiting for her.

'Shouldn't we close the window, or something?' she asked.

Julian shook his head. 'No. It's good to make love in the sun.'

'But people will see us.'

'Who, darling? It's not exactly Piccadilly Circus, is it?'

'Well, we should at least close the shutters.'

'Why, for God's sake? It's beautiful lying here looking up at that hillside.'

'But, someone might be – ' She broke off in the middle of the sentence as Julian kissed her.

Tony stood silently at the window. It was some time before he turned into the room.

'You like to see people happy, don't you?' he asked. 'Then come over here.' He unstrapped Thérèse and pulled her over to the window. 'Look at that,' he said. 'Look down there at your sister's house.' He held Thérèse's head and forced her to look. 'They're happy. Look at them.'

JACKDAW

The sun was shining straight into the bedroom. The two naked bodies were clearly visible on the bed.

An expression of loathing came over Thérèse's face. She stared intently at the two bodies. 'Filth!' she muttered. 'Pigs! Filth!'

'That's what people do when they're happy,' Tony said quietly. 'They take off their clothes and do that.'

'It's disgusting!' Thérèse shouted. She began to struggle in Tony's arms. But her eyes remained riveted. 'It's Mathilde, isn't it? I can see now. It's Mathilde.'

'Yes. Do you like her?'

'No. I hate her.'

'Why?'

'Because she had things.'

'What sort of things?'

'Things. Things I wanted. Things I could never have.'

'What sort of things?' Tony repeated.

Thérèse didn't answer. She remained still, staring down at the two lovers.

'Did she have things like jewellery?' Tony asked quietly. 'Was it that? Did Mathilde take the jewels?'

'Jewels?'

'Yes. Mathilde took your sister's jewels.'

Thérèse nodded. 'She was greedy. Greedy and ugly. I hated her. I always had. That was why I killed Minou. I remember now.'

'Minou?'

'Yes. I killed her.'

'Who was Minou?'

'I killed her because I hated Mathilde.'

'Did you kill Mathilde?' Tony asked.

Thérèse laughed. 'I know more than people think.' She rocked backwards and forwards chuckling to herself.'

'You know a lot,' Tony said. 'Secret things. Things that other people don't know. Isn't that right?'

Thérèse nodded.

'Tell me your secrets,' Tony whispered. 'Share your secrets with me.'

'Who are you?'

'Just a friend.'

'You're not a friend. You're an enemy. You are evil. That's why you're here. You have come to do harm. I know you now. I've seen you before. You're the Devil. That's who you are. You're the Devil. And you're evil. Evil! Evil! Evil!' She tried to struggle out of his grasp, but he held her tight. She began to scream louder and louder at him.

'Evil! Evil! Evil!'

'Shut up,' he said softly. 'Shut up, or I'll hurt you.'

But she continued to shout. He slammed the window shut. Thérèse struggled helplessly in his arms, and her eyes blazed at him with hatred.'

'You're the Devil,' she shouted. 'You've come to do harm.'

'Shut up!' he yelled and hit her sharply across the face. A scream was strangled in her throat as she collapsed at his feet. He picked her up and threw her on the bed. He was just about to strap her down when the telephone began to ring.

'Hell!' he muttered. He glanced at Thérèse before going downstairs.

'Hallo?'

'Tony. It's Marie. Is everything all right?'

'Of course it is,' he assured her.

'How is she?'

'Asleep.'

'Have you given her the tablets?'

'Of course.'

'Then she'll probably sleep all day. Are you all right?'

'Yes. Of course I am.'

'You sound cross,' Marie said. 'Are you sure you're managing all right?'

'I'm managing very well,' Tony replied. 'There's nothing for you to worry about. Are you both having a good time? How is your father?'

'He sends you his best wishes. I think he is feeling better today. Tony?'

'Yes?'

'I can't thank you enough for what you're doing.'

'Think nothing of it. I'm pleased to do it.'

'I'll ring you again tomorrow.'

'Fine,' Tony replied. 'But not too early. I may sleep in a bit.'

'I'll ring during the afternoon. Goodbye.'

'Goodbye.'

He was just about to replace the receiver when he heard the noise behind him. He turned suddenly. Thérèse had come into the room. She had found the knife, and she was coming towards him. Her eyes blazed with hatred as she raised the knife and struck at his neck.

19

Julian stirred and opened his eyes. He rolled over and kissed Elizabeth's breasts. 'I'm famished,' he said. 'Let's eat. Didn't you say you knew somewhere to go?'

'Yes. I've got the name in my bag.'

'Then let's go.' He looked at his watch. 'It's nearly six. We can have a bit of a drive around.' He got up and went into the bathroom to run a shower.

'I don't want to be late tonight,' Elizabeth said.

'What?' Julian shouted from under the shower.

Elizabeth appeared at the door of the bathroom. 'I said I didn't want to be too late tonight,' she repeated.

'What you really mean of course, is that you can't wait to get back into bed.'

'Not at all,' Elizabeth replied. 'I haven't spent the whole afternoon asleep like you have. You do realize that you snore, don't you? I can't bear men who snore.'

'Didn't you sleep?' Julian asked.

Elizabeth shook her head. 'No. I don't like this place much. It's got a nasty atmosphere.'

'How do you mean?'

'I don't know really. It's creepy. I just don't like it.'

'It seems all right to me.'

'There's another house at the end of this road. There was something going on there while you were asleep.'

'Such as what?'

'I kept on hearing screams.'

'Darling, what nonsense!' He came out from under the shower and took her in his arms.

'You're all wet!'

'Water is wet,' Julian explained. 'Now, what is all this rubbish about hearing screams?'

'It's not rubbish. I heard them. Coming from that house.'

'Well, let's go and investigate,' he said.

'Certainly not! But I promise you that I wasn't imagining it. I really don't like this place. It's got a horrid atmosphere.'

'We don't have to stay here if you don't like it. We can easily go somewhere else.'

'Oh, we'll see,' Elizabeth replied. 'I expect I'll get used to it.' She crossed the landing and went into the bedroom. The country around was silent and deserted. She slipped on a dressing-gown and went out on to the balcony. The house lay silent amongst its trees. She lit a cigarette and leant against the railing of the balcony.

Tony dabbed at his neck with some cotton wool. The bleeding had stopped. Luckily, he had moved aside instinctively as Thérèse had struck, and the wound had not been severe. But it had been a nuisance. Thérèse had collapsed and gone into some kind of a coma. He had carried her upstairs and strapped her into the bed.

But she had found the knife. The big knife that he had seen

lying on the kitchen table when he had entered Suzanne Declair's flat in Albi. He had taken it while she was still asleep and had hidden it in the lining of his coat. He had kept it, concealed since then under some clothes in an unused drawer in his bedroom, and had brought it with him to Marie's house.

And Thérèse had found it. He shivered as he recalled the look in her eyes as she had held the knife ready to strike. He would never have believed that a frail old woman could have had such strength. She had been like someone possessed. It had taken him all his time to restrain her. Eventually he had managed to get the knife away from her, and she had stood there screaming before having some kind of a fit and falling senseless to the floor. He realized now that he would have to start all over again.

He heard the sound of a car starting in the distance, and walked to the window. Elizabeth had just come out of the front door. He watched as she got into the car and they drove off. He looked at his watch. Half past six. They were going out to dinner. Everything was going to plan. He would have at least three hours. He slipped on a pair of gloves and picked up the knife after wiping off all the fingerprints.

Thérèse was lying on the bed, but her eyes were open. They followed him as he moved quickly around the room packing everything up.

'We've got a busy evening ahead of us, old girl,' he said. 'But first I've got to make a telephone call, and this time I'd better make sure that you can't get out of bed.' He checked that the straps were securely fastened before he went downstairs.

He wasn't away for long, but he was smiling when he returned. Everything was going according to plan. He unplugged the equipment and carried everything down to the car.

'Come along,' he said when he returned. 'You're going for a ride. I thought it was about time that you had a treat, so I've arranged a little outing for you.' He went around the room closing the shutters and windows. Thérèse's eyes watched his every movement.

Eventually he came over to the bed and unfastened the straps. She remained still bound up and struggled helplessly as he picked her up and carried her downstairs. He opened the car door and almost threw her, trussed like a chicken, into the back of the car.

He made a quick tour of the house to make sure that he had left nothing behind, and then drove down to the Malines' house.

'You've been here before, haven't you, dear?' he grinned as he got out of the car. 'I expect you can hardly wait to get back. Hang on while I open the door.' He ran up the path to the front door.

But the door was locked. Elizabeth had locked it. He bent down and looked under the flower pot. There was nothing there. She had taken the key with her. He tried the sitting-room windows, but they were all securely fastened. A feeling of panic came over him as he realized that he couldn't get in. It was the only thing he hadn't thought about. Elizabeth was usually fairly careless about locking things.

He made a tour of the house. Perhaps the back door was open. But that was locked, too. The house was all locked up. It was impossible for him to get in.

'No! No! No!' he screamed. There must be some way in. He kicked at the doors in an agony of fury and frustration. He couldn't have his entire plans wrecked by such a stupid mistake. It wasn't possible. There must be some way in.

And then he remembered the broken catch on the study window. He quickly ran round to the back of the house. The window was shut, but he was eventually able to prise it open and clamber inside. He laughed aloud with triumph as he unlocked the back door.

Thérèse struggled helplessly as he picked her up and carried her into the house.

'I've prepared a nice little room for you,' he said. 'Up in the attics. We can have some music, and then, later on, a bit of fun.' He threw her down on a camp bed that he had fixed up in the smaller attic, and strapped her down tightly. Her eyes blazed with hatred as she watched him plug in the tape recorder and attach the ear-phones to her head. A sharp spasm passed through her as the sensual music sounded in her ears.

'The *Liebestod*,' Tony said. 'Do you know what *Liebestod* means? It's the Love Death. Rather an appropriate name I thought.' He went into the large attic and crouched down over the hole in the floor. He could see the whole bed clearly below him. They hadn't bothered to remake it after they had made love. The sheets were all rumpled. Tony could clearly see where they had lain. The imprints of their heads were still on the pillows.

He sat down and waited. He knew that it might have to be for some time. But he could be patient. He had been patient for several years. He could easily wait a few more hours.

He took the piece of paper out of his pocket and read the quotation from the Empress Carlotta's last letter to her husband.

'The moment one assumes responsibility for one's destiny, one does it at one's own risk, at one's own danger, and one is never free to give it up.'

He had responsibility for his destiny. He had never abdicated his intentions, and had never been prepared to give them up, whatever the risk or danger. He had always hated Elizabeth. Hated her wealth, her beauty, her privileges. What right did she have to so much, when things had always been so hard for him? He had had nothing except for good looks. He'd never had her security. She had been brought up amongst a family who didn't know what it was like to have worries. Everything they did, they did well. But it had always been different for him. A family with no money. A father killed in the war, a grandfather who committed suicide, and a neurotic drudge for a mother. Elizabeth's family lived in a large house in Weybridge with another one in the Isle of Wight. He had always had to live in some rented maisonette in Hendon. He had had nothing. Except for his looks. And by Christ, he'd used them. It hadn't taken him long to realize that he could have any woman he wanted. And so he had taken Elizabeth. She was an only child and her father was old. He couldn't last very long, and then Elizabeth would get the lot. It had been rather a special will. Elizabeth's mother was so wealthy in her own right that the old man had not left her any money. She just got the houses and the furniture. All the money came to Elizabeth.

It had been rather a joke at first. 'Perhaps you're after the money,' Elizabeth had said. 'Perhaps I should make a will so that you won't get it all.' And she had laughed. It had been quite a joke between them. But he had never laughed. And she had never made a will.

But that bloody old cow of a mother of hers had always known. She had seen right through him from the start. They had always hated each other.

And he had hated Elizabeth. Hated her for the way she lay around the flat while he had to go out to work at some job he hated. Her father had found him a job in an architect's office, and they all pretended that he was an architect, although everyone knew that he hadn't qualified. He was just a glorified draughtsman.

But he had changed all that, and written a book. And it had been a good book. It was good because he just wrote down his thoughts. Everyone had been surprised. Fancy old Tony writing such a nasty clever book! They didn't realize that he was just a nasty clever guy. Except for Elizabeth's mother. She had put down the book and said nothing. Until he had asked her what she had thought of it. She had looked closely at him before replying. 'Well, it's just you, really, isn't it?' And she had looked so closely at him that he had had to look away.

So he had had to be patient. He had waited and waited until an opportunity had come along. He had sat at the desk in the study downstairs and made endless plans, but no chance had come along. Not until he had heard the screams upstairs in Marie's house, and had listened to the story that Monsieur

Perroton had told. Then he had known that his chance had come.

It would hardly be his fault if he were careless and Thérèse went off her head. She had done it before. He couldn't be blamed if she went rushing down to her sister's old house. It was just bad luck that there happened to be two people staying there, lying in bed together. It would literally be a Love Death. He had chosen the music well.

But he had been even cleverer. He had taken a carving knife from the flat belonging to Auguste Devine's mistress. She would have missed it, too. And Auguste was waiting now for Tony to ring him. He had telephoned Auguste about half an hour ago to say that he thought that he had found out where the jewels were hidden. He had told him to drive out to a lonely call box just outside the village. Tony would ring him up there if he found anything.

He chuckled to himself at the thought of Auguste waiting in the nearby call box. That bloody car with its ostentatious gold lion mascot would be parked outside. And the floor of the call box would be littered with cigar butts. Eventually the telephone would ring and Auguste's greedy eyes would light up. He would snatch up the phone and Tony would tell him excitedly that he had found something. Something like a shield. And he would describe the Sunburst.

Elizabeth and her fancy man would be lying dead in each other's arms, and he would leave the knife beside them on the bed. He would make sure that Thérèse wore gloves, so that there would be no fingerprints. He would tell Auguste that the Sunburst was in the house. He was bound to go up to the bedroom, and he would be bound to pick up the knife, especially as he would no doubt recognize it.

So his fingerprints would be on it, and his mistress would later give evidence that it had disappeared from her flat the day that Auguste had visited her. She obviously had so many clients that she wouldn't give a thought to the young man who had just been passing by.

Tony would have taken Thérèse back to Marie's house. He would give her a large dose of the drugs so that she would fall asleep. She might even die. In which case, so much the better. Everyone had said that she couldn't live for long. But even if she survived, it wouldn't matter. She had no memory. No one would listen to anything she said. He would put her to bed, ring Auguste and tell him to come over straight away. It would only take him a few minutes from the call box.

And then, when he saw the lights of Auguste's car in the lane, he would telephone the police. He could hear screaming, he would say. Someone was screaming down at the Malines' house. There was a car there, too. It had arrived about ten minutes ago. Perhaps the police should investigate.

It was a perfect plan. Auguste had a history of mental illness. It wouldn't be the first time that something like this had happened. But it would be the last. Madame Marty had made that quite clear. It was completely foolproof. Auguste would explain how he had been tricked, but no one would believe him. Tony had only to deny ever having spoken to him. It would be impossible to trace the call.

If things did get nasty, he had only to admit that Thérèse had become violent and gone rushing down the lane. It would then come out that she had done it before and that she had killed Mathilde. Tony had a feeling that everyone in the village had always known what had happened, but that they had kept silent for Marie's sake. They would no doubt do it again.

He was completely safe. The plan was foolproof. And the joy of it was that he had two options. Auguste or Thérèse. He had killed no one. And the police would find nothing to incriminate him. Granted there would be some stereo equipment, but everyone liked to listen to music, and no one would take any notice of anything that Thérèse might say.

There could be a few questions about Elizabeth. But Tony would explain that he had continually tried to persuade her to come out and join him. He had rung her and said that he had to be away for the weekend. Then everyone would understand

and sympathize with him. They would think that she had deserved to die. And it would all settle down again, and he would get Elizabeth's money. And the jewels.

There were still the jewels. They must be buried in the garden. There was no other possible place. Mathilde had been seen digging there. That was where the Jackdaw had put them.

Jackdaw. Tony grinned to himself. We're all Jackdaws. All of us greedy. Mathilde, Auguste and himself. Probably he most of all, because he wanted everything. He, more than anyone, probably deserved to be called Jackdaw. But no one would call him that. They might snigger behind his back and call him a cuckold, but he rather doubted it. Everyone would be kind and sympathetic to the handsome, bereaved young widower.

There was a sound from the small attic. Thérèse was struggling in the bed. She opened her mouth and let out a piercing scream. Her eyes were blazing with fury, and her fingers were clawing at the wall behind her.

'What's the matter?' Tony asked. 'Has the concert come to an end? Is that what was upsetting you? You needed some more music, didn't you?' He bent down and restarted the tape. 'How about a little drink as well?' He picked up the bottle of whisky and thrust the neck of the bottle down the old woman's throat.

She shook her head violently from side to side as she swallowed the neat whisky.

Tony bent over her and laughed. 'Don't you like it, then?' he asked. 'They say in England that whisky makes you frisky. It does you the world of good. Makes you feel nice and lively. Now, you don't want to let me down, do you? We've got a little job to do together tonight. And we want to do it well. We don't want to make a mess of it, do we?'

Thérèse moved suddenly, knocking the bottle out of Tony's hand. There was a crash as it fell on the floor and rolled into the corner of the room, spilling whisky all over the place.

'Now, look what you've done, you careless bitch!' He struck at her face in an outburst of temper. Thérèse struggled violently, her eyes ablaze with hatred.

'It's Mathilde!' she screamed. 'Mathilde!'

'You hated her, didn't you?' he taunted.

Thérèse nodded violently.

'You hated her.'

Again the violent nods. The bed shook as Thérèse nodded her head up and down, hitting herself against the wall behind her.

'You hated her,' Tony repeated. 'And so you killed her.'

Thérèse opened her mouth and let out an unearthly scream. 'Yes!' she shouted at the top of her voice. 'Yes! Yes! Yes!'

'You picked up a knife?'

'Yes!' Her head banged repeatedly against the wall. 'Yes!'

'And you stabbed her. You stabbed her over and over again as she lay in that bed. Is that right? Is that what happened? Is that what you did?'

'Yes!' Thérèse screamed. 'I hated her! I always hated her! That's why I killed Minou.'

Tony knelt down beside her and whispered in her ear. 'You can kill her again. You can do it again.'

Her head suddenly turned towards him.

'Yes,' he nodded. 'You can do it all again. We can do it together. I will help you.'

The agonized mad eyes gazed enquiringly at him.

'She will be coming back,' he whispered. 'Coming back at any moment. And she's got a man with her. You can see them. I've made a hole so that you can watch them. You can see her undress. See them both naked.' Tony's voice shook with insane jealousy as he continued. 'They will lie there together with nothing on, with their bodies touching. The man will caress her, give her pleasure. She will groan and cry in ecstasy as his hands move all over her body. You will see this. You will be watching. You will see how happy he makes her. How her body will arch with pleasure. How she will cry with joy when he touches her.'

'I hate her,' Thérèse muttered. 'Hate her! Hate her!'

'And you're right,' Tony continued. 'You're right to hate her. Because she is selfish and greedy. Why should she be happy when you're not? She doesn't care about you. She never has. She only thinks about herself. She's only ever cared about herself. It doesn't matter to her that you are alone and insecure. Because she is all right. She has everything she needs. She doesn't care that you have to go out and work all day. That you have to sit at some boring desk doing work that you hate while she does nothing.' His face was distorted with fury as he began to shout at Thérèse. 'You have to spend your days in that office surrounded by people who bore you while she does nothing. That doesn't matter to her. She takes all that for granted. That's just what men have to do. That's what they're for.'

'She's evil,' Thérèse moaned, shaking her head from side to side.

'Yes. She's evil. And she must be killed. You must kill her again.' He picked up the knife from the floor. 'You must use this.'

Thérèse's eyes gleamed as she stared at the blade. He had spent hours patiently honing it until it was razor sharp on both sides. The light flickered on the shining steel.

Tony ran his fingers carefully along the edge. 'It's a beautiful knife,' he whispered. 'I've sharpened it specially. You can plunge it into her. Penetrate her body with it. You can be like that man that she lies with. You can plunge yourself deep into her soft seductive body. You too can see how she cries and writhes when you enter her. You can listen to her cries. You will be powerful and strong, and you will plunge the knife into her again and again. And into the man as well. We mustn't forget him. They must both die. They are both evil and selfish. They must both be killed. Do you understand?'

Thérèse nodded. 'Yes,' she screamed. 'They will die. I hate them. They have never cared for me. Why should they be happy?'

'That's right,' Tony replied. 'They've never cared anything for you.' He paused and listened intently.

Thérèse was banging her head against the wall behind her.

'Shut up!' Tony shouted. 'For Christ's sake, shut up!' He

quickly turned out the light and went to the window. He could hear the car approaching up the lane. There was a sudden shaft of light from the headlamps as the car turned the corner.

'Here they come,' he whispered. 'They've arrived. Now we must be quiet. They mustn't hear us. They mustn't know we're here. There mustn't be a sound.' He took a handkerchief out of his pocket and stuffed it into the old woman's mouth, fastening it with a silk scarf tied behind her head.

She struggled helplessly as he undid the straps and carried her into the large attic. He laid her face downwards on the floor over the hole, and lay on top of her pinioning her with all his weight so that she couldn't move.

'Look through that hole,' he whispered. 'Look through that hole so that you can see them.'

The room below was dim. But they were just able to see the bed.

A car door slammed outside and they could hear voices. Tony reached out his hand and felt for the knife.

There was the sound of the front door being unlocked.

'They're coming,' he muttered.

There were sounds of footsteps coming up the stairs, and the door of the room opened. The light was turned on, momentarily dazzling them with its glare. Thérèse struggled helplessly, but Tony kept all his weight on top of her.

'That was a good meal,' Julian said as he loosened his tie.

Elizabeth crossed to the windows and began to close the shutters.

'Do you have to do that?' Julian asked. 'It's still bloody hot.'

'People can see,' Elizabeth replied.

'For God's sake, darling. There's no one around. Keep them open. I like the air.' He switched on the bedside lamp and turned off the main light. 'There. That's better.' He had taken off his shirt and was beginning to loosen his belt. 'Come on,' he he said. 'Get that lot off.'

Elizabeth turned to him and smiled. 'Don't be so impatient. I should have thought that you'd already had enough today.'

'I've never had enough.'

She laughed. 'You're very greedy,' she said.

'We're all greedy. It's a greedy world.' He crossed the room towards her and began to unfasten her dress. 'I'm greedy for you,' he murmured as he undressed her. She laughed as he fumbled with the straps of her brassière.

'Come to bed,' he whispered. 'I want you.' He took her by the hand and led her across the room. He knelt on the bed looking down at her. Their hands caressed each other's bodies.

Suddenly, Elizabeth moved. 'What was that?' she asked.

'What was what?'

'That noise. I heard something.'

'There wasn't any noise,' Julian assured her.

'There was. I heard it.' She sat up on the bed listening. 'It was a thump. Up there.' She pointed up at the moulding on the ceiling.

'You're imagining things. There wasn't any noise.'

'But there was. I promise you.'

'It was probably a mouse or something.'

'I don't like this place,' Elizabeth said. 'It's got a nasty atmosphere. It gives me the creeps. I don't want to stay here.'

'Very well. We'll go tomorrow. We'll find somewhere else.'

Elizabeth relaxed and lay back amongst the pillows. 'Yes. I'd like that,' she said. 'I really don't like this place at all. It's horrible. I think nasty things have happened here.'

'Then it's about time that something nice did,' Julian murmured as he gently lowered his body on to hers.

Gently, gently, they moved together, their hands caressing, their lips touching. They moved together, conscious only of their pleasure, aware of nothing but their joy. Quicker and quicker they moved as their passions increased. Deeper and deeper they grew into each other, aware of nothing but themselves, longing only for their ultimate fulfilment.

They didn't hear the thud. They were aware of nothing until the door burst open and the screams rang in their ears.

Elizabeth had a moment's terror as Julian's body suddenly arched above her, splattering her with his blood. She opened her mouth, but her screams were smothered as Julian's body fell across her face. She gave a sudden agonizing moan as the knife plunged deep into her stomach. Again and again the knife descended, thrusting deeper and deeper into the two bodies. The blood spurted across the carpet as Thérèse struck again and again at the two dead bodies. She screamed and shouted as she plunged the knife deeper and deeper into the two limp bodies.

Tony stood by the bed and watched. Suddenly Thérèse stopped. She turned towards the door.

'What has happened?' she asked.

For a moment Tony was unable to speak.

Thérèse looked down at the bloody knife in her hand. 'What have I done?' she asked.

'You've killed my wife,' Tony said.

'Your wife?'

'Yes. You've killed her.'

'She was your wife?'

'Yes.'

'It wasn't Mathilde?'

'No.'

'But you made me kill her?'

'That's right.'

'You made me kill your wife?'

'Yes.'

'You must have hated her.'

'I did,' Tony replied.

He began to smile.

'Thérèse looked puzzled. 'And so you made me kill her?'

Tony nodded.

She turned towards him. 'You're evil,' she said. 'I was right. You are the Devil. You're evil.'

'Yes, I suppose I am,' Tony replied, grinning at her.

'Then you must die,' Thérèse said quietly. 'It wasn't her that was wicked. It was you. You are evil. And you must die.' She slowly began to move towards him.

He felt a moment's panic as he saw her lift the knife ready to strike.

Suddenly he lurched sideways, picked up the bedside lamp and threw it in her face. There was a crash as the light-bulb exploded on the floor, throwing the room into sudden darkness.

Thérèse put her hands up to her face, and dropped the knife at Tony's feet. Quickly he moved his feet to prevent her picking it up.

She stood there helpless for a moment. There was a moan as she slowly sank to the floor.

Tony leant against the wall. Gradually he became aware of Thérèse's body lying at his feet. He kicked her gently, but she didn't move. He went to the door and turned on the light.

She was lying in a crumpled heap on the floor. He bent down and felt her pulse. It had stopped beating. He picked up her head. Her lifeless eyes stared helplessly at him. She was quite dead.

He paused for a moment to recover himself, then quickly peeled off the gloves from Thérèse's hands. The knife was lying on the floor by the bed. He bent down, picked up her body and carried it to the door. He paused for a moment to glance at the bodies on the bed before turning out the light. Quickly and silently he carried Thérèse out to the car, and shut the front door.

It only took a moment to reach Marie's house. He ran inside and picked up the phone. Auguste answered immediately. It was all so simple.

'You've found the Sunburst!' Auguste exclaimed. 'I'll be right down.'

'The Sunburst?' Tony asked. 'What's that?'

'Wait until I arrive,' Auguste replied slamming down the receiver.

Tony smiled as he went out to the car. He quickly carried the lifeless body upstairs and laid it carefully on the bed. The room was exactly as Marie had left it.

He peeled off his gloves and hid them amongst his clothes. He was amazed how calm he felt. He didn't even need a drink. He went out on to the landing to watch for the car.

He had hardly any time to wait. He saw the sweep of the lights as the car turned at the crossroads. It came to a halt outside the house. He could see Auguste running up to the door.

Slowly he turned and picked up the telephone.

The Malines' house was ablaze with lights. Tony could see the men moving slowly from room to room. Auguste was sitting by the bedroom window with a man standing beside him. The man appeared to be speaking. Tony could see Auguste continually shaking his head.

It had been so simple.

He went down into the kitchen and took a bottle of champagne out of the refrigerator.

For a moment the hillside was quiet. Then something moved amongst the long stalks of barley.

Slowly the girl got to her feet. She paused for a moment with her hands to her mouth, before walking down towards where a policeman was standing in the lane.

Epilogue

Bouchout, 1927.

'Her Majesty would like to say goodbye.' The Baroness stood smiling at Angèle. 'She has asked to see you alone. Try not to be too long with her. I'm worried about her. I'm afraid that she has caught a cold. She shouldn't really have gone for that drive yesterday. But she insists on seeing you.'

Angèle put down the book she was reading and sighed. 'Oh dear,' she said. 'I hate goodbyes.'

She walked down the long corridor to the Empress's rooms. The woman was standing outside the door.

'I've been told to wait outside,' she said sulkily. 'If anything happens, you can call me.'

Angèle knocked at the door and entered. She curtsied towards the bed.

'Come in,' the Empress said. 'Come and sit by me.' A chair had been placed beside the bed.

'So you're leaving?'

Angèle nodded. 'But not for long,' she said. 'I will come back to see you.'

The Empress shook her head. 'No, my dear. I'm an old woman, and my time has come. I saw the Emperor this morning, and he told me so. I haven't very long. That is why I wanted to talk to you. I have loved you, my dear. You have been very good to me. I wanted to give you things. I have them, you know. I know where they are. But I was wrong. I should not have taken them. They were not mine to take. I had no right to them. They only brought harm. I didn't know that at first. They warned me about it, but I would not listen. I kept on telling them that I must have them. We needed the money to save my husband's empire. I had to have them, I said.

'My husband's secretary was a Mexican, and he warned me. 'You will be cursed,' he said. 'The Gods will put a curse on you.' But I would not listen. And so my husband died, and I became a prisoner. But still I would not listen.

'They were so beautiful. I liked to look at them. I used to stare at them for hours. They were all I had left. I gave Elizabeth something. She had always liked pretty things. She was a pretty thing herself. She was Empress of Austria, you know. Married to my husband's brother. But she died. Murdered, like my husband. I had given her something. And she was wearing it when she was killed.

'And that other woman. She had something, too. Something for her son. She had it made into a ring. She told me later that he always wore it. And he was murdered. They were all murdered. Everyone was murdered.'

'Don't distress yourself,' Angèle whispered.

The Empress turned towards her. 'I love you, my dear,' she said softly. 'I always wanted a child of my own. But it was denied me. I want you to be happy. I was wrong to take them.'

'Hush,' Angèle said, getting up and taking the Empress's hand. 'Hush. Rest. You'll be tired.'

'I was going to give you things,' the Empress murmured. 'But they were not mine to give. And they always brought unhappiness. Always. There was a curse on them. I was wrong to have taken them.'

'Sssh,' Angèle whispered.

'I was greedy. I know that now. The Emperor told me so himself this morning. We were all greedy. We had no right. So we were hated by the Gods. Hated for our greed. It is a terrible thing to be hated. I see that now. I should never have taken them. They have only brought unhappiness and tragedy.'

The Empress's eyes filled with tears. She leant forward and embraced Angèle.

'I have grown to love you so, my dear,' she said. 'You have taught me so much. You are so good and kind. You deserve only happiness. It is better that I give you nothing.'

'I want nothing,' Angèle assured her. 'I have your love. That is much more important. Now, you must rest.'

The Empress sighed. 'Yes. I must rest. I must be ready for the Emperor.'

Angèle leant forward and gently kissed the old lady's cheeks. 'Goodbye,' she whispered.

The Empress closed her eyes. Angèle turned at the door, but the old lady was already fast asleep.

The woman got up from her chair outside as Angèle passed. Her eyes were full of envy as she watched her go down the long corridor.